'There's nothing else for it.
walk.'

'Walk?' She watched incredulously as he dismounted, came towards her, his cape flapping noisily in the wind, and lifted her down.

'Have you any better suggestions?'

Her eyes widened with apprehension and appeal. 'But I can't.'

'If we stay here we die. I don't choose to die. You please yourself.'

With that he left her. She stood motionless for a time, small and helpless in her blue bell-shaped coat and bonnet with the large bow under her chin and fair curls escaping and tumbling over her forehead. A dusting of snow whitened her as she stood gazing in disbelief at Gunnet's retreating figure.

Then panic jerked her into action and she ran, stumbling, falling, getting to her feet, struggling forward again and shouting.

'Gunnet, wait! Don't leave me. Gunnet, do you hear? Don't you dare leave me alone.'

He stopped and turned a sardonic gaze on her as, forgetting modesty in the anxiety of the moment, she lifted her skirts and struggled towards him with ungainly, plunging steps.

THE DARK SIDE
OF
PLEASURE

Margaret Thomson Davis

A STAR BOOK
published by
the Paperback Division of
W. H. Allen & Co. Plc

A Star Book
Published in 1988
by the Paperback division of
W. H. Allen & Co. Plc
44 Hill Street, London W1X 8LB

First published in Great Britain by Allison and Busby Ltd
1981

Copyright © 1981 by Margaret Thomson Davis

Printed and bound in Great Britain by
Anchor Brendon Ltd, Tiptree, Essex

ISBN 0 352 32247 0

This book is dedicated to
Mr Glasgow – Jack House

PART ONE

Chapter One

There it was again – that look Augusta had detected before. How dare this insolent coachman make her feel so flustered, staring at her from where he waited. She tried to discountenance the fellow with a disdainful gaze, but she found herself blushing and had to lower her eyes.

Her face hidden by her poke bonnet, Augusta followed her mother across the pavement from the straw-hat maker's. At a discreet distance came the footman, laden with their purchases: not only hat boxes were balanced on his outstretched arms but also larger boxes containing their new gowns.

Reaching the coach, an elegant buttercup-yellow and black carriage, the older woman bunched her skirts with mittened hands and stepped inside with a rustle. Before Augusta could do the same, Gunnet the coachman gripped her arm and levered her upwards. His touch whipped her blood into such a fire of distress she was agitated enough to try to complain to her mama. But her mama was chattering on at such a pace about their new outfits that it was impossible to get a word in.

'It is such an important occasion,' Mrs Felicity Campbell insisted. 'We must look our very best. Think of it, Augusta! First there will be the review of the troops in Glasgow Green. Then a great procession through the streets, then parties to attend in honour of His Royal Majesty King William. Isn't it exciting? Mercy!'

A sedan chair had impeded the path of the coach and distracted her attention. 'Would you look at the impertinence of that! These highland chairmen have no respect. Why doesn't Gunnet just whip them out of his way? I'm sure our regular coachman would not have allowed us to be so inconvenienced.' Mrs Cameron fluttered her handkerchief in front of her face and closed her eyes.

'Is that Mrs Binny, Mama, coming out of the mantua-maker's?'

'Mercy upon us, so it is!' Mrs Cameron settled back against the cushions.

'Didn't they assure us that they were not having any new gowns for the Coronation celebrations?'

'They did indeed. Oh, the slyness of the creatures! They have been seeking to persuade us to wear old gowns so that they might make us suffer some disadvantage. But do not worry. Neither Miss Mary Binny nor her sister Fay could outshine you in beauty, Augusta. No matter what splendid gown they surprised us with.'

There could, in fact, be no denying that Augusta was beautiful. Her complexion had a milky sheen enhanced by the earth-red colour of her bonnet and the blue gloss of ribbons tied under her chin. The bunches of ringlets that peeped out and dangled high over her temples were golden, whereas her mother's hair was brown sprinkled with grey. Both women had fine haughty eyes, but Augusta's were as blue as sapphires while Mrs Cameron's were a speckled brown.

Felicity Cameron gossiped about the Binnys all the way to the Black Bull in Virginia Street. Then just as they were turning the corner both she and her daughter gave little squeals of fright and clung to each other when their coach nearly collided with another. The *Tallyho* from London was rolling in with its guard tooting his horn, its coachman desperately urging the horses on to complete the last few yards of the journey although the animals were tired and hanging low in their traces, heads drooping. Passengers, black-smeared with dirt and looking like frozen crows, perched on the roof huddled in capes, long scarves, top hats and firmly tied bonnets.

Augusta, after she and her mother had smoothed themselves down, recognized the coachman as one of her father's many employees and also the husband of their cook Nessie Cruickshanks who lived somewhere in the dungeons of Cameron House. The man was of the old school and held a very poor opinion, so her papa said, of the new flashman types – men like Gunnet, who despite his coarse features was one of Mr Cameron's most elegant dragsmen. These younger coachmen had discarded the bulky benjamin overcoat as well as the old wide-brimmed hat. Well-born gentlemen now admired the trade and viewed it an honour to sit up on the box beside this new breed of coachman and be allowed to take the rein. Even Augusta's brother Roderick often journeyed on the box with Gunnet, chatting knowledgeably to him as if he was an equal.

'Mama would not be pleased at you being on such familiar terms with a servant, Roderick,' she had protested.

'Make no mistake about it, dear sister, Luther Gunnet is no common serving lout. He is a fine fellow and a swell dragsman. Why, I've seen him with one easy flick of his whip pick a fly off the ear of his nearside leader.'

'A very grand, silver-mounted whip, I've noticed. Something that no servant, no matter how smart a fellow, could ever afford to purchase.'

'I admit it,' Roderick grinned, 'it was a gift from yours truly, and why not? It's the fashion for gentlemen to give patronage to their favourite coachmen.'

'I'm quite sure you couldn't afford it either, Roderick. One of these days Papa will refuse to provide any more for such extravagances or to pay your gambling debts. Then you will wish you had been wiser and saved money instead of squandering it. And no good can come of giving expensive gifts to a man like Gunnet.'

She would have liked to say more, to have revealed her strange unease at the dark eyes keenly probing her, despite the creases that held them narrow and half-hidden. But she did not know how to voice her complaints about the servant without compromising herself. What anyway would or could her brother do? No, far better to say nothing. But even now she trembled in confusion and her cheeks burned.

'Augusta, my dear, what are you thinking of?'

'Why, nothing, Mama; nothing, I do assure you.'

'We are here. Why don't you alight?'

With a loud rustle of skirts and padded sleeves Augusta hastened from the coach.

'Mercy upon us, there is no sign of your papa. It is too bad of him. He knows we do not like to be kept waiting. We shall seek him out in his office.'

Augusta resisted the urge to look round at the coachman, grateful of the shield her poke bonnet gave to her face. She hurried after her mother across the hotel yard with its line of mud-caked coaches and steaming, snorting horses at as smart a pace as her little flat cross-banded shoes and her long skirts and petticoats would allow. Serving maids in frilly mob caps watched her progress from the hotel windows, gazing enviously at her blue-spotted dress with its sloping shoulders and sleeves enormously wide at the elbows, and at Mrs Cameron's green pelisse and pink feathered bonnet, until both ladies disappeared from view under the covered archway that led to the cluttered yard where Mr Cameron, the coach proprietor, had his offices.

Various employees in the yard lifted their caps or knuckled their foreheads and called out respectfully: 'Mornin', Mistress Cameron. Mornin', Miss Cameron.'

Inside the office building clerks perched on high stools at slope-topped desks also saluted or gave obsequious bows. Mrs Cameron, followed by her daughter, swept past them and straight into her husband's private sanctum without knocking.

At the sudden eruption of colour in his dark mahogany-panelled office, Alfred Cameron leapt to his feet in dismay.

'Mrs Cameron, can it be that time already? It cannot, surely! I would not have kept you waiting for the world . . .'

'Mr Cameron has forgotten us!' his wife exclaimed.

'No, no!' Cameron strode towards her and guided her into a chair. 'A somewhat annoying matter of business distracted me.'

'I feel quite faint with fatigue, Mr Cameron. I have been subjected to the common rough and tumble of the streets these past two hours in my efforts to ensure that I will be a credit to you during tomorrow's celebrations . . .'

'Mrs Cameron, rest assured I will be proud of you as always. How could I be otherwise? There isn't another man in Glasgow can boast of such a beautiful wife.'

He was an ox of a man in his mid-forties with shifty eyes, side-whiskers and moustache of polished brass. His broad face with its humpbacked nose, flat at the end under which his bottom lip stuck out fleshily, would have made him look more like a pugilist than a businessman had it not been for his expensive clothes and confident bearing. He did not appear too sure of himself now, however, confronted by the small figure of his wife. He was a man of avid appetites, the most obsessive of which was that for his wife's body. It was a continuous struggle to keep his desires within respectable bounds and she tormented him greatly by withholding herself at the slightest whim.

Now she delicately strained away from him, averting her face. 'Augusta, my dear,' she appealed with a flutter of her eyelashes, 'assist your poor mama to her carriage.'

Cameron opened the office door, his face sagging with wretchedness, but he quickly recovered to growl at one of the clerks in passing and set them all scratching, heads down at their ledgers.

Once in the carriage Felicity melted with a faint smile. 'What business could it be that so distracted your mind, Mr Cameron?'

'Nothing to worry your pretty head about, Mrs Cameron. Just a lot of foolish talk about railways.'

'Railways?' His wife looked puzzled.

Cameron absently fondled his moustache. 'It's a kind of iron road. Thank goodness you haven't seen the mess of the countryside these Irish navvies have been making. Digging here. Knocking down there. Building ugly monstrosities here, there and everywhere.'

'Mercy!'

'They've had railways at the pits for a while, of course. Trucks on iron rails pulled along by horses. That's all very

10

well, but now they're opening this new railway between Glasgow and Garnkirk and it's going to be worked by one of those new-fangled steam engines.'

'Steam engines?'

'I don't want to shock you, my dear, but it's a noisy, filthy monster that eats coal and belches smoke and flame and will be most dangerous to life and limb for anyone who goes near it.'

'Mercy upon us, Mr Cameron, such things shouldn't be allowed! Why don't you do something?'

He patted his wife's hand. 'Such foolishness can't last. And I'll take care you won't be troubled with steam engines, never fear. Now, tell me about your purchases. Did they please you? Are you excited about tomorrow, Augusta?'

'Oh, yes, Papa. We are going to watch Lieutenant Fitzjames parade on the Green, then later he is joining us at the Tontine.'

Her father laughed. 'There will be many more than Lieutenant Fitzjames parading there tomorrow but I have no doubt you will have eyes for only one.'

Augusta flushed and gazed down at her lap.

'A capital fellow,' Cameron went on, 'and he comes from such a wealthy family. I even forgive him for being English.'

Augusta was comforted to be reminded of Lieutenant Fitzjames's fortune. Soon she would be far away from Glasgow and enjoying the protection of a husband of substance and with servants of her own choice. She assured herself of this every time she felt beset by foolish fears and uncertainties.

The coach stopped and they stepped out on to George Square and made their way up the double outside stair to Cameron House. When Tibs Gunnet, the coachman's sister, opened the door Augusta, upset at being reminded of the coachman and his dark provocative eyes, swept past her, ignoring the girl's nervous bob of a curtsy.

★ ★ ★

Somewhere among the babble of the crowded Glasgow streets, Blind Alick, with head cocked and hair spiking from his hat, was scraping at his fiddle. The tinny notes wailed above the clamour of the street-sellers.

'Half-penny, half-penny milk-o!'

'Flowers, penny a bunch!'

'Hot pies! Hot pies!'

Luther Gunnet decided to buy some pies to share with his mother and young brother and sister. He had told them he would be home tonight, and tomorrow morning he would be able to take them to see the grand procession to celebrate the coronation of King William IV. He had no intention of staying in all night, though. Jody, one of the chambermaids at the Tontine Hotel, would be waiting for him, propped up in bed on one elbow, her tangle of hair and her bare skin gleaming in the light of the candle . . .

He was tempted to forget his promise to go home, but relented on thinking of how much his family would enjoy the parcel of pies under his arm. This way and that he wended through the crowd with as much skill and panache as if he were still at the reins of a coach and four. Crossing the rough causeway of Argyle Street he went swaggering towards the Stockwell.

Earlier, rain had gusted along Stockwell Street, but now knots of people emerged from the gloomy shelter of closes or out of the flickering lights of clubs and taverns. Under the blue glow of gas lamps and against walls men leaned wearily. Children sat huddled in doorways or stood begging. Women, old before their time, bent into shawls and shuffled along. A whole army of young prostitutes, flaunting their silks and satins and brightly rouged cheeks, paraded in efforts to attract attention. These women lived alongside the Gunnets in the rabbit warrens of tenement closes around the Briggait, the Saltmarket, the Gallowgate and the High Street. Luther had grown up with them and gone to school with them. He remembered the times when their parents had been transported or hanged or had died of some disease or abandoned them, or when their families just fell into such dire poverty that the girls and often the mothers too were forced into thieving and prostitution in order to survive.

The best of luck to them was what he thought, though he had had to be careful not to say anything of the sort when his father was alive. His father had been a hand-loom weaver, a proud and honest man who had toiled to keep his family if not in luxury at least fed and respectably clad. He had set great store by school learning. Whereas nearly all the children in the neighbourhood were forced through necessity to start work at seven or eight years of age, Luther and his sister had attended school until they were twelve. Then Tibs had gone into service at the Cameron House. Luther had gone on to college for a few years, until his father's health had begun to deteriorate. The doctor had long said that it was consumption but it was the cholera that killed the old man in the end.

Anyway Luther had given up his book-learning in order to help supplement the family income, and not just willingly but with alacrity. He had never been as convinced as his father that education was the only way to do well. To accumulate money was Luther's idea of getting on in life, and he wasn't accumulating any money while imprisoned behind the grim walls of the college in the High Street droning out Latin verbs. In the few hours each day after he escaped from his studies he used to haunt the Cameron stables at the Black Bull. Sid Cruickshanks, the coachman who was married to the cook at Cameron House, had taken an interest in him and, over the years, had taught him all there was to know about horses and how to handle a coach and four. Luther had also spent many hours in the company of the other coachmen, listening to their stories of the road and their endless discussions and criticisms of the technical aspects of driving.

These same 'lords of the road' had eventually agreed that he had the most vital requirements for the job, keen eyes, strong arms, light hands, good nerves, even temper and plenty of practice. To his delight and great satisfaction, he was recommended to Mr Cameron when the latter needed a new coachman after the death in an overturning accident of coachman Bob Smithers.

His parents had both been against the job, for different reasons. His father had believed that a clerk's position in the Ship Bank would have been more in keeping with Luther's college education. His mother worried because of the danger: so many coachmen had been injured or killed on the box. Then there was the amount of time he would be away from home, the low taverns he would be forced to frequent and the bad company, bad language and bad habits he might acquire. Eventually Luther had wheedled his parents into agreeing.

'Coaching has changed out of all recognition.' He struggled to spark them with some of his enthusiasm. 'It isn't like it used to be at all. It's an art now. A highly respected art.'

They had given him no encouragement but at least they had withdrawn their objections, or, more accurately, had ceased to voice them. When later he had paraded before them in all his splendour, they had been bewildered and overawed. He sported a well-brushed white topper, crisp linen with high stand-up collar around which was tied a black silk cravat. His trousers slimmed down to his ankles and strapped underneath his instep. His frock-coat pinched in tightly at his waist and curved out at the chest to reveal a wide expanse of pearl-buttoned waistcoat. He was clean-shaven but had a coarse bush of black hair and sideburns to match, and brows jutting over what many a female had referred to as wicked eyes. He was a fine figure of a fellow and he knew it. So did every wench in every tavern from Glasgow to London.

Of course he never spoke to his parents of the times he enjoyed with women. Nor did he ever mention the many ways he made extra money. If he picked up a passenger on the road who wasn't entered in the waybill he pocketed the fare. Poaching did a thriving business and he obliged by carrying wild fowl and game at a price. He also made a

14

considerable profit by the more legitimate means of buying articles cheaply in their place of origin and selling them often at a huge profit in Glasgow, or he bought things made in Glasgow and sold them at a profit in some other town. The boot of his coach had transported delectable goods like cheeses, fresh salmon and barrels of oysters bought on commission for tradesmen or private individuals.

All this as well as his normal gratuities – and they were often very handsome – meant that he could not only keep his mother and the two younger members of the Gunnet family but put a bit of money away in the Ship Bank. He had no intention of burying himself for the rest of his life in a hovel in the Briggait.

He turned into the street, swearing for the hundredth time that one day he'd get his family out of this place and provide them with a house in a decent area – perhaps a cottage along Anderson Way where there would be room to move. Here the crowds were even denser than in Stockwell Street, partly because the Briggait was so narrow and partly because so many of the inhabitants of the hovels were glad to get out to the street for a breath of air. At least in his place there were only his mother, his younger sister Rose, his brother Billy and himself. Tibs stayed in the Cameron House except on her night off; and of course work kept him away too as often as not.

Women in shroud-like shawls lined the inner side of the pavement, leaning against walls as if for shelter and support. Some languidly gossiped, others stared, dull-eyed and silent, like a row of skeletons in some long-forgotten tomb. The street's narrowness made it cold and shadowed, even in daylight, and the clanging of horses and carts reverberated on the cobbles. It was dark now and gas jets and shop windows and taverns cast out talons of light.

He lived in the first close next to Biddy's old clothes shop. Coats, jackets, petticoats and gowns dangled from a long shelf which stretched above the door and windows; the garments covered the place and made it like a cloth jungle that stank of sweat. Dodging his head to avoid the low roof, he clattered into the entry of the close. A foul stream of water hissed and spat. He was glad to reach the other end of the passage that led to an open yard. But around it buildings leaned near to one another and lanes, known as wynds and vennels, no more than cracks between the houses, led off the main yard. From these lanes trickled subterranean-type paths that only someone like himself, born and brought up in the area, could ever hope to find their way around.

The entrance of his own building took on a ghostly light when he opened the door. A candle flame shrank back shivering in the draught. Closing the door, he crossed the lobby and made an exuberant entrance into the kitchen.

'Ma, me old darlin'! It's your handsome broth o' a boy Luther, begorra and bejabbers!'

Swivelling him a reproving glance, his mother said, 'What would Mr Cameron think if he heard you speak like that? Just you remember your father.'

Luther knew what she meant. His father as well as his mother had always put great store not only by giving proper respect to one's master but also keeping oneself of good character and suffering trials and tribulations with patience and dignity. One of the trials of the Briggait was the Irish immigrant population. His father had never had anything to do with them. They had brought such desperate over-crowding to the street and took part in so many of the street fights after drinking in the taverns. His father had never frequented taverns, or gone to cockfights or to the theatre, or travelled or done anything at all except work. From dawn till dusk he sat absorbed at his loom. The monotonous clank and clatter was woven into the fabric of Luther's childhood but with threads of magic too, as he'd watched the materials grow like coloured cobwebs under his father's hands.

'To hell with Cameron,' Luther said. 'Now who wants pies? Hot and juicy and delicious!'

His mother turned from the pot she had been stirring over the fire, one hand on her hip, her back kept stiff.

There was still the look of a handsome woman about her, despite the stands of hair drifting greasily forwards over her tired eyes.

'That wicked lack of respect to your betters will get you in trouble yet.'

'I'm as good as any man and better than Cameron,' Luther aimed his hat at young Billy's head. It landed on target, sucking the boy's face inside but not far enough to cover his toothy grin. 'And anyone who disagrees with that doesn't get a pie.'

Billy ran towards him, tilting the hat so that he could see. Rose pattered after him on bare feet like pink seashells.

'No one's better than you, Luther,' they squealed.

'I'm warning you,' his mother said grimly. But Luther was laughing along with the children and swooped Rose into his arms to stuff a pie against her mouth and moustache her with grease. After tossing her down again he switched his attention to Billy.

'Here's yours, squire. You look as if you need all you can get to put a bit of flesh on your bones.'

'I did well at my lessons, Luther. The dominie says I'll make a professor yet.' Billy's eyes shone expectantly up at his brother.

Luther looked suitably impressed. In fact he reeled back on his heels as if completely knocked off-balance by the momentous news.

'A professor in the family? I always knew you were a genius, Billy-boy. Here, have two pies.'

Mrs Gunnet gave him another reproving stare. 'You'll be giving that boy a swelled head.'

'Well, he needs an oversized noddle to hold all his brains, don't you, squire?' He rubbed his brother's head so energetically that Billy missed his mouth and stuffed some pie in his ear, making Rose splutter with laughter.

Sal Gunnet tutted as she ladled out bowls of soup. 'Stop it, Luther. Say Grace then eat your soup. Come on, Billy, and you too, Rose. Sit at the table and less of your nonsense.' Sitting down herself she bowed her head and waited.

Rose clambered up on to a chair. Then, barely visible except for her mischievous eyes, she sat with shoulders squeezed up and lips pressed together in an effort to contain both pie and giggles. Billy wriggled his bottom on to his seat, his eyes shining up at Luther who gave him a wink before praying in solemn chant.

Afterwards Mrs Gunnet informed him, 'I've plenty of water in. There's enough for each of us to have a wash ready for tomorrow.'

'You shouldn't have carried all that. I could have done it.'

'I knew it would be turned off by the time you got here.'

'It's a pity Tibs won't be off, Mother,' Luther said. 'She'll miss all the fun of the procession.'

'If she's needed by her mistress, it's with her mistress she ought to be.'

'I don't see why her mistress should need her tomorrow. Her mistress and her daughter will be out enjoying the celebrations. I saw the pair of them earlier today. A couple of right empty-headed idiots!'

'Luther, how dare you be so wickedly disrespectful! The trouble with you is you don't know your place. I was always a good servant and proud of it. I was always loyal and respectful to my mistress and when I left I was given a letter to testify to my good character. I could get a job anywhere just by showing that letter!'

She had shown it to them many times, lifting it reverently out from the wooden box where she kept a lock of hair from each of her dead babies, her mother's wedding ring and a dried flower. The letter was wrapped in a piece of silk for protection but it had still turned yellow and was falling apart at its folded edges.

'Mother, you deserve a lot more respect than Mrs Cameron or her daughter. I've seen more than a few pampered horrors in my line of business but those two are without doubt the world's worst.'

18

'Luther!'

'Don't worry,' he said. Then with another wink at Billy, 'I always behave like a perfect gentleman to the ladies.'

Chapter Two

What Luther liked about Jody was the way she could be so relaxed and yet so responsive. As she lay back with legs spread wide and eyes dreamy, she looked completely passive yet totally sensual. Leaning over her, he kissed her on the mouth while his hand caressed her. In a while he slid over her, and locking him close with both arms and legs she curved to meet him in the frenzy of passion that engulfed them both.

Afterwards she sank back and soon drifted smilingly into a deep sleep. He lay beside her, his body exhausted but his mind restless, until eventually he surrendered himself to oblivion.

When he awoke he lit another candle and consulted his watch. Five a.m. He had slept no more than three hours but for him it was enough. Stretching luxuriously despite the icy air he glanced sideways at Jody. She did not move even when he rose, struggled into his trousers then removed his coat from the bed before leaving.

Trongate Street was bald and silent when he emerged from the Tontine Hotel but as he walked along, his feet cracking on the cobbles, candles were beginnning to wink in black cavities of windows and dribble yellow light down walls. On a doorstep of a grocer's shop two girls were crouching, one laying her head on the shoulder of the other, trying to sleep. As Luther turned down Stockwell Street a gas lamp elongated shadows of two men and a cart coming out of one of the closes. The cart was heaped with filth and dung and filled the street with an obnoxious stench. Luther returned the men's greetings as he marched past with his hands stuffed in his pockets and his hat jauntily perched on the back of his head.

When he arrived home his mother was up and polishing the bars of the kitchen fire. Billy and Rose were contented balls of sleep in their set-in-the-wall bed. A stub of candle withered on the table and the kitchen was depressingly cold.

'Good morning, Mother.' He kissed the top of her head then lit another two candles and put them on the dresser. 'It's going to be a splendid day for the procession. Not a spot of rain in sight.'

'I'll have the fire going in a minute, son.'

He could sense her excitement. Kneeling down intent on the fire she kept her back and head held stiff but even so he detected the tremor of anticipation and pleasure at their planned outing. He was glad that he had promised to accompany her. She had few outings or company of any sort and must often feel lonely.

The fire crackled, flurrying out light and heat.

'That's better.' Luther rubbed his hands and held them out as if admiring them.

Soon the oatmeal that had been steeping all night was put on to boil, and water too. Soon the children had bounced from the bed, their feet slapping across the floor. Soon the morning shadows from the yard were filtering in and making the square of glass set deep in the wall turn a wispy grey.

'Where are we going first, Luther?' Billy jumped up and down with excitement after everyone had washed and breakfasted.

'To the Green, of course, squire. All the military are going to be in the parade,' he enthused, 'the Rifle Brigade, the Hussars, the Glasgow Sharpshooters, the Highland Regiments . . .'

'Come on, Rose,' his mother urged, having donned the bonnet and shawl she kept for Sundays and special occasions, 'put the hood of your cloak up. It's cold. And, Billy, tidy yourself up at once. Fasten your waistcoat. Do I look respectable enough, Luther?' her faded eyes anxiously sought his from the shadows of her bonnet.

20

'Mother, you're the most beautiful girl I know.' Luther flicked his topper in the air, caught it neatly with his head, gave the crown a slap and offered his mother his arm.

The back court was busy with people now. The crowds swept towards the close, leaning, hunching forward to enter its low tunnel then straightening as they discharged into the Briggait at the other end.

Luther felt exhilarated as he and his family went down to Clyde Street and walked beside the river towards the Low Green. They passed the court and jail buildings that faced on to the Green, and crossed over to join the multitude that was as thick as a field of corn.

Above the babble they could hear the yelling of sergeant-majors and the sound of pipes and drums and bugles lustily blowing but they could see nothing until, using his iron-hard body as a battering ram, Luther forced a path to the front. His mother nearly lost her bonnet and shawl in the process. Billy was almost separated from them and had literally to fight his way to keep up. Rose began to cry with fear at being buried in a forest of legs. But it was worth it in the end when the magnificent spectacle of soldiers and cavalry opened up before them. A vast panorama of colour rippled like a huge flag agitating in the wind.

Men in kilts and scarlet tunics and tall fur bonnets moved shoulder to shoulder behind officers in white hackle plumes and gold-fringed epaulettes, brandishing long swords. Other soldiers in red and blue coatees and blue trousers and tall peaked hats crowded past, clutching rifles and bayonets. With careless confidence, straight-backed men in capes and high-collared tunics rode noble-looking horses that tossed their heads and pawed the ground and air, as conscious as their riders of attention and admiration.

Luther hitched Rose up into the crook of one arm, settled Billy in front of his legs then hugged his other arm around his mother's shoulders.

'What did I tell you, eh?' he smiled.

* * *

'Ah, my dear Mrs Cameron, I swear I have never seen a day shine forth with such great splendour,' Mrs Binny gushed over the luncheon table in the large room of the Tontine Hotel where the Lord Provost and bailies and local dignitaries had gathered for an early luncheon.

'I know I'm just a simple soul, Mrs Binny, but I do believe this sort of thing spoils the workpeople and gives them wrong ideas. All the shops and places of business are closed and every seamstress and shop assistant is out on the streets.'

'Ah, my dear Mrs Cameron, it is all in a good cause – the glorification of our noble sovereign.'

Felicity Cameron smiled sweetly and fluttered her eyelashes at the other woman. 'Mercy, I hope my servants will think none the less of his Royal Majesty, God bless him, for remaining at their duties in Cameron House. After all, one must pursue one's family's interests, Mrs Binny.'

She patted her ringlets and the ruby and diamond brooch at her throat. 'And I do try to regulate my household by economy – in money and time. I never visit the servants' quarters, for instance. I have trained Augusta to be my deputy in such matters.'

'A most charming and delightful deputy,' Lieutenant Fitzjames said. Augusta modestly lowered her eyes. But his scarlet tunic with its gold embellishments glimmered through her lashes, pleasing her. She fingered the delicate gold chain at her neck, then the locket that held inside it a snippet of her fiancé's hair.

They planned a summer wedding and the Fitzjames family would be travelling up from London for the occasion. And what an occasion it was going to be! She and her mother never tired of discussing the arrangements. Her father had assured them that money was no object – 'Nothing but the best is good enough for a Cameron. People will expect us to put on a good show.' Her mother said the wedding would be the sensation of the city. Musicians would be brought from Edinburgh. The materials for the wedding outfit would be specially purchased from France.

There would be the most splendid banquet. But of course before that they were to go down to London to spend Christmas with the Fitzjameses and discuss and finalize the details of the wedding . . .

Augusta was aroused from her reverie by the Lord Provost proposing the first toast.

'. . . and I am sure all now present will accord with me when I say that every act of His Majesty's reign has been distinguished by the kindest regard for the best interests of his people; and that the fervent wish and prayer throughout the nation is that he may long wear the Crown with which he is this day to be adorned – our beloved sovereign, William the Fourth, four times four. . . .'

His Lordship then continued: 'The amiable and estimable virtues of our gracious Queen are so universally acknowledged that I require only to wish that she may long live to be the solace of our sovereign, and a bright example to her sex. Our beloved Queen Adelaide, four times four. . . .'

The next toast was to the Princess Victoria, followed by others to the Royal Family, the British Constitution, Earl Grey and His Majesty's ministers, the Imperial Parliament, the Army and the Navy and the Sheriff of the County.

After the toasts many of the ladies and gentlemen left the hotel to watch the procession from the pavements and other vantage points in their own or friends' houses. Others, including the Camerons and Lieutenant Fitzjames, repaired to the hotel's Coffee Room, the windows of which looked on to the High Street. The Tontine was on the corner at Glasgow Cross and from its windows the four streets leading from the Cross could be seen: Trongate Street, Saltmarket Street, High Street and Gallowgate Street.

Along the Gallowgate came a dense forest of flags, each flag bright with sketches of different scenes and mottoes to represent the particular trade of that part of the procession. The spectacle, with its hullabaloo, the cheering, the clatter of horses' hooves, the cracking of flags, the uproar of emotion, awakened in Augusta such sensual excitement she could hardly contain it. It burned in her eyes when she

23

stared up at Lieutenant Fitzjames willing him to share in her intoxication. But the lieutenant's pale eyes betrayed a slight shrinking of embarrassment and she immediately lower her lashes.

Eventually, when the whole procession had passed, the gentlemen assisted the ladies into their pelisses. Augusta snuggled happily into hers before lifting her muff. Lieutenant Fitzjames offered her his arm and they followed her parents out to the yard of the Tontine where their carriage was waiting.

The parade was passing along George Street when they reached the square, and a dense mob of spectators had spilled down the Queen Street side of the square completely blocking the entrance to Cameron House which was situated at the corner.

'Mercy!' wailed Mrs Cameron. 'What will become of us?'

Cameron tugged down the coach window, jerked out his head and shoulders and bawled up at the coachman: 'Crack the whip! Shout them out of the way. Run them down if necessary. If you can't get your mistress safely home you are no longer in my employ. Now, let's be hearing from you!'

He thumped back in his seat growling, 'How dare that rabble venture near my door.'

His words were all but drowned by the great screech of the coachman and the slashing of his whip and the whinnying of the horses, which was followed by a panic of screaming from all sides. But the coach moved forward and soon Felicity and Augusta were able to make a dignified exit across a path on the pavement cleared for them by the physical exertions of the footman and the coachman, the sharp commands of Cameron and the supercilious looks and disdainful flapping gestures of Lieutenant Fitzjames's gloved hands.

Inside Cameron House the servants had been enjoying the procession from the drawing-room window and on hearing the jangle of the front door bell they scattered pell-mell down to the kitchen, leaving a breathless and dishevelled Tibs to open the door. She curtsied several times as the Camerons and the lieutenant entered but none of them noticed her and she thankfully scuttled away to the nether regions.

The parlour bell rang as she burst into the kitchen and Fiona McPherson the parlour maid hurried past to answer it, intent on composing her coquettish tip-tilted features into a serious mask of polite enquiry.

'McPherson, remove these and then bring tea,' Augusta commanded as soon as the girl entered the parlour.

'Yes, miss,' Fiona curtsied low before gathering up the pelisses, the feathered hat, the topper, the high-crowned military hat and the gloves. She curtsied again, pertly, then quit the room.

'Augusta, there is something about McPherson that I find distasteful.'

'Do you wish me to dismiss her, Mama?'

'Oh, I suppose not. It is such a nuisance to get decent servants nowadays. So many people are being lured away into factories. And now Mr Cameron tells me of steam monsters and railways and hundreds of men being employed to knock down buildings and dig through hills to clear a path for them. I really do not know what the country is coming to.'

'What worries me,' said Cameron, 'is the noise. It will upset the cows and hens which means the country will be short of milk and eggs.'

'I agree, sir,' said Lieutenant Fitzjames. 'Wholeheartedly. No railway will ever be allowed to cut through Fitzjames land.'

A tap on the door heralded Fiona with the tea. With excruciating care so that there was not the tiniest tinkle she lowered the tray on to the fireside table.

'Shall I pour, Mama?' enquired Augusta after the maid had wafted from the room.

'Would you, dear? You will have noticed how invariably kind Augusta is, Lieutenant Fitzjames.'

25

The lieutenant gave a slight bow. 'I am the most fortunate of mortals.'

'I shall be brokenhearted and helpless without her,' Mrs Cameron continued.

'Madam.' A slight movement of the fingers of one hand and another tiny bow indicated Lieutenant's Fitzjames's grief.

Cameron said, 'Your parents will be mightily impressed with my daughter's beauty and accomplishments when they meet her at Christmas, I'll warrant.'

'How could they be otherwise, sir?' Fitzjames allowed himself the ghost of a smile in Augusta's direction.

The fire burning brightly reflected warm movement in the shiny material of her dress although she was sitting now with perfect stillness except when her white neck angled forward and her lips slightly pouted to sip her tea.

Sometimes she felt somewhat affronted by her fiancé's casual and often lethargic manner. On one occasion she had broached the subject to her mother, who had assured her that this was the sign of a true aristocratic gentleman. A circumspection of conduct must be observed at all times and to be ladylike Augusta must behave with the same restraint of decorum. She took another sip of tea. Then she forced her gaze safely away from the lieutenant's polite smile.

Chapter Three

A mountain of luggage swayed on top of the Cameron coach as it rattled over the cobblestones. Nearing the Black Bull, it passed the early morning mail coach which was setting off along Trongate Street, carriage lamps flickering. It overtook a lumbering covered wagon driven by an old man who raised a hand in salute.

Gas lamps glittered coldly like blue diamonds and the hard frost made steam clouds of the horses' breath. Gunnet, dressed for the cold, wore leather breeches and black top-boots, a five-tiered macintosh cape, top hat and hogskin gloves. Jim Jimieson, the lanky red-headed footman, was on the box beside him, similarly attired but with two tiers to his cape.

Inside the coach, looking like a red-faced bear, Cameron sat hunched up in a fur-collared coat. The Cameron ladies were not only well protected but well nigh invisible, in large poke bonnets, voluminous cape coats and enormous muffs enveloping hands and arms. A fur rug spilled across the floor and covered all their feet.

'I'll be only too glad when we have arrived, Augusta,' said Mrs Cameron. 'I am looking forward to the prospect of spending the festive season in London with your dear lieutenant and his esteemed family. But I am certainly not looking forward to this journey.'

'Would you care for a sip of brandy, my dear?' enquired her husband.

'Not at the moment, Mr Cameron, but I dare say I will be glad of its reviving properties before long. Mercy, I do hate these long journeys. I get so exhausted.'

Past the Cross now and away along the Gallowgate with work-people flitting like shadows. Past the houses. The flare of the coach lamps on the hedges. Beyond, the darkness of the unknown.

Gradually, as the blackness softened into grey streaked with orange, hills and trees took shape, floating out of the mist like wraiths. The coach kept up a steady speed, its regular movement rocking the Camerons off to sleep. But as daylight faded the coachlamps into insignificance, Felicity stirred.

'Mr Cameron, you are snoring,' she complained irritably.

'Eh?' he spluttered and jerked.

'You were snoring loudly, sir.'

'Sorry, sorry,' he grunted, in none too good a humour himself.

'Mercy, I ache all over. When do we reach an inn, for pity's sake?'

Cameron peered from the window in an effort to judge

where he was. Then he fished his watch from his waistcoat and studied it.

'Any time now.'

Sure enough, the sound of voices was heard shortly afterwards, and Augusta could see a landlord with a white apron tied around his middle, waving a welcome. Behind him was a whitewashed building with brown shutters and a sign on which was painted a golden cockerel.

'Hello there, Luther!' the man was shouting. 'How goes it?'

'It's like this, Ben,' Gunnet's deep voice answered. 'I'd go a damned sight better after a tot of rum.'

The landlord laughed. 'You're not on the stage, then?'

'No, this is the Cameron coach. I've Mr and Mrs Cameron and their daughter inside. See that they're well served.'

'That I will, Luther.' He waited deferentially while Jimieson opened the coach door and they alighted. 'Welcome to the Golden Cockerel,' the landlord said. 'If you would be kind enough to follow me.'

Inside the building they were led to a room with a cheerful fire and white walls on which hung rows of paintings of horses and coaches. A guard's 'yard of tin' horn adorned the wall over the mantleshelf. In the centre of the room a round table covered with a white cloth was set with a platter of bread and a roast of beef.

'Sit yourselves down at the table, Mr Cameron, ladies. I'll see about vegetables. And a bowl of hot soup would go down well, no doubt.'

It was a simple meal but they were hungry enough to enjoy it and feel refreshed, and they returned to the coach in a cheerful frame of mind. Even the sight of Gunnet enthroned high on the box did nothing to spoil Augusta's good humour. Soon they were off at a brisk trot.

A frosty sun glittered over the countryside for a time but was eventually hidden by a curtain of sleet. Mr and Mrs Cameron nodded off again and Augusta did not bother to waken them to see the stagecoach that passed them travelling north. It had several people huddled together on the roof looking very miserable and bedraggled.

But some time later their own coach gathered speed and the horses' hooves thundering madly awakened her mother and father.

'Mercy upon us, Mr Cameron, he is racing. He is!' Felicity's voice climbed in panic.

'There is no other coach on the road that I can see,' said Cameron, fighting with the leather strap in his efforts to lower the window. 'What the devil are you playing at?' he bawled up at the coachman as soon as he managed to twist his head out.

'There's a steep hill ahead,' Gunnet shouted back. 'I need to "spring" the horses to give them a good start up the slope. It's either that or you all get out and walk.'

Cameron thumped back on his seat. 'There's no need to worry,' he said. 'It's all right.'

'It is not all right!' Mrs Cameron wailed. 'He is going far too fast. He is unnerving me, Mr Cameron.'

In an effort to comfort her mother Augusta said, 'Hold my hand and close your eyes. I will tell you when it is safe to open them again.'

Despite her brave words, her heart pounded with terror. However, after a while the horses had resumed their more even trot and the two women could relax again. With chatter about the Fitzjameses and their London mansions, they passed the time quite pleasantly.

The sleet whitened and fluffed into snow, making the countryside as pretty as a picture. Trees spread ermine tracery against a blue velvet sky. Before they knew it they had reached another inn and were refreshed by hot tea and toasted muffins and large portions of boiled ham before setting off again. This time the coach lamps were lit for it had grown dark, though a moon gleamed down and reflected on the vast silent expanse of snow.

At the next stop they slept overnight and set off early on a crisp white morning. Soon the wind began to rise, swirling the flakes before it like feathers. They began to pile up

29

round the window and stick to the glass. Eventually it was snowing so heavily that it was almost impossible to see out of the coach, despite Augusta's persistent rubbing at it with a gloved palm. The virgin white outside made the brown velvet interior darker and tinier. The odour of leather and dust thickened and became oppressive.

Augusta's head ached as she struggled to subdue panic. She had never liked small enclosed places. Her father was dozing again, his chin sunk deep in his fur collar, his fleshy underlip sticking out.

Her mother was saying, 'And of course the Fitzjameses will see that dear Roderick obtains a good position . . .' and Augusta thought how she missed her brother now that he was away at university; on the rare occasions he came home it was obvious that he was Mrs Cameron's favourite.

Abruptly Felicity stopped speaking, riveted her attention on the buttoned velvet of the coach and listened.

'Why are we going so slow now? That driver is just being perverse.'

Just then the coach gave a lurch. Then it jerked forward and quickened, only to bump them about and make the seats feel iron hard.

'Mr Cameron,' cried Felicity in alarm, 'Mr Cameron! Mercy upon us! Wake up, Mr Cameron. What is happening now?'

Cameron gave a start. 'What is it?' he darted a look around. He rubbed first one window, then the other, dodging his head about in an attempt to see. 'Looks as if we're in the middle of a blizzard.'

The coach jolted again, throwing the women backwards and forwards and almost dislodging their bonnets. They squealed in apprehension, which turned to alarm when Cameron opened the window and a gust of wind swirled snow all over them.

'What are you doing, Gunnet?' he yelled. 'Can't you be more careful?'

'I'm doing my best,' Gunnet hollered back. 'I can't even see the leaders, never mind the road.'

'Well, you'd better stop at the first inn we come to.'

'One thing's certain – we can't stop here!'

After the window was safely secured again Cameron busied himself ridding the ladies of the offending snow.

'What is happening?' complained his wife. 'He was eager enough to hurry some time back. Why is he being so awkward? Surely there is no need to jostle us about like this? I thought he was supposed to be your best driver, Mr Cameron.'

'To be frank, my love, it would be impossible for anyone to see where he is going in this weather. I'm afraid we'll just have to suffer the discomfort as best we can until we reach an – '

Suddenly the coach gave a terrible jump and seemed to slither sideways.

They heard Gunnet roaring at the horses, the sharp crack of his whip and the beasts whinnying. Then the coach swung wildly, flinging Cameron on top of the two women. It teetered at an alarming angle, then crashed over on to its side. Piercing screams welled up from the tangle of arms and legs as Cameron's heavy body slammed his wife and daughter into the space between the seats.

Outside, all was chaos. The two lead horses were rearing up, shrieking with terror. The two 'wheeler' animals had been pulled down by the weight of the coach and were kicking frantically, trying to regain their feet. Jimieson who had fallen forward between them was being kicked by the flailing hooves.

Milk-white ground frothed into vermilion as Jimieson's head was beaten to pulp by the iron-shod hooves. Gunnet, catapulted into the snow, lay for a moment stunned by the fall. Then he staggered up, shaking himself as if to clear his brain.

'Christ!' he groaned on seeing Jimieson, and raced over to pull him free. But the man was dead.

Going back to the coach Gunnet heaved himself up until he was on his hands and knees beside the door which was now the roof of the coach. Hampered by the snow and wind he nevertheless managed to jerk it open, and it crashed back to reveal a jumble of bodies heaped in the narrow space between the now vertical seats. Cameron was on top and beginning to struggle to raise himself. Gunnet reached down, grabbed his arm and dragged him out of the coach.

'My wife,' Cameron was almost weeping, 'my poor wife . . .'

'I'll get her.' Gunnet leaned down again but Augusta was dazedly lifting herself from on top of her mother's twisted body so, holding her round the waist, he hoisted her clear and deposited her on the snow, where she steadied herself against the roof, the wind whipping at her loose coat.

Her father was flat on his belly on the side of the coach with Gunnet who was hanging head and shoulders inside the open door.

'I'll have to be careful. She's unconscious,' he told Cameron.

'Don't touch her,' Cameron interrupted. 'I'll see to my wife.'

'All right. I'll unhitch the horses.' Gunnet leapt down.

Still in a daze, Augusta watched him struggle with the animals and afterwards go over to Jimieson's body, bring back a pistol from inside the man's cape, stride back and without hesitation aim and fire at the squealing horse that lay struggling on the ground. At this she broke into hysterical screaming and weeping which stopped just as suddenly with her astonishment at Gunnet's passing words:

'Be quiet, you fool!' he snapped before clambering on to the coach again. Cameron had somehow managed to squeeze himself underneath his wife and cradle her in his arms. Felicity Cameron had regained consciousness and was sobbing wildly into his shoulder.

'There don't seem to be any bones broken,' Cameron said, his eyes strained and anxious. 'But she's badly bruised and in pain.'

'If you raise her so that I can get a proper hold of her we can get her out between us without . . .' Gunnet suggested, but the rest of his sentence was engulfed by Mrs Cameron's screams.

'I can't move! I can't move!'

'But, my love,' Cameron pleaded, 'if I could get you on one of the horses with me we could soon reach an inn and you could be properly attended to.'

'I can't move. I am in agony. How do you know that I have not broken every bone in my body? I cannot move and I will not move.' Her voice rocketed into a scream again. 'I will not move!'

'Gunnet, where's Jimieson?' Cameron asked distractedly. 'Can't you send him for help?'

'He's dead.'

'O God! My daughter – is she all right?'

'Yes. Mr Cameron, it's too risky to stay here. I know how snow can drift. The best chance for all of us is to take the horses and keep moving until we come to an inn.'

At this Mrs Cameron's screams loudened.

'I can't move her while she's in this state.' Cameron struggled to make himself heard. 'You'll just have to go. Take my daughter. Make sure she's safe then bring back help.'

Gunnet hesitated then shrugged, before securing the door and jumping down to where Augusta was hiding close to the roof, trying to protect herself against the storm.

Chapter Four

'Fix your bonnet on properly and let's go,' said Gunnet.

As Augusta secured the bonnet back on her head she was telling herself no, her ears weren't playing tricks, the coachman really was talking to her like that. She was about to burst out with an indignant objection but as she stepped out from her shelter the wind buffeted and frightened her and she was glad of his steadying fingers digging into her arm. When she realized he was leading her away from the coach towards where the horses were tethered, however, she began holding back.

'Where are you taking me? I want to stay with Mama and Papa.'

'Well, you can't.'

'What do you mean?' she wept as he dragged her roughly towards one of the horses. 'I want to go back inside the coach with Mama and Papa.'

'There's no room in the coach now. We'll have to take our chances and make for an inn. Come on, I'll give you a hand up.'

Before she realized what had happened she was perched astride the horse and her lace-edged drawers were showing at her ankles. She gave a cry of distress and struggled to tug her skirts down despite the wind fighting to whip them up even higher.

'For God's sake,' Luther shouted, 'what's the use of bothering about that at a time like this? Do you think I've never seen a woman's drawers before? Just concentrate on hanging on and follow close behind me.'

He left her sobbing in confusion and set off on another horse. A few minutes later he turned and when he saw her still helplessly sitting where he'd left her he slewed his horse and angrily returned.

'Did you not hear what I said?' he bawled as close to her face as he could reach. 'Hang on and follow me.' With that he made a loud, snarling noise and aimed a blow at her horse's rump, sending the beast suddenly galloping away.

Then his horse sped in front of hers, but before long both animals were slowed to trotting pace then to a stumbling walk by the blizzard conditions and the state of the ground. The road had disappeared and the whole countryside was hushed by a thick carpet of white.

Looking back, Augusta could no longer see the coach. She wondered how long they had been travelling. Exhaustion and cold were making her feel dizzy. She longed to ease her aching body, thaw her frozen limbs at a fire, give herself up to the bliss of a feather bed. Several times she had been tempted to ask Gunnet if he knew where they were and if he thought shelter was near at hand. But when she caught glimpses through the speckling snow of his broad back, so alien and uncaring, she felt frightened and couldn't make a sound. Drifts deepened until the horses began to flounder and throw up their heads and whinny in protest, nostrils flaring and eyes red.

She began to cry again when the animals refused to breast an icy wall.

'A lot of good that'll do you,' said Gunnet.

She wiped at her eyes with the back of her hand. 'It's no use. It's too deep for them. What are we going to do?'

'Just be quiet and keep trying.'

Weeping bitterly she struggled with the horse, kicking it as hard as she could to force it forward until at last Gunnet said,

'There's nothing else for it. We'll just have to get off and walk.'

'Walk?' She watched incredulously as he dismounted, came towards her, his cape flapping noisily in the wind, and lifted her down.

'Have you any better suggestions?'

Her eyes widened with apprehension and appeal. 'But I can't.'

'If we stay here we die. I don't choose to die. You please yourself.'

With that he left her. She stood motionless for a time, small and helpless in her blue bell-shaped coat and bonnet with the large bow under her chin and fair curls escaping and tumbling over her forehead. A dusting of snow whitened her as she stood gazing in disbelief at Gunnet's retreating figure.

Then panic jerked her into action and she ran, stumbling, falling, getting to her feet, struggling forward again and shouting.

'Gunnet, wait! Don't leave me. Gunnet, do you hear? Don't you dare leave me alone.'

He stopped and turned a sardonic gaze on her as,

forgetting modesty in the anxiety of the moment, she lifted her skirt and struggled towards him with ungainly, plunging steps.

'It's up to you,' he said. 'I told you we've got to keep going.'

'There's surely no need to go at such a pace.'

'Once we slow down, the next stage is stopping to rest.'

'Well, what would be wrong with that?'

'Before we would realize what was happening we would be overcome by sleep, a sleep we would never awaken from. I've seen it happen. Come on. We mustn't weaken.'

She followed him as best as she could, keeping her skirts hitched up because otherwise she couldn't walk without tripping and falling. When she had fallen her cries of distress did not bring Gunnet to her assistance and she had been forced to struggle to her feet by herself, her clothes becoming wetter each time.

Sometimes the wind dropped and the air cleared of snow and she could at least breathe easier and see where she was going. But her leg muscles felt as if they were being torn apart. Each heavy, dragging step had become agony. Pain was now twisting up her back and her whole body felt strained beyond endurance.

Sobbing burst out like anger. Her clothes, especially her drawers, were soaked and turning to ice against her skin. She was wet and cold and miserable and absolutely exhausted. It was impossible to go on like this. They had reached a hillock on which bent a few trees as if ready to snap with the weight of snow on their branches. Leaning against one she found its support an exquisite relief.

'Gunnet,' she called. 'Wait. I can't go on any further. I just haven't the strength.'

'You can do anything if you've a will to. *Will* yourself.'

'How can I?' she said brokenly. 'That takes strength as well.'

'Even you can find that kind of strength.'

'No, I can't.'

'The alternative is to give up and die.'

'No, it is not. You have strength. You can help me.'

'I am helping you.'

'You are not helping me.' She raised her voice in anger despite tears of weakness. 'You are no use at all. You ignorant brute of a man. It is well seen that you are a common servant and not a gentleman.'

'Oh, yes,' he gave a burst of derisive laughter. 'I know what you expected, you spoiled, pampered little brat. You're a fine one to talk about being useless. You've never done a day's work in your foolish, shallow life. Well, you're not getting what you expected from me, not here, not now. So, come on.'

He strode away beyond the trees and disappeared down the other side of the hillock.

Fury as well as fear spurred her on. Ignoring the agony it caused, she forced her body to propel itself after him.

'How dare you speak to me like that! My father shall hear of this.'

'Your equally pampered and stupid mother has probably signed your father's death warrant by keeping him back there,' he shouted without turning round.

'You wicked cruel man. How could you say such a thing?'

'Because it's the truth.'

'I do not believe you. Papa knows what he is doing. He would not endanger Mama's life. They will be sheltered there, warm and safe under the fur rug. Oh, how I wish I was with them!'

'Make no mistake about it, I wish you were there too!'

The sky had become heavy and metallic and was glowering down at them as if it too was black-hearted and angry.

'It'll be dark soon,' she accused. 'And then what'll we do?'

He did not reply and she shouted again:

'Gunnet, answer me!'

'Give your tongue a rest.'

'How dare you! How dare you!'

Her words feebled as her strength was taken up in

concentrating on withstanding the bluster of wind that tugged at her clothes and the new biting strength of snow that attacked her.

The blizzard grew to furious proportions. She could no longer see Gunnet. Like a blind woman she stumbled along with no idea in which direction she was going. The wind tore at her coat, ripping it open, snapping it behind her like a flag and leaving her vulnerable to icy wetness. With strength she never knew she possessed she fought against the elements. She fought beyond her strength until she seemed to become mad – not insane with reckless fury like the storm but buffeted and bewildered into a kind of airy-headed idiocy. Even the pain left her. A numbness crept over her limbs.

The numbness was a blessing, a sweet relief. It brought with it soothing drowsiness, a warm blanket of sleep into which she gratefully sank. Then through the heavy black velvet under which she sheltered, she did not know nor care for how long, she began to feel ripples of disturbance and unwelcome pain. From far-off a voice penetrated her sleep.

'Wake up! Come on!'

She was being shaken. Head lolling about, she groaned in protest.

'I'll carry you but you mustn't sleep. Fight it, do you hear?'

A particularly vicious shake brought a glimpse of Gunnet's face close to hers. Yet she could do nothing to protect herself. She was only vaguely aware of being swung into the air and tossed across his shoulder. Her head and arms dangled down and for a few minutes she remained dazedly conscious before succumbing to sleep again. A cry from Gunnet pierced the woolliness of her mind. She thought he said something about a shepherd's bothy or a hut for storing hay but his voice was a long, long way off and she no longer cared about it.

Some time later, annoyance dragged her unwillingly back to consciousness and pain. She was lying on a bed of straw and Gunnet, on his knees beside her, was rubbing her bare feet with snow. Her skin had the sickly white colour of death. She shivered with distaste.

'I'll have to get these wet clothes off,' she heard him say.

Her eyelids were heavy and she kept drifting far away. Yet his voice kept reaching her, goading her to make the effort to open her eyes. It was during one of these moments of muzzy consciousness that she saw him pull off her undergarments and then start to unfasten her dress. A sense of outrage struggled to reach the surface. She made an attempt to move, to push him away, moaning in rising alarm and distress.

'That's right,' he said. 'Come on. Fight me. Anger will help to get your blood circulating again.'

Now he had her in his arms and was peeling off her icicle of a coat and dress.

'How dare you,' she managed. 'Take your hands off me.'

'If these wet clothes are left on, you'll freeze. I'll wrap you in my cape.'

Tears trickled down her cheeks and she closed her eyes, surrendering to oblivion, unable to face the shame of his gaze on her nakedness. Cleaving to the darkness, despite the fact that he was shaking her again, she withdrew far away from him in her mind. Then gradually she became alive to a strange excitement. The enormity of realizing that Gunnet was wrapped close to her inside the cape, his skin hot against hers, was confused by a tingling ecstasy as his fingers explored her most secret places.

Gasping, and in a frenzy of will, she fought to push him back. His creased eyes with their mocking smile remained close, came closer, his voice softly intimate.

'I thought that would waken you up.'

She meant to cry out in protest but his mouth silenced her. Astonished at the delight his kiss brought she did not struggle against it at first but became, for a few minutes, completely absorbed. Even the sounds of the storm outside were erased. Until suddenly out of the sweet silence came a welter of emotions that she had never experienced before. Like a delirium their strangeness agitated her and frightened her and she felt compelled to protect herself against them. Once more she began to fight him. Ignoring the pain in her limbs she lashed out with them and struggled to toss her head from side to side. He laughed quietly, not breaking the intimacy, the secret world they were cocooned in.

Then as his mouth found hers she melted, and his hand cupped her breast and gently kneaded it and plucked and pulled at its nipple. A vein of heat stretched down from her breasts and spread over her lower abdomen like a pain. She moaned with the ecstasy of it and spread her thighs wide, desperate for relief; and it came when something plunged hard inside her. At the same time the ecstasy increased like waves of madness, forcing little breathless screams from her, high-pitched with astonishment and delight, completely scattering thought. And eventually she collapsed, loose with exhaustion.

She must have slept, for the next thing she knew was the sun streaming into the hut. Gunnet was nowhere to be seen and the door was lying open. A piece of paper rustled inside the cape when she moved and finding it she read: 'I've hung your clothes on the side of the hut. The sun will soon dry them. This hut suggests there's a farm nearby. I've gone to look over the other side of the hill.'

She dressed automatically, her mind still submerged in physical gratification. The warm sun seemed to expand through her like joy and she gave herself up to the thoughtless, sensual moment, her face raised and eyes closed.

When she opened her eyes again she observed an unusual sight. A strange contraption was being pushed towards her by two horses. What looked like two broad pieces of wood, standing on end and joined at the front in a pointed nose, were cutting through the snow. The horses were dragging behind them an enormous block of wood that was flattening the snow. On top of the wood and holding the reins a ruddy-faced man was perched on a chair. Following the whole contraption rode several horsemen. As they came

40

nearer Augusta recognized one of them as Gunnet. He spurred his horse ahead and when he reached her he said:

'I'll get one of the others to take you to the farmhouse. I must find your father and mother.'

Chapter Five

Although cramped and stiff, Mr and Mrs Cameron had survived the ordeal remarkably well. The snow had drifted up around the coach but had not completely covered it; in fact it had protected them from the bitterly cold wind and insulated them from the worst of the storm.

The coach, righted with the help of the farmer and a couple of his workers, and supplied with a fresh team of horses from the same source, had not suffered any serious damage so after a period of rest and refreshment they were able to continue on their journey. Eventually, without further mishap, they arrived on the outskirts of London and were soon entering a district of very elegant houses. Turning into one of the most impressive driveways, they pulled up in front of the Fitzjames residence.

Augusta had sat for the remainder of the journey without saying a word, not moving a muscle. She had not yet recovered from the shock of all that had happened, and still quickened in terror when thoughts of the blizzard penetrated her defences. She had to keep assuring herself that it was in the past and that she was perfectly safe now. What had taken place with the coachman during the night was too shocking to contemplate. She erased it, pretended it had not occurred at all. Gunnet had never looked at her since the journey was resumed, nor at any of the inns on the way had she allowed her eyes to stray in his direction.

Now, as the coach and four entered the gates and cantered along the drive towards Fitzjames Hall, she forced her head up and the sight that met her eyes helped divert her mind from its turmoil.

Mrs Cameron, despite her fatigue, was also rallied to

attention by the grandeur of the place with its east and west wings and pillared frontage. She exclaimed to her husband in delight at the lines of footmen in powdered wigs and white gloves who were waiting to receive them as the horses came to a halt in front of the entrance.

They were helped to alight and led into the house. Still half-dazed but somehow managing to retain a stiff, dignified composure, Augusta followed her mother into an assembly hall ornamented with a wrought-iron staircase, oil paintings in gilt frames and statues draped in white. The stairs led up to the right then strung across the hall to the left, parallel with a landing fronted by pillars which soared upwards to a curved ceiling painted in delicate shades of pink, green and blue.

Eventually she reached a bedroom dominated by an exotic bed with a gilt canopy hung with drapes of deep peach and green. A maid provided water to wash away the dust of the journey, and also unpacked her clothes and helped Augusta to do her hair and change into a fresh gown. Then she rejoined her parents on the landing and they were all escorted to a lofty room that sent Mrs Cameron into a paroxysm of excitement. The footman had barely finished announcing their names when she hastened forward, eyes darting appreciatively about and crying:

'Delightful! Delightful!'

Mr Cameron went booming across, hand outstretched, to meet his host and hostess, ruddy face bursting with enthusiasm.

'A grand place you have here. To be frank and honest I've never seen such a grand place in my life, and we have some fine houses in Glasgow. I've a fine house myself.'

Lieutenant Fitzjames wandered forward to breach the second in which his parents gazed down at Cameron's hand as if it was vaguely revolting.

'Allow me to present my mother and father . . .'

Mrs Fitzjames offered limp fingers. She was a tall woman who looked as if she refused to acknowledge the existence of anyone below the level of her nose. Her husband had a

42

long face like a horse. They both had a weary, disinterested appearance as if, beneath an all too thin veneer of polite attention, they were miles away across a vast no-man's land.

Augusta perceived, however, an occasional glimmer of interest in her direction and once Mr Fitzjames had murmured to his son:

'A fine beauty. Ought to carry on the family name with some pride.'

She felt some relief that she seemed to have gained acceptance. But a worrying tenseness remained on her parents' behalf. The Fitzjameses seemed to be treating them with almost insulting coolness. Not that Felicity, fussing and plucking at her skirts, patting her ringlets and fluttering her eyelashes, seemed to have noticed. Her father also seemed completely oblivious to anything being amiss as he relaxed back on the sofa puffing at his cigar.

Augusta's concern only pricked the surface of her mind, however. Her recent experience had distanced her from herself. On the outside a beautiful mask managed occasionally to smile and murmur polite answers if anyone spoke to her. This outside self sat straight-backed at the piano in the noble drawing-room, fingers caressing the keys as she sang and Lieutenant Fitzjames turned the pages of her music.

Inside, far away in darkness, there wandered an unrelated, bewildered creature. She ignored it. She listened to the wedding plans being discussed. She learned with wonder that as well as a town establishment she and the lieutenant were to be given the Fitzjameses' country seat when the lieutenant resigned his commission. Yet still the animal creature wandered like a lost soul.

A ball had been arranged the next evening to officially celebrate the couple's engagement.

'Mercy,' cried Felicity, as later in her bedroom deliberations were held about which gown would be most appropriate to wear, 'there will even be lords and ladies there. Oh, isn't it exciting? Oh, Augusta, aren't you absolutely thrilled.'

'Yes, Mama.'

Felicity clasped her hands together and hugged them under her chin.

'Oh, I can hardly wait to be back in Glasgow to tell everyone. Can't you just see their faces? They will be ill with envy. Absolutely ill!'

Next day they rode through the park. Then there was the shopping expedition, and the thrill of the teeming London streets viewed from the luxurious safety of the Fitzjames carriage. Then the immediate preparations for the ball and the heady excitement of the occasion itself.

Amidst all this, Gunnet and the incredible journey from Glasgow were swept further and further away.

The ball was so breathtaking in its grandeur that Augusta at last felt liberated from her secret nightmare. The nightmare was conquered by fashionable gowns shimmering all around, blinding her, enclosing her in the magic of a rainbow. It was chased like a shadow by blazing jewellery and chandeliers bright as stars. It was charmed away by elegant, attentive gentlemen, and none more elegant or attentive than her own Lieutenant Fitzjames. It was swirled to airy nothing in his arms, to the lilt of a Strauss waltz.

By the time the ball was over and she had returned to the privacy of her bedroom at Fitzjames Hall, she was as excited as her mother. The only thing that clung from her recent experiences was a sensuous stirring, a glow, an awareness of pleasures she had never known existed before. But without allowing the coachman to take shape and defile even the vaguest part of her mind, her instincts rushed in to assure her that this was part of what marriage would mean. Already the lieutenant had stolen quite a few kisses but they had been politely restrained, formal. This was the conduct most befitting to a gentleman. He had kissed her hand, her brow, her cheeks, even her lips, and she had reacted with appropriate degrees of coyness and modesty. A gentle, respectful and affectionate relationship developed between them that was a great comfort to Augusta.

Gradually she also established some sort of rapport with Mrs Fitzjames and if not open admiration and esteem at

44

least a probationary acceptance. This was indicated by the fact that when the visit came to an end and they were bidding their goodbyes, the limp hands were once again offered to Mr and Mrs Cameron but Mrs Fitzjames honoured Augusta by bestowing on her a kiss on the cheek, a cold, fleeting kiss but a kiss nevertheless.

The rows of footmen were once again standing to attention as they approached the Cameron coach and one of them helped the ladies to climb in before bowing and backing away.

'You lucky girl!' her mother cried ecstatically as the coach clattered off. 'Oh, aren't you a lucky girl, Augusta?'

'Yes, Mama,' she said. And she was truly grateful.

Chapter Six

Felicity fluttered among her guests like a butterfly in a flower garden. The drawing-room was a tableau of colour. Mrs Laidlaw-Smythe looked magnificent in gold silk brocade trimmed with black. Her hair was drawn severely up from her imperious face and knotted on top of her head, and she held her lorgnette constantly at the ready. Her daughter Polly cringed nearby in coffee-coloured silk with layers of cream frills that tried to cover her lack of bosom.

Plump Mrs Binny wore turquoise silk and her daughters Mary and Fay sat close together looking like sweet peas in heliotrope taffeta and yellow satin. Even Miss Ina Fotheringham and her twin sister Kate, gaunt, sour-faced spinsters, looked rather fetching in their gowns of eau-de-nil muslin and sherry-coloured velvet.

They all were drinking tea from fragile, fluted cups, while the gentlemen of the company were still in the dining-room enjoying brandy and cigars.

It had been a triumph of an evening. The cook had surpassed herself with the dinner, but quite apart from the food it had been most delectable to discuss Augusta's forthcoming marriage. The ladies politely smiled and made appropriate murmurs, but they were ill with envy and struggled bravely to conceal it. Augusta couldn't help admiring them for accepting her mother's invitation in the first place and subjecting themselves to the torture of hearing all about the grandeurs of the Fitzjames way of life; to sit through the whole evening and manage with tolerable success to cling to dignity and decorum was truly remarkable of them in the circumstances.

Certainly Felicity Cameron's delirious joy and delight must be a sore trial to her guests. She looked so light-hearted it would have surprised no one if the diminutive figure in the gown of rose pink silk had suddenly taken flight and soared up to the ceiling. Her ringlets bounced this way and that as she sought to make absolutely certain that each of the ladies had everything provided.

'Mercy upon us, Miss Fotheringham, your cup is nearly empty. McPherson, attend to Miss Fotheringham at once!'

'You are too kind.' Ina Fotheringham's tight mouth somehow tugged into a smile.

'Mercy! Are you quite comfortable there, Harriet? McPherson, bring another cushion for Mrs Laidlaw-Smythe.'

Murder glinted from Mrs Laidlaw-Smythe's lorgnette but her voice retained its polite Edinburgh accent. 'I am perfectly comfortable, Felicity. I do not believe in cushions. They are not conducive to a good straight back.'

'You are right, of course. I am such a simple soul I tend to stray from these excellent edicts. Shall I take poor Polly's cushion away, dear?'

Polly who had almost folded up into the cushions sprang back before her mother could fix a furious lorgnette upon her.

'There is no need, Felicity,' said Mrs Laidlaw-Smythe. 'Polly simply ignores what she has no wish for. The men that girl could have had! But she is just not interested.'

'Such a pity,' sympathized Mrs Cameron. 'I'm so thankful Augusta accepted the dear lieutenant's offer. Did I tell you that the Fitzjameses have a country seat too? Such acres and acres of land as far as the eye can see. Mr Cameron will want to go there for the hunting, of course, but I prefer the delights of London. The theatre, the opera, the magnificent shops. Such clothes you just would not believe. Oh, mercy, what fashions! We have nothing like that here. Mrs Fitzjames insisted that I come to visit as often as the fancy takes me.' Felicity patted her ringlets. 'Such a charming woman. And, of course, they all adored dear Augusta and went into such raptures about how exquisite she looked, and how well-bred and virtuous she was.'

Indeed Augusta at that moment looked very pretty with the crown of tiny flowers perched on top of her golden ringlets and a virgin white dress flattering her rose-petal skin and bright eyes.

Mrs Binny, purple with both fury and heat, flapped her fan energetically in front of her dumpling face.

'Dear Mrs Binny,' Felicity cried, 'you are suffering from the heat. McPherson, help Binny to a seat further from the fire. Mercy, I know only too well what it is to suffer from heat. At the grand ball the Fitzjameses gave to celebrate Augusta's engagement of marriage to their dear son I danced so much and the enormous ballroom was so crowded there were times I thought I was going to faint. Of course, it was not only the heat, as you can imagine, it was all the excitement too. Why, there were so many lords and ladies there I felt quite flustered. And of course they all remarked on what a delightful match the happy pair made . . .'

Remembering the ball and the thrill and splendour of London, thinking of how she was actually soon to belong to that magnificent world of which her mother had been chattering at such length, made Augusta feel delightfully happy. In fact Felicity Cameron's joy transported them both into a euphoria which lasted for days after the dinner party. It was only spoiled by vague feelings of malaise that gradually created an irritation of temper that Augusta could not control.

At breakfast one morning while her mama was chattering

47

blissfully, a wave of physical nausea made her cry out in distress.

'Oh, Mama, will you stop going on so! You are making me feel quite ill with nervous excitement.'

Felicity was struck dumb with astonishment at her daughter's unaccustomed impertinence and before she could recover speech Augusta had pushed back her plate and rushed from the dining-room.

Upstairs, Augusta wrung her hands in irritation and regret. But it had been impossible to hold her emotions in check. Now it was becoming more difficult to control the waves of nausea that were threatening to engulf her. Suddenly she pattered across the room to the wash-stand which held the pottery bowl and jug. Just in time she removed the jug before vomiting into the bowl. Then she leaned against the wall as cold perspiration forced its way like pins and needles through her pores. She felt weak and drained. It really was too bad of Mama to upset her like this. Averting her face from the revolting contents of the bowl she went to the bell-pull to summon the maid.

When Tibs came hurrying into the room, Augusta pointed to the bowl. 'Take that away, please, and see that it's cleaned properly before you bring it back.'

'Yes, mistress.' Tibs gave a quick little bob before rushing to do as she was told.

After she had gone, Augusta lay down on the bed for a few minutes to make certain she had recovered properly before returning downstairs. She would have to apologize profusely to her mother. She was ashamed at her most regrettable lack of control. At last she felt strong enough to get up. Smoothing down her slate-blue dress and straightening the flat white collar that covered her shoulders, she tipped up her head and in a determined effort to retain her dignity swished from the room.

Chapter Seven

'The problem is space,' sighed Felicity. 'When Mrs Laid-law-Smythe and Polly come through to the wedding they will just have to share a room.'

'I suppose we must invite them?' murmured Augusta. She was still feeling far from well. On several occasions during the past few days the sickness had returned to distress her though she had not mentioned it to her mother.

'Of course, dear. Harriet is one of my oldest friends.' Studying the guest list, Felicity nibbled the end of her pen before continuing. 'You see, there's Mr and Mrs Loudon from Inverness. We will need a bedroom for them.'

'Oh, Mama, we hardly know them. I thought you didn't even like Mrs Loudon.'

'Mercy, of course I don't like her, dear. She's a most obnoxiously vain peacock of a woman. I'd love to have seen her face when she read my letter of invitation. I told her all about the Fitzjameses, of course.'

In the silence that followed Augusta willed herself not to succumb to the strange giddiness that was now besetting her. With at least outward calm she continued to stitch at her embroidery. The parlour seemed hot and airless. Tibs had built up the fire and the light from it was jerking the room about. Augusta blinked then raised her head to aim an eye-stretching stare at the painting on the wall opposite. She willed herself to keep the picture in view, to use it to steady herself. But even as she watched it, the painting rippled and distorted as if she was viewing it through a running brook. Then it flew away into nothing.

The next thing she was aware of was that she was lying on the sofa with McPherson bending over her, flapping her apron. She gazed up at the servant in bewilderment.

'What happened?'

'You fainted, Miss. You gave your mama a terrible fright. The master is attending to her now.'

With McPherson's help Augusta struggled to a sitting position. Her mother was reclining on the chair opposite sipping a glass of brandy, her father anxiously standing over his wife.

'Mama, I'm so sorry. I don't know what came over me.'

Cameron screwed round a harassed face. 'Are you all right now?'

'Yes, Papa.'

'Mercy, it really is too bad of you, Augusta,' wailed Felicity. 'I know the wedding is an exciting prospect but that is no excuse to allow your emotions to overcome you like this. My heart is still fluttering at the fright you gave me. I don't know what I would have done if your papa had not been here.'

'I am sorry, Mama. Really I am. I don't know what . . .'

'Oh, come on, girl. You've caused enough trouble,' said Cameron. 'It's time we went through for dinner.'

The thought of food stirred up nausea in Augusta. 'I'm afraid I don't feel very hungry. May I miss dinner and retire early instead?'

Felicity sighed. 'Oh, very well.'

Augusta rose, testing the ground with her feet as if it were dangerous. Then she pattered over to her parents and kissed them to bid them goodnight. It was like kissing stone statues. It occurred to Augusta that they had never shown her much real affection. That they loved each other she had no doubt, but she wondered for the first time if they truly cared about her.

In her room, she summoned Tibs to help her undress, lecturing the girl severely about having laced her stays so tight she had been made to feel faint. Yes, that was the explanation, she told herself. Left alone, Augusta lay back in the bed. Her eyes strayed over the room. On the flat top of the dressing-table stood the silver candlesticks and her ornate silver-backed brushes and tortoiseshell combs with their silver handles, her scent bottles, her ring stand, and her pretty cabaret de toilette of china. All were part of her life and she found pleasure from recognizable things like these among her new perplexities.

Eventually she drifted off to sleep, until the rattling noise of curtains being drawn awakened her. Then Tibs was lighting the fire and putting a hot water can next to the washstand. Augusta watched the girl bring a clothes-horse from a cupboard and hang clothes on it to air ready for when she arose to wash and dress.

For no apparent reason the sight of Tibs distressed her and panic rose with sickness in her throat.

'Bring me the bowl – quickly!' Augusta's sudden spasm of retching made Tibs dart into action and get the bowl under her face just in time.

'Oh, dear, oh, dear,' she wailed. 'Shall I fetch the mistress?'

'No.' Augusta flopped back against the pillows in wretchedness and exhaustion. 'Perhaps a cup of tea might help. Bring me a tray, please.'

'Yes, miss.' The girl flew for the door still clutching the bowl.

The tea did help and, surprisingly, so did the biscuits that Cook sent up. After nibbling at a couple of them and sipping the tea, she felt in fact perfectly restored. But she arose with care and took her time over dressing.

Downstairs in the dining-room she was able to greet her parents in her normal manner as if nothing was amiss, although her father remarked on how little she ate for breakfast.

After he left for his office, she and her mama went through to the parlour, and it became evident that Mrs Cameron had more to discuss than what shopping and sewing they still needed to do for the trousseau. Her mother propped herself up with cushions on the sofa, clutching a lace-edged handkerchief and with a bottle of smelling-salts to hand. Augusta sat on the chair opposite and picked up her embroidery.

'Put that down at once,' Felicity said. 'I want to talk to you.'

'Yes, Mama.' Augusta arranged her embroidery on the little table at the side of her chair then sat with hands folded neatly on her lap.

'Have you been sick?'

'I have, Mama. It has been most distressing. I didn't mention it because I didn't want to worry you.'

'In the mornings?'

'At other times too, but mostly in the mornings.'

Felicity held her handkerchief to her temple and closed her eyes for a long moment, Augusta watched her with interest.

'Augusta,' she continued eventually, 'have you missed your . . . your monthly indisposition?'

'Why, yes, Mama.'

'Oh, mercy upon us!' Felicity's suddenly loudening voice disturbed and confused Augusta. 'Mercy upon us, you must be with child!'

'But, Mama –'

'There are no "buts" about it. Of course we will seek confirmation from a doctor but it is only too obvious. Oh, what are we going to do?'

Augusta, having no idea, kept silent.

'Augusta, how could you?' Felicity wailed.

'How could I what, Mama?'

'You know perfectly well what I mean. Oh, to think you could be so immodest. To think you could have allowed the lieutenant to take such liberties.'

'But I didn't –'

'There's no use trying to deceive me any longer and there's no use trying to excuse yourself by blaming the lieutenant.'

'No, I wasn't –'

'It is entirely up to a lady to set the standards of modesty and decorum. You should never have allowed him to touch you.'

'To touch me?'

'What I cannot fathom, Augusta, is where and how you got the opportunity. You were practically never alone with the lieutenant.' Mrs Cameron closed her eyes again. 'You didn't . . . you couldn't have allowed him into your bed one night? Oh, mercy, mercy, the wicked wantonness of it!'

Augusta sat still and stiff-backed. But colour had drained from her face and her eyes had melted and widened into abstraction. The nightmare was creeping back. It was a dangerous animal lurking in the black shadows of her mind. Frightened, she strung out thoughts like rosary beads. *It couldn't be true. It mustn't be true. Such a thing was impossible.*

'Your father will have to be told. We will have to decide what to do,' her mother was saying. 'Send one of the maids to tell Mr Cameron to return here immediately.'

'Are you sure that is necessary, Mama? Papa might not take kindly to being sent for.'

'Of course it's necessary. Do as you're told at once, Augusta.'

'Yes, Mama.' She went over to the escritoire where she penned a brief note and sealed it in an envelope. Then she corssed to the bell-pull.

Very shortly, McPherson entered and after a graceful curtsy stood dutifully waiting.

'Tell Tibs to deliver this note to the master in his office,' Augusta said.

'Yes, miss.' McPherson took the note and bobbed down and up again before leaving.

After she had gone, Felicity moaned, 'Oh, mercy upon us, to think that the servants will know. Oh, I cannot bear the shame of it. I shall be ill. You selfish, ungrateful girl – did you not even think of ordering me a cup of tea to help comfort and revive me?'

'I'm sorry, Mama.' Augusta returned to the bell-pull. Both a mental and physical agitation were building up in her so that she no longer felt in command of herself. She was a small craft at the mercy of a stormy and uncharted ocean.

In between sipping her tea, her mother kept moaning and holding her handkerchief to her temple and repeating:

53

'What are we going to do? What are we going to do? The lieutenant will have to be told for a start. Oh, the shame of it! When I think of how Mr and Mrs Fitzjames will never again be able to regard you as sweet or innocent or modest, since you are none of these things, you dreadful, shocking creature . . .'

Beginning to sniffle, she laid aside her cup to dab at her eyes and revive herself with smelling-salts. 'How could you do this to me, Augusta? All the arrangements will have to be changed. The wedding date will have to be brought forward. I can't bear it . . . Gossiping tongues will wag. Something must be done to allay people's suspicions.'

Suddenly she sat erect. 'The lieutenant could arrange for an immediate posting abroad. Yes, that would be a believable excuse. The wedding date would quite understandably then have to be brought forward.' She relaxed back against the cushions. 'Thank God! But, mercy, what a rush it's going to be.'

Just then Cameron strode into the room.

'What's wrong, Mrs Cameron? Are you ill? I have come as fast as I could. I knew you would not send to my office unless something serious had happened.'

'Oh, Mr Cameron!' Felicity's tears returned and she stretched out her arms to her husband.

He hastened to sit beside her on the sofa and nurse her close to him. 'Tell me what is wrong. Why are you so distraught?'

'You will find this hard to believe, Mr Cameron,' Felicity sobbed against his chest, 'and I am sorry that you have to hear it, but hear it you must. Tell your papa, Augusta. Go on. Tell him!'

'Mama says I am with child, Papa.'

The clock on the mantelshelf ticked loudly through the horrified silence. Cameron's face sagged with shock and his fleshy lips hung open. Eventually, his eyes shifting about, not looking at either woman, he spoke.

'Is this true?'

'Oh, I don't think there's any doubt about it,' Felicity replied.

'My own daughter,' Cameron's voice gathered righteous indignation, 'guilty of fornication! Despite the good Christian upbringing I've tried to give her. You know what it says in the Good Book?' he turned, eyes now bulging with anger, on Augusta. 'You know what it says about filthy fornicators?'

'Mercy upon us, Mr Cameron, talk about the Bible or anything else won't help us now. We got to *do* something. The wedding date will have to be brought forward for a start.'

'How do you propose we do that?'

'You'll have to write the lieutenant a letter and send it off immediately by special messenger.'

'God know how long it will take even by special messenger. The weather is still not dependable.'

'But it would be better than waiting for the Mail, would it not?'

'I suppose so.' Cameron poured himself a large whisky, then went over to the writing-desk. He thumped down on a chair in front of it.

'Forgive me, Papa – ' Augusta began.

'No, I shall not forgive you, Augusta. Your behaviour has been unforgivable. And you have caused your mother and myself great and quite unnecessary distress. A few months was surely not too long to expect you to wait before sleeping with Lieutenant Fitzjames?'

Augusta had begun to tremble so much the tight grip of her hands seemed the only thing that was holding her together. Even her clusters of ringlets were shivering.

'I didn't sleep with Lieutenant Fitzjames, Papa.' Eyes, enormous and vulnerable, waited in apprehension.

'Spare us the sordid details,' Felicity cried. 'What does it matter where it happened?'

'But, Mama, doesn't it matter if the lieutenant knows it wasn't him?'

'You stupid girl! Of course he'll know it was him. He had his way with you, hadn't he?'

'No.'

'Could you credit such deceit? Could you credit it, Mr Cameron? As if we haven't been deceived enough already.'

'It wasn't my fault, Mama. I tried to stop him.'

Cameron groaned. 'I think she's gone wrong in the head as well. First she says he didn't, then he did, then – '

'It was the night of the blizzard, Papa. It was Gunnet I was with.'

In the silence that rocked the room, Felicity's face acquired an idiotic expression. Cameron rose, looking stunned in disbelief.

'Gunnet? You mean Gunnet is responsible? You mean it's his child? Gunnet?'

All of a sudden Felicity let out a high-pitched wail, making Augusta leap to her feet in alarm.

'The coachman? A common servant?' her mother screeched.

'Oh, Mama, please . . .' Augusta ran across the room to try to loosen Felicity's clothing or do something, anything to help her, for her hysterics reached such abandon that she was making strange noises that sounded indeed as if she had taken a fit.

'A common servant! Everybody will know. Get her away from me. No wedding. Nothing but shame and disgrace. Keep her away from me. Don't let her touch me. I never want anything to do with her again.'

Cameron strode over, jerked his daughter roughly aside and then, to her astonishment and pain, crashed the back of his hand against her face.

'You filthy slut! Get out of this house and don't come back.'

The loathing in his eyes shocked her. She remained staring up at him in bewilderment until he grabbed and forcibly hurtled her from the room.

In the cool, quiet hall she could still hear her mother's screams, now muffled by the heavy doors.

In a daze she wandered from the house, through George Square and away down Queen Street. A cold wind knifed through her dress and ruffled her curls, but she was hardly aware of it. It was as if she moved in a dream. Then some children running past bumped into her, making her clutch at a shop door lintel to save herself from falling. It was then that she realized she was in Argyle Street.

She gazed around. Never before in her life had she been out alone, and never without a carriage. The teeming thoroughfare with its side streets and wynds leading from it looked alien, threatening. She felt lost on the edge of a dark continent.

Chapter Eight

A tangle of noise and strange cries swirled around her.

'Buy a trap! A rat trap! Buy my trap!'

The man had a nose black with warts, a long chin and small, shifty eyes like those of the rat he was carrying in one of the cages slung over his arm. Augusta averted her gaze from the revolting apparition. A dog was following the man, barking loudly and ceaselessly.

Jostled along by the crowd, Augusta became more and more aware of noise. It battered at her temples and reeled inside her head. Towering tenements on either side of the cobbled street contained the bedlam-like prison walls.

The Tron Church across the road with its square, dumpy tower jutting out from the tenements made the thoroughfare narrower at that part of the street. Further along on the side on which she was walking she passed the elegant arches of the Tontine Hotel. Beyond that reared the Tolbooth clock, chiming high above the heedless milling throng. Past the Cross she found herself in Gallowgate Street. The very name frightened her and she hesitated, allowing herself to be pushed aimlessly this way and that.

Suddenly a deafening cheer arose from the crowd. It confused her more than ever until she saw the reason for it

57

in the shape of the Royal Mail coach with its four steaming black horses racing towards the Cross with the guard blowing lustily at his bugle.

Then she was swept onwards like a leaf in the wind in her green dress, and the coach disappeared from her bewildered gaze. Now the tenements looked meaner. Archways or tunnel-like openings in the buildings led to narrow passageways between them. Along these passages a forest of poles jutted from windows on either side. On the poles flapped rags of wet clothing.

The shops became smaller than those of Argyle Street and Trongate Street. Ancient shops with bow windows with tiny panes of glass had shutters folded back against the walls. Shops like caverns had no windows at all. In the shadows of one of these she saw a cobbler bending low over his lathe. A hooked nose stuck out grotesquely from his close-fitting leather hat, making him look like an evil gnome. A grocer's shop now, the smell of food adding pangs of hunger to her distress. She stopped in utter helplessness, not knowing which way to turn, and rain came whipping along with the wind to prick her face and make her blink. Within minutes her ringlets were straggling wetly across her cheeks and trailing down on to her white collar. The dampness of her dress made her shiver.

'This is my pitch!' a woman's voice suddenly shouted close to her face. 'F... off, you cow, or I'll scratch your eyes out.' The woman grabbed her arm and pitched her forward with such force that Augusta stumbled and fell. Some people in the crowd laughed and no one came to her assistance until as she was struggling up from the muddy ground a voice cried,

'Och, would you look at the poor wee sowl.'

An arm went around her and helped her to her feet.

'Holy Mother of God, you shouldn't be out on a day like this and without even a bonnet to your head or a shawl to your shoulders.'

Augusta stared at her rescuer. A witless grinning face

stared back. She had seen it before but couldn't remember where.

'Come away with Biddy. Mistress Nessie'll give you a seat at the fire.'

Augusta allowed herself to be led back towards the Cross and then along Trongate Street and Argyle Street.

'Nessie sent me to the Colonel's Old Shop for sugar,' Biddy the skivvy confided. 'It's in the Gallowgate and it's cheaper, so it is.'

She went on chattering but the rain and wind snatched away her words as soon as they were uttered. Augusta did her best to stumble along beside the girl. Her mind was now completely paralysed by her physical discomforts. Her white kid shoes with their soft soles and dainty cross-straps tied round her ankles were like paper against the cutting edge of stones. Mud filled them, squelching icily between her toes. Her dress flapped wetly against her shivering body and she had to keep tearing the plaster of hair from her face so that she could see where she was going.

Up Queen Street now and into George Square, the sight of the house blanking her mind with confusion. Before she could form coherent thought, Biddy had hurried her into West George Street and cut to the left again into a courtyard where a steep flight of stone stairs led down to a doorway she had never seen before. When it opened she found herself in the kitchen quarters of Cameron House. Even this was not a familiar place. She had seldom set foot in it, preferring to summon the servants to the parlour when she had to pass on any of her mother's orders.

The Cameron kitchen was a warm cavern. From inside the house it was reached by a door underneath the hall staircase that led down more stairs to another door, opening on to the kitchen area. At the other end a door led out to the stone stairs and yard. The window next to the back door looked out on to these stairs and so didn't get much light, but the blazing fire at which Nessie the cook laboured brightened the place and gave it a welcoming glow.

A long scrubbed wooden table in the middle of the floor

was surrounded by plenty of chairs, one of which with wooden arms and a knitted cushion was Nessie's throne. There, between the serious business of stirring pots and rolling pastry, she rested her bad legs. The stone flagged floor was cruel to the rheumatics and varicose veins. The shelves and a dresser nearby were adorned with russet and cream patterned crockery. The light from the open range reflected cosily on dinner plates, side plates and saucers propped up on end, and cups and jugs dangling on hooks, and soup and vegetable tureens crowding the top of the cupboard with a brass oil lamp.

A tap under the window indicated that water had been piped into the kitchen but water did not always appear when the tap was turned on, and this unreliability proved an excruciating worry when any of the Camerons demanded a bath and enough water needed to be carried upstairs to one of the bedrooms to fill the tin bath. A much smaller room off the kitchen was where Nessie and her husband Sid Cruickshanks slept and kept their personal belongings, while the rest of the servants slept in cupboards of attic rooms under the roof of the house.

On seeing Augusta now, Nessie's eyes squeezed shut and bulged open again so energetically that her cap, inside which was bundled a surfeit of white hair, wobbled about on her head. Sid removed the pipe from his mouth, contemplated Augusta's bedraggled figure then replaced the pipe and studied the door behind her. McPherson, immaculate in a bombazine dress and white apron, stood staring at Augusta with a faintly contemptuous air.

'Would you look at the poor wee sowl?' Biddy announced to them. 'Out without a bonnet or a shawl, so she was.'

Nessie was the first to recover. Bustling over to Augusta she led her to the high-backed chair by the fire.

'Fiona,' she snapped, 'go upstairs and pack a bag with Miss Augusta's things. Her hair brush and comb. All her toilet things and her nightdress and underclothes and dresses and cloaks. As much as you can get in.'

'I can't do that!' McPherson protested. 'What's the mistress going to say?'

'Do as you're told and less of your cheek. The mistress never goes into that room. Anyway, they're Miss Augusta's things and she needs them down here. Tibs, stop that whimpering. Go and put clean sheets on my bed. And you, Biddy, fill a hot-water jar. I'll make her a hot drink.'

'You're surely not going to let her go to bed in your room?' McPherson said. 'You're surely not going to let her stay here!'

'Och, and why not, eh?'

'There'll be trouble for us all if the master and mistress find out, that's why not.'

'They needn't find out if we're careful,' Nessie said.

Nessie was busy squeezing lemon into a jug. 'Away and get the young mistress some dry clothes before she catches her death.'

'Mistress?' said McPherson. 'Not any more, from what I've heard.'

Sid separated himself from his pipe. 'The way I see it is, just because a lady's suffering unfortunate circumstances it can't be said she's not a lady. It seems to me she's a lady born and nothing can change that.'

McPherson swished away without a word.

'Here's your hot drink, Miss Augusta.' Nessie was bending over her and Augusta had the impression of a mobile face flushed with firelight and silvered with tufts of hair.

'Och, she's shivering owr much to hold it, so she is.'

Biddy's face alongside Cook's now, grinning toothlessly.

Hands steadying hers and assisting the cup to her lips. The glorious comfort of the steaming liquid. But still she shivered and shook and gazed helplessly around.

'Of course,' Sid said between slow puffs at his pipe, 'it's not going to be easy.'

'There's extra mattresses,' his wife assured him. 'We can make up a bed on the floor out here for ourselves.'

'I meant it's not going to be easy to keep the young mistress hidden. Not for any length of time, it seems to me.

61

The way I see it, it's not just Biddy we would have to worry about. It would be Fiona McPherson as well.'

Tibs came running from Nessie's room. 'I've made the bed.'

'Don't just stand there hugging that hot-water bottle like a daftie,' Nessie snapped at her. 'Put it between the sheets.'

The bewhiskered face bent over Augusta again, the bulging cap above it balancing like a white dumpling on a frill.

'Don't worry, Miss Augusta, you'll feel better when you finish that up and get into a nice warm bed.' Then to Sid: 'I can deal with Fiona.'

'Yes, you're a capable woman,' Sid conceded to the door. 'And I'm not saying Fiona's a bad girl. No, I'm not saying that at all. But you know and I know who she's soft on.'

'Don't mention that rascal's name,' Nessie warned, hitching up her face. 'Just wait till he comes back! Just wait, that's all.'

Gently she raised Augusta and led her across the kitchen and into a windowless room hardly bigger than the cupboard in her bedroom upstairs where her trunk and old rocking-horse and other miscellaneous possessions were stored.

'Tibs,' Nessie called, 'come on and help me get these wet clothes off. And, Biddy, bring her other things through as soon as Fiona comes back.'

The room was lit by a candle stuck on a cracked saucer on a table beside the bed. By its dim flickering light, Augusta made out an old double bed, a chest of drawers, a small hanging looking-glass very clouded and cracked, and a pegged board screwed to the wall on which dangled a few articles of clothing. Above this was a shelf which held some boxes. On the plain wooden floor was a rag rug.

'Here's your nighty, Miss Augusta,' Nessie was saying. 'Get her other arm into it, Tibs. And stop your blubbering, girl, you've nothing to cry about. You should think yourself lucky the master hasn't remembered who you are. Maybe he never did know or surely he would have flung you out as

62

well. Biddy, don't just stand there, turn the bed down and we'll get Miss Augusta into it. She must have a fever, she's shivering so much.'

The bed was lumpy and uncomfortable but Augusta was glad to be cocooned tightly between its sheets and blankets. The voices of the servants receded and approached nearer, faded and grew stronger, ebbed and flowed, she had no idea for how long. She thought she heard herself moan and cry out too, and she had vague sensations of hands holding her down and arms raising her up and something cool soothing her brow. But it was part of a strange hazy world that had no reality in time or place.

Then suddenly her eyes opened and saw that she was lying in a small dark box that could hardly be called a room. The door was ajar and orange light from the kitchen was trickling in. She could hear voices with startling clarity and they made her struggle to a sitting position, her heart thumping in her throat.

'She can't possibly stay here any longer,' Cook was saying. 'Do you want us all to get sacked? That's what will happen if we're found out. And we can't just put her out. What's she going to do? She's a lady. She can't do anything. She'll die out on the streets. And I'll have no more of your stories about saving her life. It's your fault she's in the state she in. Are you going to let her die now? That's what I'd like to know.'

Gunnet's deep voice shouted angrily:

'Christ, what am I supposed to do? Her father's sacked me. I've my family to worry about. To hell with her!'

'The way I see it,' Sid Cruickshanks deliberated, 'you and you alone are responsible, Luther. It seems to me there's no getting away from the fact. She's your responsibility. You'll just have to worry about her as well.'

'She's going to have your baby,' Nessie emphasized.

There was a long silence, then Luther groaned: 'Oh, all right. I'll take her to the Briggait. My mother can see to her.'

Chapter Nine

The only thing Augusta could do was to remain as silent and as aloof as possible. She did not in fact know how a lady should behave or what a lady should do in such circumstances. She had no terms of reference. Nothing she had ever spoken of, nothing she had ever read, gave her any point of guidance, any clue, any idea whatsoever.

Standing in the candlelit kitchen among the servants, dressed in her bonnet of fawn velvet, tied under her chin with brown and orange ribbons, and her coat with its luxurious fur collar, she felt the whole situation was beyond her. The urge to burst into tears was all but overwhelming. Yet she realized that she had no alternative but to go with Tibs and Luther Gunnet.

Ever since she'd wakened and found herself in Nessie's room it had seemed too ridiculous to be true. She still felt dazed inside. Disbelief, partly born of stubbornness, clung on. She just refused to believe such a thing could happen to her.

That morning she had felt physically recovered and had savoured the breakfast cook had given her in bed on a tray decorated with a pretty lace cloth. There had been kidneys and bacon and egg and toast and muffins and marmalade and a pot of refreshing tea. When Tibs brought warm water, she had washed and dallied over the choosing of what to wear as if she was going for her usual drive with Mama. Tibs had laced her stays and helped her to don petticoat after petticoat, then her fawn silk dress. Then she'd tied her ringlets up with ribbons to match.

Afterwards she had sat in the windowless room reading a novel by candlelight until cook served lunch on the table by the bed.

In the afternoon Tibs packed all her things except her fur-trimmed coat. It was pinched in at the waist and widened towards the hem and she felt it looked very fashionable especially with the large puffs of the upper sleeves.

As soon as day had begun to fade into night Luther arrived. His voice startled her back to reality. Listening to him talking in the kitchen to Cook she was tempted to make a scene, lock herself in the room, have hysterics, refuse to move. Yet at the same time she knew it was impossible to do any of these things.

So now she was standing with as much pride and dignity as she could bring to her aid, her trembling hands well hidden in her muff. On one side of her hovered Tibs clutching a bag containing articles of clothing. Luther Gunnet on her other side also held a bag filled with her belongings. She was about to leave her home here in George Square with these two servants and go to their home, she knew not where. The Briggait had been mentioned but this name meant nothing to her.

Augusta hesitated then said, 'You are a good servant, Cruickshanks.'

'Thank you, Miss Augusta.'

Nessie came as near to curtsying as her bad legs would allow her but had to immediately steady herself by grabbing at the table.

Gunnet groaned. 'Oh, come on, for God's sake.'

Cook, obviously detecting, to Augusta's shame, the fear in her eyes, said, 'Don't worry, Miss Augusta. You'll be all right with Mrs Gunnet.'

Augusta disdainfully shook off Gunnet's hand which was now attempting to drag her unceremoniously from the kitchen. And before he could touch her again she swept out on her own.

Darkness halted her. The moon was playing hide and seek high above. Standing outside the kitchen door facing the wall beneath the yard felt like being trapped at the bottom of a deep, narrow well.

'The stairs are on the right,' Gunnet said. 'Hold on to my arm.'

Ignoring him she removed one hand from her muff to

65

daintily edge up her skirts so that her feet could feel the steps without tripping.

Tibs whimpered, 'They're slippery, Miss Augusta.'

'If she slips and falls it'll be her own fault,' Gunnet said.

With concentrated care, taking one step at a time like a child, Augusta managed to reach the top.

Round into West Goerge Street now, into the square and down Queen Street. As she passed the front of the house her throat constricted and tears almost betrayed her. She was frightened. The man taking her away from everything safe and comforting was a coarse stranger.

'Hurry up,' he was saying now. 'There's no use pitter-pattering along like that as if you're scared a bit of dirt will spoil your slippers.'

Not having any wish to demean herself by arguing with him in front of Tibs she said nothing. But she hated him for making her walk. Surely he could at least have provided her with a sedan chair. Obviously, being the ignorant brute that he was, he had no idea of what a lady needed not only to protect her person but her sensibilities.

Argyle Street and the Trongate were crowded but it seemed a different and more ominous throng than during the hours of daylight. It was a strange, terrifying world. Gas lamps and the occasional lantern attached to the walls of buildings cast ghostly fingers along creaking shop boards, shadowing doorways and endless threads of closes and wynds. Passing these places as she hurried along the main street between Luther and Tibs, she caught glimpses of ragged gossipers at the tops of stairs and at the bottom of closes and wynds. But she tried not to look to either side of her, concentrating instead on the ground immediately in front of her feet.

When Tibs and Luther suddenly crossed the road she was forced to raise her eyes fearfully to evade the coaches and horses and rough men with sedans jumbling noisily and dangerously along. Once across, they continued down a side street.

'Where are we now?' she asked Tibs.

'Stockwell Street, Miss Augusta. This leads straight down to the river. The Briggait cuts off at the bottom. We won't be long now.'

'This is the close,' Luther said at last.

In an inclined posture he groped his way into a dark tunnel-like place, the stench of which made her feel sick.

Tibs's voice echoed eerily all round. 'We won't be long now, Miss Augusta.'

Keeping between Luther and Tibs she crossed the open courtyard to the left until they reached a door set back in the shadow of a wooden stairway. Luther pushed open the door and indicated that she should enter. Fighting to keep her apprehension in check and ignore her palpitations of alarm she felt her way into first of all a lobby no bigger than a broom cupboard and from there into a low-ceilinged room less than a quarter of the size and in no way as congenial as the kitchen she had just left. From the dismal light of a couple of candle stubs and a smoky fire she could discern two set-in-the-wall beds, a wooden table and a few stools around it. Two chairs covered with woollen cushions sat on either side of the fire. A dresser with shelves held a few pieces of crockery arranged neatly with cups and saucers at either end and a bread plate standing up in the middle displaying its blue willow pattern and brown cracks. The room appalled Augusta with its poverty and lack of warmth and comfort.

Standing over by the fireplace was a woman of handsome features who had obviously made some attempt to look presentable. Her skin was shiny and red in patches as if she had been scrubbing it. Her hair, the same mousy colour as Tibs's, was pinned back but looked as if it had been done very inexpertly and without a mirror. Two children leaned shyly against her skirts. The woman pushed them aside and curtsied with surprising grace.

Luther said: 'This is my mother and my sister Rose and my brother Billy. I'll put these things through in the room.'

'Tibs,' said Mrs Gunnet, 'take Miss Augusta's coat and bonnet and muff. Put them in the cupboard in the parlour.'

Then turning to Augusta, her eyes veiled with painful embarrassment yet with her head held high, she said, 'We have quite a comfortable parlour, and you are welcome to use it. It will not be what you're accustomed to, of course. But at least it is better by far than anything for miles around here. I have a respectable home.' She stopped as if in mid-sentence and turned her face towards the fire.

Tibs said hastily, 'I'll take you through, Miss Augusta.'

Augusta followed Tibs across the kitchen to the door through which Luther had just emerged. He seemed even bigger in the tiny hovel. His wiry bush of hair nearly touched the ceiling and his shoulders looked of enormous width. She drew delicately back from him as he passed her and followed Tibs into the parlour.

'Shut the door,' she told the girl.

'Yes, Miss Augusta. Shall I unpack your things now?'

'Very well.'

She sat down on a chair beside the fireplace, oppressed by the smallness of the room. For a few minutes she watched Tibs scurrying about unpacking her clothes and hanging them up or folding them into drawers then pushing the bags underneath the cotton valance of the set-in-the-wall bed. She noticed with some relief that the patchwork quilt, or what she could see of it in the shadows, looked clean enough.

'Will that be all, Miss Augusta? I'm here all night, you see. I don't need to go back to work until five-thirty tomorrow morning. So if there's anything else . . .'

'Why isn't there a fire in here? I am cold.'

'Oh . . . oh . . .' The girl's face screwed up in distress. 'I'm sorry, Miss Augusta. I'll . . . I'll . . .' Suddenly she turned and flew from the room. There was a worried murmur of voices and then scraping noises. Then the door opened and Tibs came anxiously running in, holding out a shovel full of red-hot coals. The parlour fireplace was set with paper and after Tibs emptied the coals on top of it there was soon a decent glow of heat.

Augusta said, 'Be sure to shut the door when you go out.'

'Yes, Miss Augusta.'

Tibs curtsied before leaving and shutting the door behind her.

Left alone, Augusta took stock of her surroundings by the light of the two candles. The walls were whitewashed and the floor, like the furniture, gleamed darkly with polish. In front of the fire at her feet lay a rag rug with a black centre and a black border. The chair she was sitting on was a rocker on which was tied a maroon woollen cushion. On top of the mantelshelf a pewter candlestick wavered like a grey ghost illuminating a text which read in Gothic letters: GOD BLESS THIS HOME. Another candlestick billowed its yellow skirt on top of the chest of drawers and glistened her brush and comb set. In the centre of the room a small table hid under cream tatting and at the opposite side of the fire bulged a black, buttoned horsehair sofa. The only other furniture consisted of four chairs, two of dark oak and two upholstered in blurred tapestry. These few articles cluttered the place and used up nearly every inch of floor-space.

Sitting primly with head held high and hands folded on lap she tried to keep her eyes fixed on her silver brush and comb set. But desolation and fear kept caving her in. All the ramparts of her life had gone and she did not know what threat tomorrow might bring.

In this clutter of a place she could not settle to read. Yet she did not dare allow herself to think. At last she called out:

'Tibs!'

'Yes, Miss Augusta,' Tibs hastened breathlessly into the room.

'I think I will retire now.'

'Yes, Miss Augusta.'

The fire had sunk low and she felt cold as she allowed Tibs to undress her and put on her nightgown, then twist pieces of tape in each of her ringlets to secure them. But she felt too depressed even to bother telling the girl to bring more coal. Instead she climbed into the bed and slid under the blankets and quilt.

Tibs snuffed out the candles. 'Goodnight, Miss Augusta.'

'Goodnight,' Augusta murmured faintly.

It was very dark and strange. She pulled the quilt over her head and, hiding beneath it, sobbed brokenheartedly.

Chapter Ten

'Miss Augusta?'

The voice with its questioning yet withdrawn tone disturbed her sleep. She did not recognize it, and for a few seconds she felt bewildered and too frightened to open her eyes. When eventually she peeped from above the bedcovers Augusta realized that the candles had been lit again and Mrs Gunnet was standing by the bed. Her hair had not been brushed and, although still screwed up and pinned, strands had escaped and strayed down over her ears.

'I've brought you a cup of tea.' Eyes were guarded in a face set hard. She was a big woman but not fat.

'Where is Tibs?'

'She's gone to work. Yesterday was her night off. She won't be back now until next week.'

'Oh.' Augusta struggled into a sitting position and immediately discovered that the room was bitterly cold.

'The fire is not lit. How can my clothes be heated? How can I venture up? Well?' she asked Mrs Gunnet who was hesitating in a wretchedly indecisive manner.

'There's a bit of fire in the kitchen.'

'What use is it there? Light a fire in here as well.'

Still the woman hesitated, her face strained. At last she turned, went over to kneel in front of the fireplace and began raking it out with her hands.

Augusta finished her tea, which at least warmed her inside and quelled the nausea that had begun to rise. She called Mrs Gunnet to remove the cup then from beneath the comfort of the bedclothes watched her take what seemed an age in folding and tying strips of paper and packing them into the grate. After carefully sifting out cinders Mrs Gunnet arranged them on top of the paper. This task having been completed she rose and disappeared through to the kitchen, leaving the door ajar.

Augusta was just about to call a rebuke when the sound of Luther Gunnet's voice arrested her. He was speaking to his mother in the kitchen.

'What are you doing?'

The answer was an embarrassed half whisper: 'I'm lighting a fire in the parlour.'

'What for?'

'For Miss Augusta of course. So that she can get dressed.'

'If she has to have a fire to dress in front of she can either come through here or light one in there herself.'

'Luther, don't be ridiculous. She's a lady. She's never been used to anything like that.'

'She'll have to get used to a lot more than that. And anyway, we've never been able to afford a fire in the parlour before and we can afford it less now. You know that perfectly well, Mother.'

'Yes, but you can't expect her to understand . . . Luther, where are you going? Luther?'

Augusta stared wide-eyed at the figure dwarfing the doorway before hiding her head under the quilt. She felt humiliated at being seen with her hair twisted round tapes and sticking out grotesquely. Then to her horror the bedclothes were suddenly ripped back not only from her head but from her whole person.

Mrs Gunnet came rapidly into the room. 'Luther, what are you doing?'

Ignoring her, Luther said to Augusta: 'It's time you were up. But first let's get something straight. There are no servants here. You have no right whatsoever to expect my mother to run after you. If you want a fire lit you do it yourself. But coal costs money and, thanks to your father, I'm not earning any just now.'

Mrs Gunnet was surreptitiously trying to tug the quilt

from his hands in order to cover Augusta again but he pushed her aside.

'Mother, we're not exactly strangers. She is expecting my child.'

'Have you no shame?' his mother asked.

'Not as far as she is concerned. Now, Augusta – '

'*Miss* Augusta!' Augusta managed an imperious tone despite her crimson cheeks and trembling lips.

'Augusta,' he repeated firmly, 'my mother and I are going through to the kitchen. We'll expect you to join us for breakfast in not more than ten minutes.'

'I'll stay and help her to dress,' Mrs Gunnet said.

'It's time she learned to dress herself.'

Gripping his mother by the arm he forced her from the room. On his way out he tossed the bedclothes on to the sofa and Augusta had no alternative but to get up. Shivering with anger as well as cold she first of all struggled with the tapes covering her ringlets. Once freed from this indignity she hurriedly wriggled from her nightgown. Then not without difficulty and much fumbling she dressed herself in her dark green gown with the white collar. But although she was cold and hungry she could not bring herself to eat at the same table as Luther Gunnet. She sat down on the sofa, clasped her hands tightly on her lap and tried to be brave. Eventually Luther returned, followed by his mother. Mrs Gunnet never fidgeted or fluttered or gave any of the usual physical signs of agitation yet an aura of extreme distress managed to emanate from her rigid body.

'Luther, please, for my sake . . .'

'It's you I'm thinking of, Mother.'

He towered above Augusta whose hair still looked somewhat awry. She had not been able to fasten all the buttons at the back of her dress and Mrs Gunnet leaned across and deftly did them up.

'Why aren't you through at the table?' Luther demanded.

'I wish to eat here on my own.'

Mrs Gunnet said: 'I can easily bring her porridge in here.'

'Why should you?' Then to Augusta, 'If you don't come through and eat with us then you don't eat at all.'

'Luther, she's got to eat for the child's sake. And . . . and I'd rather have it this way. I value my privacy too.'

'All right. But it's not going to work forever. Sooner or later she's got to fit in.'

After he strode from the room Mrs Gunnet opened the shutters to reveal a window at which hung a pair of net curtains. Immediately Augusta became aware of noise that she had not noticed before. The clatter of coaches and carts and wagons. The gruff urgings of drivers. The shuffling of feet and the whisper of clothing.

'Is that the Briggait out there?' she asked Mrs Gunnet.

'No, Miss Augusta, that's Stockwell Street. We're on the corner, you see. The close is on the Briggait. I'll get your porridge.'

The bowl in which the porridge arrived was made of thick undecorated crockery and the equally primitive looking jug held watery milk.

'Is there no cream?' she asked in surprise.

Hearing her, Luther called from the kitchen. 'Just think yourself fortunate that you've anything to eat at all. If I don't find work soon we could all starve.'

His mother's face stiffened. 'Luther!'

'Well, it's true. And it's her bloody fault. That's what sticks in my throat. Her and her stupid family.'

Mrs Gunnet said: 'I'm sorry about the cream, Miss Augusta. And I know there should be other things too. Eggs and meat and muffins and marmalade and the like. I have been in good service and I know how everything should be done. But we are poor people, you see.'

'Come away and have your breakfast, Mother. There's no need to apologize to her.'

Mrs Gunnet held a chair at the small table in readiness for Augusta to sit down. Then after settling her comfortably she went out, shutting the door behind her. Nevertheless Augusta caught some of the woman's words to her son.

Words like 'tragedy' and 'responsibility'. Then the son's voice raised in anger.

'If I wasn't accepting my share of responsibility she wouldn't be here. But this could ruin my bloody life, Mother. If I let it. But I'm damned if I'm going to let it!'

Augusta's hand trembled as she raised the spoon to her mouth. The noise of the man's voice on the one side and the violent sounds of the street on the other made her feel like a fragile butterfly in between, something so out of place that it could be destroyed simply by finding itself in such an alien environment.

Tears choked hard in her throat but she was hungry and she continued to spoon porridge into her mouth and make the effort to swallow it down. Then she sat like a child staring at the empty bowl. The low-roofed room closed in on her. The whitewashed walls had a streaky, bluish tinge in daylight, reminiscent of the diluted milk. They were like stable walls and cluttered within them the furniture gave the room the appearance of a seedy back shop. It had been good once; each sagging chair had obviously belonged to a respectable home at some stage in its life. The chest of drawers had once graced some civilized bedroom. The little oak table had stood on a carpeted floor and been a useful place to rest a lady's embroidery frame or china teacup. Now the pieces of furniture were only shabby homeless articles long ago abandoned and crushed together like junk.

She rose eventually and squeezed over between the chairs to stand at the window. The scene outside was blurred by the net curtain but she did not pull it aside. A rough, noisy throng crushed terrifyingly close to the glass. She shrank back quickly and retreated to the rocking-chair. Trying to concentrate on her novel she struggled to ignore the rumble of noise from outside and the cold wrapping around her like a wet shroud. Mrs Gunnet came in later to make the bed, empty the chamber pot and take away the dirty dishes, but made no attempt to communicate with her. Augusta watched the older woman. She worked quickly and deftly like someone who had been well trained. It was on the tip of her tongue to ask if a fire could be lit but caution restrained her. She did not know if Luther was still in the kitchen and she had no wish for another distressing scene.

After what seemed like an age Mrs Gunnet returned with a cup of tea and a plate of bread and cheese. The afternoon dragged on and she was forced to don her coat and hug her fur muff to prevent her hands from freezing. Darkness gathered in the room. She thought she heard children's voices and surmised that the young Gunnets must have returned from school. She tiptoed over to the door and listened harder to try and find out if Luther was also there. Then plucking up courage she eased open the door. Mrs Gunnet was sitting erect beside the fire, hands clutching each arm of the chair, feet set firmly on the wood floor, head tipped back. Her eyes, though closed, seemed twisted with pain and as if instinctively sensing Augusta's presence she immediately opened them and stood up with a proud grace.

'Yes, Miss Augusta?'

The two children hurried over to lounge half-hidden behind her chair. Luther was nowhere to be seen.

'Even with my coat and muff I am frozen to the marrow of my bones and I have not even had the civilized comfort of a wash. Surely I can have some of that fire to heat this dreadful room? And unless I get a hot bath I shall probably die of cold.'

'I would have seen to the fire, Miss Augusta – only Luther said . . .'

'I do not care what your son said!' Augusta shivered with anger now as well as cold. 'I need to have a fire and a bath of hot water.'

Mrs Gunnet took a moment or two before saying, 'I'll bring the fire through but I don't know how I can manage the hot water.'

'Heat it, of course.'

'It's not just that. We haven't a tap, you see. It's a pump out in the yard.'

'Well, bring it in from the yard. Get the children to help

75

you. They can be fetching some in while you're seeing to the fire. Oh, do hurry, for goodness sake. I've never been so wretchedly cold in all my life.'

Another few agonized moments of hesitation before Mrs Gunnet nodded. Then she bent down and began digging the shovel into the grate. In a few minutes the fire in the parlour was lit and a tin bath placed in front of it.

'I've one kettleful hot just now. I'll empty it in.'

After she'd done this she told the children: 'Rose, you manage the kettle, and Billy, you take the bucket, and mind how you go in the dark.'

With frozen clumsy fingers Augusta struggled to undress herself. For one thing she wanted to make sure she got a bath before Luther Gunnet returned. For another, she was impatient to feel the comfort of the hot water thawing her icy limbs. However, she was forced to give up her desperate fumblings with the back buttons of her dress and ask Mrs Gunnet to assist her with them.

She was sitting blissfully in enough hot water to lap against her thighs when she was startled by an outraged voice shouting,

'Mother, why the hell are the children struggling outside in the dark with kettles and buckets?'

There was no reply and suddenly the parlour door crashed open and Luther entered. Augusta screamed and squeezed her eyes tight shut as if by doing so she could will him to disappear.

Mrs Gunnet's voice came close to her ear and tugged a towel protectively around her nakedness. 'She – sh! It's all right, Miss Augusta.'

Augusta opened her eyes wide. 'No, it's not all right. How dare he invade my privacy like this?'

Her indignation faltered with fear when she saw Luther's face. In his eyes was a malice so concentrated it paralysed her.

'How dare you,' he said, 'make slaves of my mother and brother and sister!'

Mrs Gunnet kept her gaze averted from him. 'I don't mind, Luther . . .'

'I mind!' he interrupted. 'I mind a great deal and I will not have it. Go through to the kitchen, Mother.'

Augusta gave a cry of panic and clutched at the older woman's arm. Frantically she tried to stop her from rising.

'Mrs Gunnet, I forbid you to leave me!'

'You have no right,' said Luther striding over and wrenching off her clutching hands, 'either to order my mother to do anything or to forbid her to do anything. Get that into your empty, useless head!'

'Luther, Luther,' his mother repeated in a tight monotone.

'It has to be done, Mother. For her own sake as well as for ours.'

Then suddenly she was jerked to her feet and before she knew what had happened she was sprawled across Luther's knees and her naked thighs were stinging under the vicious blows of his palm.

Chapter Eleven

Lying back in the black pit of the bed, in the stale-smelling stable of a room, she tried not to cry. Desperately che clung to anger to harden away fear.

How dare Luther Gunnet frighten her! How dare he hurt and humiliate her! How dare he shatter her whole life! She could not, would not tolerate it. He had bullied her into coming with him while she was ill and in a state of shock. He had literally dragged her off. He had wrenched her from her beautiful, civilized home and imprisoned her in this dreadful hovel.

That last time at Cameron House she should have run upstairs from the kitchen and sought the protection of her mama and papa, if she'd only had her wits about her. Their fury and disappointment would have subsided by then and they would surely have realized that what had happened

77

was Gunnet's fault, not hers. That night of the blizzard she had fought him with all her strength but he had overpowered her. They must realize the truth of this by now. They too had been in a state of shock and confusion before, but now they would have had time to think.

Augusta's heart began to fill with hope. If she returned to George Street they would take pity on her.

'Please, please, Mama and Papa,' she would say, 'forgive me for unwittingly causing you such worry and distress. But, oh, how distraught I have been too . . .'

They would make everything all right again. She willed time to pass quickly until it was morning and she could be away.

At last a feeble wisp of light threaded through a crack in the shutters. She arose in an agony of impatience but was forced to feel her way slowly and cautiously across the room since it was still dark. After much fumbling she managed to unlatch the shutters and allow the small window to shoot beams of dusty brilliance into the room.

Outside, Stockwell Street had already awakened. Hurrying past were women in shawls, carrying shopping baskets, black-faced chimney-sweeps, men in ill-fitting fustian clothes, ragged children with eyes dazed by fatigue.

From the farrier's building came the resounding clanging of iron and the shuffle of horses' hooves. A cart rattled over the cobbles; its racket battered about inside the room, louder and louder before gradually dwindling away again. A carriage swayed and creaked and thundered and blocked out light.

Cold chilled through the soles of Augusta's feet and her cotton nightgown. She took a spasm of shaking and hurried, moaning a little, to where her clothes were strewn on the sofa. Not yet adept at dressing herself, she was near to tears before she managed to don her gown. At last she won the fight with buttons and tyers and, quite faint with the need for a cup of tea, gave her hair cursory attention before opening the bedroom door.

She saw him immediately. Dressed in a loose-fitting white

shirt he sat at the table with is mother and the children. Each had a bowl of watery-looking porridge in front of them. They were eating with no sign of enjoyment. The tiny room was lit by a candle stub stuck in a saucer. A smoky fire blackened the kettle and the teapot on the hob.

Luther's eyes pierced her like barbs of hate, making her clumsy as she lifted a cup from the dresser and carried it over to the hob. Nervously glancing at the table she saw no signs of any milk or sugar. Without a word she carried the steaming brew into the other room and shut the door. Sipping at the tea, she willed herself to ignore its revolting taste and not be overcome by the wave of nausea that so often buffeted her in the mornings. Nevertheless it seemed to warm and strengthen her and after she'd finished it she donned her brown hooded cape and waited behind the door, hugging the cape around her and praying for sounds of Luther leaving the house.

At last she heard the outside door bang. Hurrying to the window she peeped tentatively out. Soon Luther came into view, tall and muscular among the crush of people. Growing bolder and moving nearer to the glass her eyes clung to him as he strode further away up the street. He still wore his hat at a jaunty angle and moved with a careless swagger. He was an insolent wicked man who needed to cool his heels in jail. Merely to deprive him of his employment wasn't a stern enough measure with which to punish him. She would tell her father so.

Having assured herself that Luther had completely disappered, she left the room. Mrs Gunnet's even voice halted her in the kitchen.

'You cannot go out alone. It isn't safe for a lady to be on the streets by herself. I will come with you.'

Augusta hesitated, remembering the rabble outside and the dark, stinking yard and close that she would have to pass through before even reaching the street.

'Oh, very well. But do hurry. I am eager to be home.'

'You mean to George Square?'

'Where else?'

Lowering her eyes but not her head Mrs Gunnet picked up a shawl and tossed it round her shoulders. Her face had a sickly pallor and her mouth was set in a thin bitter line.

As soon as Augusta stepped outside she was glad she had let the older woman accompany her. The yard was a gloomy underworld from which there seemed no escape. For a few seconds she felt totally confused.

'This way,' Mrs Gunnet said.

Augusta followed her out to the Briggait. Scant light filtered into the narrow street but in a minute or two they had turned up the Stockwell which at least was bright and busy. Soon they were making their way along the much wider and more familiar Argyle Street with its colourful coaches and proud prancing horses. The glass of shop windows winked friendly invitations, creating a kind of joy inside Augusta. In her imagination she savoured again the life to which she had been accustomed. What shop would she visit today? What new bonnet or gown would she order? What acquaintances would she and her mama call on? With whom would they sit and gossip and sip tea?

Round into Queen Street now with its elegant mansions kept apart by private lanes and fronted with double stairs separated from the street by iron railings. Into George Square at last, and there was Cameron House. Reaching the front door Augusta said.

'Thank you, Mrs Gunnet. You may return to your home now.'

Mrs Gunnet stood in utter stillness for a moment, then without looking at Augusta and with not a word she turned and walked away.

Augusta rattled the door-knocker and waited impatiently until it was opened by McPherson, immaculate in a blue and white striped morning gown. The maid stared in astonishment at Augusta's dishevelled hair and untidy appearance. She was not wearing a bonnet and the hood of her cape had blown back. The crumpled collar of her dress protruded from the top of the cape and her face looked far from clean.

'You are blocking my path, McPherson,' Augusta said. 'Stand aside, please, so that I can enter.'

All expression smoothed from the maid's face and she said politely:

'You are no longer welcome here, mistress.'

'That is not for you to say.' Augusta pushed past her. 'Where is my mama?'

'In the parlour. And she has said . . .'

'Thank you, McPherson. We shall ring for you if we need you.'

Stubbornly Augusta waited until McPherson had withdrawn before she hurried across to the parlour.

Her mother was reclining on the sofa, covered by a knitted blanket. Immediately on catching sight of Augusta she screamed in hysteria:

'What are you doing here? How dare you come back! Leave this house at once!'

'But, Mama, please,' Augusta struggled to make herself heard. 'Surely, at least, we can talk.'

'Talk, talk, that's all I hear is talk,' Felicity cried out, 'you wicked wanton creature. Better you were dead and buried. You have ruined everything for me. Even my own dear son has deserted me. Fled to the colonies to escape the disgrace you have brought on us, and to start a new life. But what about me, what about my life?'

'We haven't talked at all,' moaned Augusta. 'You don't understand. I want you to know how terribly sorry and distressed I am. I have been forced to live in the most intolerable condition in the Briggait. It is a frightful place, I cannot bear it.'

'They never stop talking,' Felicity ranted on. 'They simper and whisper behind my back and torment me most cruelly to my face. I am tormented beyond endurance till I shall surely die.'

'Mama, please listen to me. It was not my fault. He was too strong for me. There was nothing I could do. I'm frightened and desperately unhappy. I need you and Papa to protect me.'

'They simply delight in it. Oh, the cruel barbs; the knives slyly pushed in and twisted unmercifully.' She waved a handkerchief wildly in front of her face. 'I cannot bear it, I cannot bear it. My whole life has turned to ashes because of you. Get out of my sight: I want nothing more to do with you.'

'Mama, you cannot make me go back to the Briggait. You do not know what it is like. It is just too horrible to describe.'

'Only the other day Mrs Laidlaw-Smythe called with her daughter Polly. All the way from Edinburgh, just to crow about that girl's propriety and delicacy and good taste, her modesty, decorum and unsullied virtue. How she rubbed it in, saying it was all the result of good breeding, of course.'

Augusta couldn't believe her ears. Her very soul clung frantically to the safety and comfort of the room. It was like the difference between heaven and hell. Every part of her being savoured the thick carpet, the easy chairs, the footstools and the big black marble clock with its pillared front that tick-tocked leisurely and tranquilly in this haven of comfort.

Then in the towering mirror, ornamented with gilt shells and pink cupids, she suddenly caught sight of herself, and was shocked beyond measure at how alien she looked in these surroundings.

Small and with tousled hair and anxious, dirt-smudged features she realized that the person she saw no longer belonged in this safe and luxurious world. She was already lost. Yet it was too terrible a fact to face.

Panic-striken she shouted at her mother: 'This is my home!'

'They all blame me. They all talk as if is my fault,' Felicity wailed. 'It is so wickedly unfair. My social life is an ordeal instead of a pleasure now. I cannot face my friends.'

'Oh, what does it matter about your stupid friends or their silly spiteful talk? What does it matter?'

'Such selfishness. Such wickedness. She does not care about my sufferings!'

'Mama, you do not know what suffering is. You have always been pampered and sheltered. You do not even know where the Briggait is. You do not know what I am talking about.'

'I have been so ill I have not been strong enough to put a foot on the floor without help. I have been too weak to reach my carriage. I have not been out to buy one new bonnet or gown. I have not had one moment's pleasure.'

'Is that all you can think about. I'm with child. I'm at the mercy of that dreadful man. He has even struck me, Mama. He has beaten me. I'm living in a hovel. I'm cold and hungry and frightened. I'm begging for your help and protection and all you can talk about is not getting out to buy a new bonnet?'

Her mother was never going to help or protect her. The conviction made Augusta wild with grief. She caught a glimpse of herself in the mirror again. There she was – for ever and ever – a dirty-faced trollop from the underworld, an untouchable. In tragic rage she snatched a brass ornament from a nearby table and hurled it at the mirror.

A deafening explosion lengthened into a medley of clattering and tinkling sounds as splinters of glass showered the mantleshelf, the clock, the ornaments, the tiles on the fireplace, the brass fender.

'McPherson! McPherson!' Mrs Cameron's screeches rivalled the noise that Augusta was now making as she jerked the whatnot from its corner, causing its load of *objects d'art* to fly from its shelves and spray the room like bullets.

The door burst open and McPherson entered to stride immediately over and grab Augusta by the arm.

Mrs Cameron kept babbling, 'McPherson, protect me, she's a madwoman. Get rid of her. Get her away from me!'

Augusta fought to free herself of the maid's strong grip. 'How dare you! Leave me alone!'

Despite her struggles and her angry commands, however, McPherson hung grimly on and managed to drag her from the room and jerk her unceremoniously across the marble-floored hall towards the front door.

Longing to be upstairs in her own bedroom, Augusta wept in tragic despair. Pushing her roughly outside the maid delivered the final insult:

'I hope you think he's worth it, you dirty little whore!'

Chapter Twelve

Augusta fled in the opposite direction from where she'd come. Eyes wild, she forced herself on until the steepness of the hill rising above the north side of the square snatched her breath away and the fight for air became more urgent than her grief and humiliation. She flung back her head, gulping hugely, nostrils dilated.

It was a long time before she managed to calm down and when she did and her convulsions had at last subsided she stared dazedly around, trying to get her bearings. The few elegant villas and gardens straggling the hill had dwindled away to nothing. She found herself alone on a wide expanse of rough grass high above the town. On the right a wooded area darkened the landscape. Some distance ahead a road cut across and faded into the trees. But before completely disappearing it passed a sombre building set well back and barely visible. It had a chilling yet familiar look.

Standing with the wind tugging at her cloak and whipping her hair across her face Augusta remembered that she had once taken a country ride with her parents along that road. Her papa told her it was called Asylum Road and the ugly building was the lunatic asylum. She and her mama had withdrawn deep into the coach so that they would not be offended by the sight of the place.

She averted her gaze now but more in fear that she too was going mad. So much had been happening to her. Her whole life had quickened, turned upside down. She felt bewildered. At the foot of the hill was the jungle of Glasgow, packed to suffocation and half-hidden under a pall of smoke. Surely this could not be the Glasgow she had always known? She was eighteen now and could still recall being taken country walks first by her nurse, then by her governess Meredith who taught her about the trees and hedgerows and wild flowers that started right at their back door. Even Queen Street was pastoral. Surely it was not so long ago that from her bedroom window she had watched the kilted cowherd driving the cattle down towards Argyle Street? She stared at the tall chimneys thrusting up like black fingers pointing at the sky. In the distance the River Clyde, slate-coloured on this sunless day, twisted alongside densely packed roof-tops. She saw where the Old Bridge spanned the Clyde and knew that it was to there she must return. It seemed incredible now that she had passed along Clyde Street in her carriage on her way to Glasgow Green to watch, from the carriage window, the troops parading on the Green. She had actually passed Stockwell Street and the Briggait without even noticing they were there. Fighting for control of her emotions she dried her face as best she could with her cape and reluctantly, oh, how reluctantly, began her descent back down the hill.

As her frail shoes jarred and slithered on the slope and their ribbon cross-straps cut into her ankles she blamed Luther Gunnet for all her misfortunes. Her bitter resentment of him gave her the strength she needed to pass Cameron House without dissolving into tears again. She felt it unwise to risk any other route in case she became hopelessly lost. But her feet quickened down Queen Street on to Argyle Street and she pulled the hood of her cloak well forward to hide her face. All the way along Argyle Street she kept her eyes lowered, determined that no one who knew her would see her in this state.

Only when she turned down Stockwell Street did she release her hold on her cape and raise her head. Steeling herself she entered the Briggait, went through the close, crossed the yard with its mountain of rubbish and human excretion and entered the house.

Luther was shrugging into a clean shirt. There was no

sign of his mother, The children, she knew, would be at school.

'Oh, God,' he groaned at the sight of her. 'I thought we'd seen the last of you.'

'Believe me, if I had my way,' Augusta said fervently, 'I would not be here. Do you think I wanted to set eyes on you again? Or this stinking hovel?'

His eyes narrowed. 'Watch your tongue. This is my home and you've been glad of its shelter.'

'Glad?' Her voice heightened in mocking incredulity. 'Glad? How could anyone be glad to be stuck in this dungheap? No one with any intelligence or decency would want to be within miles of its revolting stench.'

'This is the cleanest house for miles. My mother sees to that.'

'Your mother,' she peeled the words of her tongue with as much distaste as her bitter suffering could muster. Instinctively she knew that to insult his mother would hurt him most and she searched for words outrageous enough to cut him deepest. But all she could think of was: 'That common skivvy!'

A few strides brought him with frightening rapidity to where she stood. She was sure he was going to strike her but such was her hatred she raised her head almost as if to welcome his blows. He stopped, hand straining in mid-air, fighting with himself.

'Still the proud lady, eh?'

'I will always be a lady. Living under the same roof as scum like you will never change that.'

'Scum, is it?' He grabbed her by the arm as she made to walk away towards the room and jerked her back to face him. 'I'd still be up on the box and everybody saluting me as the best dragsman in the country if it wasn't for you. I'd still have a pocketful of money and a beautiful girl waiting and willing in every hotel. It's because of you I've no work and my mother is out searching for the cheapest scraps she can find to eat and my brother and sister will have to give up their schooling.'

'Remove your hand from my arm at once. You're hurting me.'

'The trouble is I've been too much of a gentleman.'

'You!' she raised an eyebrow and flung the words at him derisively. 'A gentleman?'

'You neither know or appreciate how lucky you've been . . .'

'Lucky? You're mad!'

'With frustration perhaps. Both work and pleasure are being denied me. The wenches are peeved because they think I'm getting my pleasure from you. And I'm not.'

'Let go of me, I said.'

'It's time I did though. It's time you justified your keep.'

'I don't know what you're talking about. You're the one who's caused the trouble. You and your revolting animal behaviour.'

'I've had enough of this. After today you'll know what I'm talking about.'

'What are you doing?' she cried out in alarm when he suddenly threw her cloak aside then with both hands roughly caught hold of her dress. To her horror, before she could make any attempt to stop him, he had ripped the bodice open to the waist. Panic-striken she flew towards the room but he was too quick for her. Before she could shut and lock the door his boot kicked it open and he was in. With one hand he crashed it shut again.

'Get the rest of them off!'

She clutched her arms across her chest, gripping her shoulders tightly, more to contain her terror than to prevent him from seeing her chemise and the bulge of her breasts above it.

'All right, I'll get them off for you.'

At first she hardly struggled, she was so stunned as he jerked and tore at her clothes. She gave little gasps that rapidly changed to sobs and then to screams as he denuded her of her last garment.

'Scream away,' he said coolly, 'for all the good it'll do you here.'

Bumping into the conglomeration of table and chairs she tried to reach the bed for a blanket with which to cover her nakedness but he followed her and tossed it aside.

'You're no lady now,' he said, holding her at arm's length without effort, despite the wildness of her struggles. 'You look much the same as any other wench to me. You have breasts.' His hand flipped at them in a contemptuous gesture. 'Not much as far as size goes. I'll admit I've seen better.' Then his fingers explored between her legs with neither tenderness nor passion. 'Yes, you're exactly the same there as any wench I've ever known.'

His coolness was somehow more insulting than anything else she had had to bear. Twisting her head to one side she closed her eyes and wept.

'Get into bed,' he said.

She remained like a helpless rag doll, not seeing that he was stripping off his shirt and breeches but aware that that was what he was doing.

Suddenly she was manhandled into the bed. Managing to twist on to her stomach she clutched at the end of the mattress. He made no attempt to turn her towards him. Instead he hoisted up her thighs and took her from the back like an animal. She wanted to die, she could not cope with the shame. Her sobbing increased and only dull rhythmic moans escaped each time he plunged into her.

Afterwards he rolled on to his back and she slid her legs straight and closed her eyes and was silent. Eventually the bed jarred as he got up. He took a few minutes to dress, then she heard him stride across the room. The door opened and shut.

The cold made her stir eventually. She got up feeling weak and sick. Her back ached and a sticky liquid oozed from her and trickled down her legs. In disgust she rubbed at it with one of her torn undergarments before donning fresh clothes. Wrapping a shawl around her she clutched it close for comfort.

She did not know how much time passed before she heard Mrs Gunnet's voice, the sound of dishes being put on the table and the sawing of bread. She leaned her head back against the rocking-chair, nearly swooning with longing for a cup of tea. Her whole being revolted against going through to the kitchen and seeing or being seen by Luther Gunnet, yet at the same time she knew it was inevitable. When she felt sufficiently recovered in strength she would walk through that door into the tiny room beyond. She would collect a cup from the dresser and she would walk across and fill it with tea. She would take a slice of bread too. She had to eat. It was simply a matter of surviving. Surviving meant having to force herself to perform necessary actions. It meant crushing or somehow keeping all sensitivity and spiritual awareness in abeyance. It mean enduring. It meant accepting the practicalities that life insisted must be met.

For the first time she had an inkling of what Mrs Gunnet and other working-class women must have felt through the years. In this jungle world there were no choices. Priorities fell into place. Things became basic. A cup of hot tea and a hunk of bread were more important than shame or embarrassment or humiliation or even hatred.

Still feeling weak and dizzy she managed to rise and go over and open the door. She saw Luther before he saw her. He was sitting at the table, his head supported, his eyes half-shaded with one hand. Out of the corner of her eyes she saw him look up as she entered. She avoided his gaze but she could not control the trembling of her hands as she collected her meal of tea and bread and piece of cheese. She marvelled at the fact that despite her distress she could at the same time feel a pang of pleasure in finding the cheese. As soon as she returned to the privacy of her room she stuffed a piece into her mouth. She'd had nothing to eat all day and very little the previous day. Before she reached the settee she had wolfed down the rest of the cheese and started on the dry bread. She had nearly finished the meal and was gulping down some tea when Luther came in and shut the door behind him. She cowered away, hugging the hot teacup for comfort.

Keeping his hand on the doorhandle he said abruptly:

'We'd better get married. For your sake as well as the child's. I'll see to it,' he told her. Then the door jerked open and crashed shut and he was gone.

Chapter Thirteen

The minister came to the house to perform the ceremony. He was a highlander and new to the town, a shifty-looking individual in a dark coat and breeches and grubby linen. Ill-at-ease with the discord between Augusta's fine clothes and the poverty of her surroundings he did not seem sure what attitude to adopt towards her. Normally with ladies he fawned and flattered. Common women he bullied and harassed with threats of eternal damnation, accusing them of being wicked fornicators and corruptors of men since the time of their ancestor Eve.

He suspected that Augusta was pregnant and itched to launch into one of his tirades. Her aloofness, however, and the strangeness of the situation made him hesitate. The bridegroom did not seem to fit into the surroundings either. He sported very fashionable clothes with skin-tight white trousers strapped under the instep and a waistcoat resplendent with mother-of-pearl buttons. His frock-coat, thrown wide open across his chest, had huge revers and a padded collar that reached down to a nipped-in waist.

As the minister fussed and fiddled with his holy book he stole another glance up past the frilled shirt and cravat to Luther Gunnet's face. The man looked anything but happy. His features could have been carved out of solid rock. His unwavering stare was glued to a high point on the opposite wall and his voice although clear was devoid of expression as he repeated the words:

'I, Luther Gunnet, take this woman, Augusta Cameron . . .'

The girl's face was a mixture of misery and haughtiness. Her hair, parted in the middle, had a cluster of ringlets tied up with blue ribbons on either side of her head. The glossy grey dress she was wearing caught the light as if shining through a glass darkly. She wore no jewellery and her hands were entwined tightly in front of her.

Crowded into the small parlour were also Mrs Gunnet, her two daughters and her younger son. Not one of them looked as if they viewed the occasion with the slightest approval, far less happiness. Even the youngest, a girl of no more than six, was glowering and hanging back. Her brother Billy's eyes were lowered. The lad was digging and scuffing at the floor with his heel and it was as much as the minister could do to prevent himself from giving the irritating rascal a well-aimed punch.

Mrs Gunnet dressed in shapeless brown cotton, and with coarse red hands, was obviously an ordinary working-class woman. Yet there was something about her too that disturbed the clergyman. It was not so much her statue stillness, her poker-straight back or her tight thread of a mouth. Behind the stillness he imagined he caught, in her guarded eyes, one demented flicker. It increased his uneasiness and made him hasten the ceremony to a conclusion. He wanted to quit the cold gloomy place as soon as possible and return home to his open-faced, biddable wife.

After he'd gone, Luther did not follow his family through to the kitchen. He shut the parlour door and turned to Augusta.

'We're husband and wife now in the eyes of God and man. Do you understand that?'

She did not reply.

'Augusta, I want no more nonsense. No more having your meals by yourself through here. No more expecting my mother to do anything for you. The worry of all this has affected her health and if you don't care about her I do. In future I'll expect you to help her, rather than the other way around. Now, go through to the kitchen.'

She remained motionless and erect but he could see the furtive beating of her heart. It was like a pain she was trying to hide. Hands clasped, eyes staring in his direction, she managed not to look at him. Severe in her grey dress yet so small and absurdly defenceless, she made him feel a twist of pity. For the first time too, he experienced stirrings of admiration.

'We've got to make the best of it.' He had meant to soften his voice, yet the words rapped out like bullets. He was always more aggressive with her. He regretted it, struggled with it as ferociously as with a tiger on the loose, but to no effect. Bitterness and resentment against Augusta continuously fought with his other emotions. The more he determined to 'make the best of it' and contain his conflicts, the more concentrated and explosive they became.

'If I have to force you, I will,' he said. 'If I have to drag you through there, if I have to humiliate you into doing each and every task, I will. Do you believe me?'

'Oh, yes.' Her lips warped and she flashed him a contemptuous look. 'I believe you.' With dignity she crossed the room. Then she stood waiting near the door for him to open it and allow her to pass through.

He itched to strike her and it was only with a supreme effort of will that he allowed her to sweep out in front of him. She sat down in the kitchen like a queen on a throne, making Rose and Billy cringe away in embarrassment and hatred. His mother, who was stirring the pot in front of the fire, stiffened and averted her face. There was nothing he could do except repeat, this time to her,

'We'll just have to make the best of it.' Then he added, 'Show her where things are kept, Mother, and give her a share of the chores. She can be a help to you once she knows how.'

His mother made no reply. Augusta sat like a rigid doll glued to the chair. The children glowered into their laps. So strong was his frustration and so irked was he with the emotion-charged atmosphere that he burst out:

'Oh, to hell with the lot of you!' Crashing the outside door behind him he crossed the yard and was soon striding along the riverside towards Glasgow Green.

The pleasant spring day surprised him, as if he expected

the whole world to match the black mood of the house he had just left. The Green soothed his eyes with its velvet hands. Trees bursting into bud and the river's sparkle helped to prop up his spirits. A hint of swagger returned to his step. He even mustered a wink for one group of girls strolling by.

Taking deep breaths of fresh air gave him a bouyancy, a physical lightness. Nevertheless his mind remained like a heavy stone inside him.

He had Tibs to worry about as well now. He had known, of course, that she had been living on precarious and borrowed time at Cameron House but her removal as a direct result of Fiona McPherson's spite had offended him. It would be far from easy for Tibs to find another job without a recommendation. A position in a house was out of the question; but there might be a chance in the mills. Admittedly every trade was fenced round with prohibitions these days. If you weren't a relation of someone already working, for instance, in cotton-spinning, iron-moulding and mining it was impossible to get into it. The mine owners as good as owned the families of all their employees from birth and even before.

Still, Tibs, Billy and Rose must surely find some kind of work somewhere. They had to. There was no money left. He cringed inside at his own inability to provide for them. He had tried just about every family in town who owned a coach but without success. He widened his area of search to further and further outside Glasgow in the hope that some of the farmers or land-owning gentry might agree to employ him, but in each case he was met with indignation and verbal abuse. It was as if he made a habit of raping and ruining every gentlewoman who had ever come within a mile of him. He was not to be trusted, they said.

At first he tried to reason with people. He pointed out the injustice of his family being made to suffer. Why should they starve? They had done nothing wrong. 'Whatever ye sow, that shall ye reap,' he was told by the few who deigned to listen. But it was the hypocrisy which was worse. It was one thing to be preached at by cosseted matrons and smugly told that he had brought his misfortune upon himself and his family. It was quite another for some local squire's son or merchant to take a high-handed, holier-than-thou attitude. Luther knew for a fact that many of them had sired bastards by dairymaids and chambermaids and whatever serving wenches they could get their leg over. Why should men like that make him suffer? There had been no stigma, no victimization, no punishment in any form meted out to them.

His stomach turned acid at the injustice of it all. The spring day faded. The blackness of his mood blotted out the emerald banks, the diamond river, even the coloured cobwebs of girls clustering beneath the trees.

Hunger ached in his guts and he was tempted, as he emerged from the Green and shouldered up Saltmarket Street, to grab at some of the food displayed on stalls and in shop doorways. But pride prevented him from doing this too. The thought of running through the streets like a common thief was repugnant to him.

He tried to think of some way in which he could use his wits to advantage and be more certain of evading the ignominy of being caught. The mere idea of robbing one of the Cameron coaches engulfed him in a rush of pleasure. But to be a successful highwayman one needed a horse and a pistol and he had neither. A rage of frustration swept his moment of hope into the dust.

It took all his self-control to keep walking along Argyle Street instead of making for home and venting his fury in physical violence on Augusta. He believed it to be a man's right to chastise his wife, by beating if necessary, but he was afraid that in his present mood he might go too far.

Soon he had left Argyle Street behind and was trudging through the ancient suburb of Anderson. In Anderson there was now a brewery for porter, a rope works and a calico printfield. He had already tried to get work at all three and also at a nearby farm, all to no effect. He was able-bodied and more than willing to work hard, but these things apparently meant nothing against someone with a little experience and such tender years that the lowest pittance need be paid.

He sat brooding and trying to ignore his hunger until it was nearly dark. Then he reluctantly set off for home. Immediately he entered the kitchen he realized that something had happened. Augusta's eyes were huge with anger. Tibs was sobbing in the corner and Billy and Rose were dour-mouthed. But is was his mother who caused his stab of concern. She had the wild look of a trapped animal. There was an aura of suspension in the unnatural stillness of her body, yet her eyes kept furtively flickering.

'What's happened?' he demanded.

His mother half muttered to herself, 'I couldn't let the children go hungry to the mills tomorrow. The work will be hard enough. I couldn't let them go the whole day – the whole week maybe – on an empty stomach.'

'Tibs and Rose and I got fixed up this afternoon,' Billy said.

Suddenly Rose ran towards him. 'I don't want to go to that place, Luther. I'm frightened. I saw a man beating children there with a horse-whip.'

'Be quiet,' Billy shouted. 'Snivelling won't help. We don't get paid until Friday, Luther. Mum had to do it.'

'Do what, for God's sake?'

'Sell some of her fine clothes to old Biddy.' He jerked his head in Augusta's direction. 'And a mighty fine fuss she's been making about it.'

'Is that all?' Luther relaxed with relief. 'It's all right, Mother. Don't worry.'

Augusta shivered with anger. 'Oh, of course, it means nothing to you. Your mother goes into my room and, unknown to me, steals two of my best gowns and sells them.'

'That's enough. You'll eat your share of whatever money she got.'

'But she didn't know the value of the gowns. The shop she sold them to only gave her a few miserable pence.'

95

'If you're so clever why didn't you sell them and get a better price?'

'It never occurred to me . . .'

'Yes, I can believe that.' Suddenly he felt too tired to be angry with her. He could see the open bewilderment in her face and her helplessness, and despite the bitterness he felt at the ruin she'd made of his life, he felt a tenderness too. She looked more of a child than his sister Rose.

'Come on to bed,' he said, going towards the room. 'It's late.'

She hesitated as if taken back, her stare trying to read his face as he stood waiting for her in the doorway. Eventually, eyes lowered, she walked past him into the room. He shut the door then stood watching her fumble with her clothes and try to undress without him seeing her nakedness. Only after she had donned her nightdress did she remove her petticoats and drawers.

He removed his own garments and dowsed the candle. Then after he had climbed into bed beside her he gathered her into his arms. She lay stiffly, warily at first, then slowly relaxed as if all her bones were melting. He held her close and nursed her to and fro, to and fro while she moaned and wept and sobbed against his chest.

Chapter Fourteen

'I'm away,' Luther called from the doorway. 'Wish me luck.'

Augusta kept her face turned towards the wall and said nothing.

Since their wedding night there had been a kind of truce between them but it was a mockery of congeniality. She could see that beneath the thin surface of Luther's restraint there still simmered a hatred and resentment of her. Sometimes she caught the full force of it in his eyes as if he was trying by sheer strength of will to blot her out. Often she would nurse her locket in her hands and open it and weep over the silky strands of Lieutenant's Fitzjames's hair. She would remember the delicacy of his looks and his behaviour and she would dream of the luxurious home she might have shared with him and the wonderful life she would have enjoyed. Then she would catch sight of Luther's coarse hair and features and return his look of hatred. Or her eyes would fall on her already bulging belly in which lay Luther's child and she would loathe and detest it too. It was only another link in the chain that bound her.

Yet she could see that Luther also felt trapped and sometimes she experienced a bitter ache of pity for him. She tried to tell herself as she lay in bed listening to the sound of her husband's feet crossing the kitchen, then fading into the distance, that her shameful behaviour of the previous night had been caused by pity. Since their wedding night Luther had never touched her. He had lain stiffly and silently at her side until gradually his body relaxed into sleep. She could not match his stillness. Various discomforts caused by her pregnancy made her restlessly move about, turn and twist, curl up on one side or the other, thump round on to her back, splaying wide her legs. Often while he slept, she would creep furtively, miserably from the bed in the dark in order to use the chamber pot.

Often before he slept she would be disturbingly aware of him. The heat of his body so close to hers and the sensual male smell of him would cause her heart to thump with embarrassing loudness. She would struggle to calm her pulse and her uneven breathing only to have a plague of worse agitations beset her. An ache stretched at her breasts and between her legs until she could have moaned with the torment of it. Last night she had indulged these feelings in a shameful lack of decency and self-control.

Lying on her side, facing him, she had slid stealthy fingers up his arm then over his chest. Her thigh had opened and stretched across his belly. His hand had immediately caressed her leg and she had given herself up to the animal ecstasy of his touch. So delirious and complete was her abandon she hardly remembered what had followed.

Surely it had been a kind of madness. She had behaved with such a total lack of restraint and had been crying out so loudly he had been forced to hold his big palm over her mouth to silence her. Even so, his mother and the children must have heard. In shame she pressed her face deep into the pillow. At least Tibs and the children would have left for work now but Mrs Gunnet would be there. She couldn't understand the woman. She had tried to speak to her, tried to help her in the house but it was if an impregnable wall separated them. Mrs Gunnet somehow managed to act as if she wasn't there most of the time. Or she'd say, 'It's not your place to do that, Miss Augusta,' and grimly refuse to show her how to do anything. To make life even more of a misery, hunger continuously gnawed at Augusta and to assuage it she instructed Billy to get as much as he could for another of her gowns. Luther had wanted to sell his silver-topped cane to an innkeeper who had once admired it but she had gone into a tantrum to prevent him. Somehow, like her silver brush and comb set and her gold locket, it represented a solid link with the life she'd once known.

'That was a gift from my brother,' she said. 'How dare you allow it to get into the hands of some ignorant innkeeper who cannot appreciate its true value.'

She was now left with two gowns, the grey in which she had married and her green with the white collar. But she had several warm coats and her fur muff and it was warmth that mattered, she realized now.

Struggling up from bed in an agitation of embarrassment at having to face Mrs Gunnet, she donned her grey gown and swept through to the kitchen. Avoiding the older woman's eyes she went straight to the hob and poured herself a cup of tea. While she sipped it she searched for something to eat, finding only a piece of dry bread which she immediately demolished.

'Why isn't there more food?' she asked her mother-in-law. 'Didn't Billy give you the money for my gown?'

'I was going out to try and get something for tonight's supper.'

'I shall come with you. I need some fresh air and exercise,' Augusta insisted.

Mrs Gunnet nodded, and Augusta returned to the room to don outdoor clothing. When she hurried back Luther's mother was waiting with a coarse shawl draped over her head and folded across her chest.

'I don't go to the shops along Argyle Street,' she said. 'The shops are cheapest in the High Street.'

It was a dry sunny day. The yellow rays had filtered through the net curtains of the parlour, but no sun brightened the cold yard between the tenements. Nor could the stinking air be called fresh. However they were soon across the yard and through the close with Mrs Gunnet clutching tightly at her shawl and staring straight ahead and Augusta bunching up her skirts to protect them from any foulness.

At the corner Augusta was pleased to catch a glimpse of the River Clyde at the foot of Stockwell Street sparkling like a silver ribbon in the sun. Instead of proceeding up Stockwell Street, Mrs Gunnet marched to the other end of the Briggait and on ground floors of tenement buildings there were many drinking saloons and brokeries and pawn shops.

Up past the Cross now. Past the square tower with its four-sided clock and open stone crown known as the Trongate Steeple. Into the High Street. The tenements here had a high cliff-like appearance like those in Edinburgh and crow-stepped gables to the street. Basements had rough stone arches under which shopkeepers displayed their goods.

Out on the streets were trestle tables piled with pails and buckets and basins. The street was also cluttered with barrels and women selling fruit or fish from handcarts, and men pushing barrows and both men and women with bundles on their backs or trays of merchandise hanging from their necks. The closes were even narrower than those of the Briggait and there was a variety of shapes and sizes of buildings down these long closes or alleys. There, hawkers also shouted their wares, squeezing their trays and carts and barrows between hordes of men and women and children in tattered clothes. Augusta felt shocked by the sights and sounds yet so great was her relief to be out of the confines of the house in the Briggait that the sights of the High Street, horrifying though they were, did not distress her quite so much as they might have in the past.

Mrs Gunnet halted at a shop with a bow window stuffed high with packets and tins and cards advertising various goods. Without a word the older woman entered the shop. Augusta stepped in too but there was such a putrid stench in its shadowy interior that she felt nauseated and had to return outside for a breath of air. For a moment or two she supported herself against the glass of the window and idly gazed at its contents. Then an apothecary's a little further along caught her eye and she moved nearer to examine it. Through its thick glass she saw two large bottles, one filled with emerald green liquid, the other with ruby red, and between them a pestle and a mortar. There were cards too, some toppled over and all covered with dust. Peering closer to the glass, Augusta managed to read: 'Butler's Cajeput Opodeldoc – for rheumatism, sprains, bruises, and unbroken chilblains. The basis for this Opodeldoc, the Cajeput Oil, has been highly esteemed on the Continent for Chronic Rheumatism, Spasmodic Affections, Palsy, Stiffness and enlargement of Joints . . .'

An unusual and alarming sound, among the cacophony of noise pressing in on her, switched Augusta's attention from the window. At first she could not make out the origin of it. People were crushing this way and that and blocking her view. Then suddenly a large horned animal, either a cow or a bull, burst through the crowd, jostling close with other similar beasts and all throwing back their heads and issuing forth loud bellowing noises.

Alarmed by the unexpected proximity of the animals Augusta backed into the nearest close. Other people crushed in too. All were intent on either pushing at or trying to avoid some of the animals that had also turned into the lane which was no more than five feet wide. Men women and children were shouting, screaming, laughing and crying. Unable to do anything else Augusta continued to move backwards. At last she managed to edge sideways into an opening between the buildings. Here it was quiet. The sounds of turmoil became detached from her. She looked around. Ancient houses brooded on either side, some with upper floors jutting out like canopies making cold, dark, shadowy places. Roofs jutted out too, some black-thatched, heavy and low. Outside stairs were made of stone and badly dilapidated and broken. Here and there a notice board protruded on which was written 'Lodgings to Let'.

She came to the conclusion that if she took the first turning on the right that ought to bring her out to the High Street again. Then she would simply have to turn right again, to do down to where she'd left Mrs Gunnet. After taking the first turning on the right, however, she found it blocked at the end by a towering tenement. A narrow opening in this tenement led off to the left and she followed this path hoping that from it there would be a right turning. But after wandering for some distance she only found another gloomy lane like a shadow on the left. Here different paths trickled off in all directions between crooked houses with black cavities for windows. She tried to be brave and quell the flutterings of fear in her chest. Telling herself she mustn't panic or run she stopped to get her bearings. She had lost all sense of direction. She could wander round and round in circles for hours. Then darkness would come. In desperation she looked for someone to ask the way. But not a living soul was in sight. She hesitated. The only alternative was to knock at one of the doors. There must be people somewhere. Catching sight of a basement door slightly ajar, she eased her skirts up and carefully descended the steps. Then, taking a deep breath and holding herself as straight and with as much dignity as she could, gave a sharp knock. After a few seconds she thought she heard a woman's voice say, 'Come in,' but it was as faint as a whisper. She hugged her velvet coat around her for comfort. Then, deciding she had no choice, she pushed the door wider and stepped inside.

The place consisted of one tiny cave-like room with a rough earthen floor. There was no fire in the open grate and no glass in the low window through which icy air flowed freely. Propped in the corner by the window a woman sat on a bed of straw. Beside her a baby lay sleeping. For a minute or two Augusta couldn't speak. Never before in her life had she witnessed such deprivation. Not one article of comfort or convenience could be seen in the room. There wasn't even a table or a chair. No candle gave a flicker of warmth or light. Nothing covered the rags the woman was wearing except another rag – it looked like a man's coat – which concealed her legs and half covered the baby. But it was the woman herself that horrified Augusta most. Once she might have been pretty. Now no flesh padded the fine bone-structure or kept the luminous eyes in proportion. White skin, scarlet-flushed and as delicate as a butterfly's wing, stretched across the skeleton, one hand of which clutched a receptacle crimson-stained with blood.

The wasted body did not move but the eyes struggled to give the impression of polite deference.

'Can I help you, mistress?'

The problem of having lost her way seemed so trivial in the presence of this woman's tragedy that Augusta felt ashamed to mention it.

'Why are you here like this?' she said. 'Have you no one to look after you or your baby?'

'I've a good man. No better man ever came out of Ireland.'

'How can you say that? He has not provided for you. This is a dreadful place. And he has left you and the child alone in it.'

'He's out looking for work. He keeps trying every day. There's nothing left to sell. It is not his fault. Every day he

102

tries. And every night he comes home and weeps because he thinks he's failed me.'

Augusta said, 'I would give you money but I have none.'

'And every day I'm so afraid,' the woman continued with obvious difficulty in finding enough breath.

'Of being alone?'

'In case he'll steal bread. In case they'll transport him or hang him. Like a common criminal. He's such a good proud man.' Suddenly terror splintered the woman's gaze. 'You haven't come to tell me something's happened to my man?'

'No . . . no,' Augusta hastily assured her. 'I've lost my way, that's all. I just wanted to know how to get back to the High Street.'

Tears of weakness spilled from the woman's eyes and the blotches on her cheeks burned furnace bright.

'My Patrick will show you the way.'

'When do you think he'll be back? When does he usually . . .'

Augusta' s voice faltered. The woman's eyes had closed and her breathing had become more laboured. Unheeded, the baby gave a thin wail. Augusta turned helplessly away but stopped at the door and turned back again fumbling with the buttons of her coat. Before she had divested herself of the warm quilted velvet, damp icy air had penetrated her dress. Leaning over she tucked the coat around both woman and baby. The child was blue with cold but once wrapped close to its mother in the luxurious coat it sucked its thumb in blissful contentment. The woman's eyes opened and stared dumbly up at Augusta.

She retreated outside, her thoughts in a turmoil. The woman's face haunted her. Her mind opened on to a maze far more bewildering than the confusion of streets around her. Oblivious now to the cold, hardly caring any more where she was going, she followed winding threads of lanes in nerve-stretching distress. It occurred to her that there might be countless others in as wretched a condition as the woman she'd just spoken to.

103

The truth of poverty stamped itself indelibly on the empty pages of her mind. The reality of it grew like a nightmare as she wandered in timeless abstraction through the streets. She did not even notice that dusk was creeping down.

Chapter Fifteen

The building beckoned to her, drew her like a moth to a flame. It was very large and made of stone. Row after row of windows stabbed out light and she was able to read the notice above the door which revealed the name of the cotton mill at which Tibs, Billy and Rose were employed.

Relief quickened her steps, and as she entered the building she felt eager for the sight of them. For the first time she felt that she and they were part of the same family. It was a comforting thought. Once she found Tibs's unruly mop of hair and harassed face, and Billy's bright intelligent eyes, and Rose with her pink cheeks and ringlets, she would be all right.

But no sooner had she entered the mill than noise scattered her wits. It rattled and crashed and screamed at such a pitch it seemed impossible for it to continue without exploding her eardrums or disintegrating her head.

The atmosphere was at once damp and hot. Fibrous dust and the rancid stench of machine oil choked the air, sickening her. She had an overpowering impression of iron pillars and iron wheels high and low, joined by enormous leather belts continuously, rapidly whirring. Giant bobbins jumped and clattered and clanged and flew about. Tiny children walked to and fro in front of the machinery, anxiously watching it and every now and again tying broken threads. Others crawled under the machinery like nervous dogs.

A man with a fat orange-peel face and bulbous lips stalked about brandishing a horse-whip.

Augusta caught sight of girls in a more advanced stage of

pregnancy than herself struggling to lift and lay full bob-bins. She was shocked at how strained and ill they looked, shocked at the mere idea of anyone with child being expected to do any kind of work. She remembered friends of her mother who had retired to bed or to their couch for the whole nine months and had never taken the risk of even lifting a handkerchief.

'Why the hell aren't you at your machine?'

The man with the whip suddenly appeared, bawling in front of her. The sour stink of his sweat filled her nostrils, nauseating her.

'No, I don't work here.' Her shout was all but mangled in the racket of the machinery. 'I was looking for the Gunnet family – Tibs, Rose and Billy.'

'What a bloody liberty! In for a chat, are you?'

'No, I – '

'Just to while away your time and theirs?'

'No, you see, I . . .' She strained to make herself heard above the din.

'Well, Mrs, maybe you've time to waste but they haven't. They've another hour or more to go, and it'll be their last hour's work if they're not careful. I'll have no idlers here. There's plenty dying for the chance of a job.'

'Yes, of course,' Augusta called out hastily. 'I'm sorry. I'll wait for them outside.' She hurried for the door, trembling in anxiety in case she had put the children's job in danger.

The sudden change of temperature from the heat of the mill to the cold outside gripped her like a vice. Her instinct was to stay sheltered in the doorway but she was too afraid that the man would see her. Instead she pattered across a graveyard of tall wooden boxes and squat trucks and sought shelter in the shadows of a brick wall. She could hear water busily gurgling and splashing on the other side of the wall. She asumed it must be the River Clyde and, that being so, if she followed it she must surely come to the foot of Stockwell Street and the Briggait. But in which direction should she follow it? She decided it would be safer to wait for the children. Time dragged with excruciating slowness. She kept moving her weight from one leg to the other and back again. She leaned against the wall. Eventually, hunkering down, hugging her knees she used them to support her head. In wretched fatigue she nearly drifted off to sleep. Only the cold and her hunger pains kept her awake.

Then at long last she was stirred to her feet by the sound of the mill door opening and the sight of the mill hands spilling out. In her desperation to find the faces she knew, she was unaffected by the army of shivering, hollow-cheeked cripples. Her anxious eyes skimmed over ghostly faces completely lacking in the usual mobility or liveliness of youth. Her mind did not register the knees bent inwards and backwards, ankles deformed and thick, spinal columns bent forward or to one side. She did not even flinch at the maimed and mutilated, crushing past a little boy with a stump for a foot, nearly knocking him off balance.

'Tibs!' she called on catching a glimpse of the frizzy head.

It struck Augusta as odd how, on seeing her, Tibs avoided her eyes. There was an unmistakable aura of shame about the girl that had not been there before. It lay on her like a heavy cloud, dulling her gaze and dousing her usual animated agitation. Billy and Rose, although benumbed with fatigue, had none of the shame with which their older sister was obviously shrinking inside.

'I got lost,' Augusta explained as she joined them. 'I didn't know how to get home by myself.'

They made no reply and the journey to the Briggait was made in silence.

As soon as they entered the house Luther took Augusta completely by surprise by bawling at her:

'What the hell do you think you've been playing at?'

'Luther . . .' His mother see-sawed the word, lurching it out like a warning.

'Mother's been distraught with worry. We've both been out searching the town for you.'

'I got lost . . .'

106

'You got lost,' Luther sneered. 'You useless, stupid . . .'

His mother closed her eyes. 'Luther, please . . .'

'You were with Mother. Why didn't you make sure you stayed with her instead of wandering off God knows where?'

'Anyone would think I got lost on purpose.' Augusta's voice held much bitterness. 'I'm very sorry if I've caused you any trouble.'

'Trouble? You've been nothing but trouble right from the start. I'm bloody sick of you! You've had my mother in a terrible state.'

'I'm sick of your mother!' she said in a retaliation that was merely a defence against tears.

Mrs Gunnet's face distorted and she clutched at her shoulder.

'Mother, what's wrong?'

'Just a twinge of rheumatism.' She gave another gasp of pain, her features twisting with the regret of it as she fumbled into a chair. 'Your father will be in soon. Time to put the kettle on . . .'

Luther immediately swung round on Augusta.

'You're to blame for this. Tibs, make Mother a cup of tea. Maybe that'll soothe her.'

'I can do it,' Augusta started towards the kettle simmering on the hob.

'You can't do anything. Get away through to the room.'

'My place is here now. You said so yourself.'

'He's away to deliver the cloth,' Mrs Gunnet's voice turned prim with pride. 'That was a grand order he had.'

Rose began to cry and Billy said wearily, 'Stop your snivelling,' and went over to his mother, put his arm around her and hid her head against his shoulder.

The child's dirt-streaked face and thin body drooping with fatigue lit a spark of admiration in Augusta. How hungry he must be as well as tired and yet he could still show such tenderness and concern for his mother. Determined to do something for his sake if for no one else's she lifted the stub of candle to go over to the sideboard to see what food she could get ready. Tibs had made the tea and was pouring out a cupful for her mother. Luther was jabbing a poker into the fire to try and give her some heat.

'What do you think you're doing with our only candle?' he asked.

'I was just taking it over to the sideboard to see what there is to eat.'

'Oh, isn't that typical,' he gave a sarcastic laugh. 'Even at a time like this all she can think of is herself.'

Suddenly Augusta's tears would not be held back. In helpless rage she flung the candle at Luther, plunging the cave of a room into blackness except for the fuzz of yellow round the fire.

'Here's your candle,' she shouted. 'You can eat that for all I care!'

Stumbling, fumbling in the dark she found her way into the room but before she could shut the door Luther had reached her with surprising speed. His hand grabbed out at her and in the second that she felt its iron hardness she knew she was in immediate danger of physical violence, perhaps death. Animal instinct propelled her without hesitation into action. Instead of struggling to be free of him she hurled her body against his, clung round his neck, lips searching and opening.

'Luther, I'm sorry. I'm sorry.'

He gripped her by the back of the neck, making her whimper in pain but press and squirm herself all the more urgently against him.

'You fuckin' little whore,' he said close to her ear.

The shock of hearing such language was almost as violent to her person as a blow. Yet it brought a frightening thrill that intensified to hysterical passion as he kissed her. Then suddenly he tore her arms down from his neck and pushed her aside.

'You care about nobody but yourself and your own self-gratification.'

'That's not true.'

'Oh? Prove it.'

'What can I do?'

108

'What I've already told you to do. Look after my mother instead of having her look after you.'

'What happened today was an accident. It wasn't my fault.'

He gave one of his bitter laughs. 'I notice you didn't immediately assure me that, yes, you would look after my mother. But one thing you can be sure of, Augusta. If anything happens to her I'll hold you responsible.'

'That's unfair. I've tried my best.'

'Your best's not good enough. Stop your useless whining and come through and have your supper.'

The candle had been lit again and everyone was sitting round the table with plates of steaming porridge in front of them. They were obviously waiting for Luther to say Grace. Mrs Gunnet looked perfectly normal. Luther drew in a chair and sat down. Augusta went over to the fire where the porridge pot still simmered. Very carefully she dished a plateful then carried it over and placed it in front of her husband. Despite being harrowed and hurt, she experienced a little flutter of pleasure in performing the task and bustled back to the hob to ladle out her own.

'Thank you, God, for what we are about to receive,' Luther intoned.

'You used to say a much nicer longer Grace,' his mother reminded him.

'We used to have more to be thankful for.'

Augusta ate greedily and soon the porridge had filled her belly with warmth and comfort. The children spooned wearily, lethargically. Looking at them and realizing that they would have to be up and away to work at half-past five in the morning, she pitied them. At least she could stay in bed and have a decent rest. Tibs rose eventually and began clearing the dishes, and impulsively Augusta rose too.

'You've the mill to face tomorrow, Tibs, I'll see to the dishes.'

To her surprise Tibs immediately collapsed over the table in heartbroken sobs.

'Making a fuss won't change anything, my girl,' Mrs

Gunnet said stiffly. 'You've got to work and there's an end to it. Just think yourself lucky you've found a job.'

'I don't mind working,' Tibs wiped at her streaming face. 'It's not the work.'

'What is it then?'

Helplessly the girl shook her head. Augusta began gathering up the plates.

'It's a terrible place. I don't blame you for being upset. And that horrible man . . .'

Another welter of sobbing overcame the girl. 'He's the overlooker. I hate him.'

'I don't blame you.'

'Will you stop saying that?' Luther burst out. 'You're only making her worse.'

'I was trying to be sympathetic.'

'Well, your sympathy's no use. Just go through to the room out of the way.'

She was so hurt she burst into tears and sobbed in unison with Tibs.

'Oh, God!' Luther groaned.

'Don't worry, I'm going,' she managed.

In the room, she had to grope and stumble against the furniture to reach the candle on the chest of drawers. As she did so her tears dried and her heart hardened.

What was the use of crying here? she thought bitterly. A river of tears wouldn't wash this terrible place away.

Chapter Sixteen

'I'm desperate, Sid,' Luther told the coachman. 'It tears at my gut to see my family go hungry.'

They were sitting together at the bar of a low-roofed tavrn. Sid Cruickshanks had bought Luther a tankard of ale and he took a swig at it before speaking again.

'Surely there's some way you can help.'

'Coaching's out,' the old man replied eventually. 'Cameron has seen to that.'

'I know. But can't you think of anything else?'

Slowly Sid lit a pipe then through teeth clamped on the stem he said, 'There's more than you can't get work. It seems to me half the town's unemployed.' The tobacco glowed comfortingly as he sucked. 'Men especially. There's Paddies at every other street corner trying to sell the shirt off their backs for a few potatoes.'

Luther tugged his fingers through his wiry hair. 'Damn, damn, damn!'

'There's a rat match tonight,' Sid said after a while. 'If I'm not mistaken a few shillings could be made there.'

'Upstairs?'

Sid nodded.

'A dog's needed for that.'

'There's a dog at the stables. A good catcher is old Drum. That place used to be hotching with rats.'

'Would you give him to me?'

Sid shook his head.

'Well,' said Luther. 'What the hell are we talking about?'

'It might be possible to loan him to you. I say *might*, you understand. It could only be for one match, Luther. I'd be taking a big enough risk with that. You know Mr Cameron.'

'Damn bloody Cameron.'

'You can damn him all you like but the fact remains I've more to lose than you. There's my job, and Nessie's, and the roof over our heads.'

'I know. I'm sorry. It's just I'm so desperate to earn a few shillings. Augusta's had to sell most of her things. I've sold my watch and all my decent clothes. But she nearly goes mad when I try to part with the damn cane her brother gave me. She's a queer one.'

'She's a lady born and bred, and don't you forget it.'

Luther's eyes narrowed angrily but he managed in an even voice, 'What about the dog? Can I get it for tonight?'

The lean leathery jaws drew at the pipe until Luther exploded with irritation.

'For God's sake! It's only a step away. It wouldn't take me five minutes.'

'Now, just hang on. You can't set foot in the Cameron stables.'

'You then.'

'You never could content yourself for any length of time.'

'You'll go?'

'I've a coach to take to Edinburgh in half an hour.'

'For old times' sake, Sid.'

'How would you get the dog back?'

'In the middle of the night. No one would see me then. Don't worry, I'll get it back.'

For a long time the coachman hesitated before knocking out his pipe and speaking.

'I'll be honest with you. I wouldn't take such a risk for you alone. But,' he shook his head, 'I keep thinking of poor Miss Augusta.'

'All right, all right! For Augusta then.'

After the lanky figure in the long tiered benjamin coat and felt black hat wended his way through the crowded tavern then disappeared, Luther took another mouthful of ale and studied his surroundings.

The place was filthy. Even the tubs where the spirits were kept were dirty and blistered with heat from the gas, their gilt hoops now blackened. The long bar was packed with men of all classes. Gentlemen in top hats and neat-waisted coats rubbed shoulders with coachmen in livery, and tradespeople, and soldiers with their uniforms carelessly unbuttoned.

Everyone was smoking and drinking and talking loudly about dogs. Many had their 'fancy' animals with them. Under the arms of some men protruded squashed-looking bulldogs with flat pink noses. Other nursed Skye terriers curled up like balls of hair and sleeping like children. Little brown terriers were wide awake and struggling to get loose. It was as if they smelt the rats upstairs and were impatient to get at them. Breathing heavily on an old chair lay an enormous bulldog with a head far too large for its body and its forehead overhanging its flat nose. It had a sore look, with its pink-rimmed eyes and nose and tinges of the same colour at all the edges of its body. On the other side of the fireplace sat a disreputable-looking white bull-terrier with a black patch over one eye and ribs that showed like hoops. It kept watching the movements of the customers and every time the entrance door swung back it gave a warning growl.

By the time Sid came back, the bar was so solidly packed with men and dogs, and more still pouring in, that at the landlord's request they had to overspill into the parlour. Gaslight revealed dingy wallpaper on which hung clusters of black leather collars adorned with brass rings and clasps.

'Give your orders, gentlemen,' the barman kept shouting.

As they settled at one of the tables, Luther admired the dog at Sid's heels.

'Christ, he looks a fierce one.'

'Yes, you'd better be careful with old Drum. That dog would have you by the throat as quick as any rat. No, don't put a hand near him, Luther. Not yet. Give him a chance to have a sniff. Let him take his own time. I'll have one more drink with you then I'll have to go.'

The dogs belonging to the company were now being hitched on to the tables and minutely examined by all who got near them. Limbs were stretched out and fingered, legs squeezed, eyes and mouths scrutinized. Nearly all the animals were scarred from rat bites. One terrier in particular had obviously suffered much about the face and neck. Its owner proudly declared that his 'Mac' had once killed two hundred rats in six minutes.

Eventually the barkeeper gave the order. 'Shut the shutters upstairs, and light the pit.'

Immediately there was a mass exodus of thumping feet towards the wooden stairs.

'Time I was away,' said Sid. 'You keep a tight grip on old Drum, do you hear me, lad? That beast goes mad the first whiff of a rat.'

'How many do you reckon he's capable of? How many should I risk?'

Sid chewed the stem of his pipe. 'Two dozen would be a safe enough figure.'

113

'You think they'd bet on that?'

Stretching to his feet and tugging his coat around him Sid said, 'If I were you I wouldn't dare risk any more. If they find out you've no money to cover your losses, my guess is you'll not get out of here alive. But you always were one to take risks. I've given you the dog. That's the best I can manage. You do what you've a mind to.'

'I might take a chance on more. If I said double that, it would be bound to raise the stakes. And if I got him really mad . . . He looks as if he could do it, Sid.'

'Ah, well.' The coachman made to leave. 'All I can say is I'll be glad to be on the road this night. If it comes to the worst I suppose Drum will find his own way back.'

'At least wish me luck,' Luther called after him.

At the door the old man raised his pipe in a silent gesture of goodwill.

Luther rose, winding the leather thonging that held the dog tightly round his hand. The animal was beginning to wheeze and scream and pull with such force it sounded as if it were strangling itself. As he fought to control it going up the stairs Luther could hear a bedlam of squalling and barking from what had one been the drawing-room above.

The pit consisted of a small circus about six feet in diameter and fitted with a high wooden rim that reached to elbow height. Over it, branches of a gas lamp were arranged which lit up the white painted floor. At one side of the room a bed-recess afforded grandstand seats for the inn-keeper and a couple of his most valued customers. The rest of the men clambered up on tables and forms and hung over the side of the pit itself.

Dogs were struggling in their masters' arms and straining at leashes and making such an earsplitting din that the innkeeper had to bawl:

'All you that have dogs, you'll *have* to make them shut up.'

But when a rusty wire cage filled with a dark moving mass of rats was brought forward, it was as if all hell had been let loose. Luther was jerked about in his fight to control Drum who by this time was in a perfect fit of excitement, foaming at the mouth and stretching his neck forward until it seemed that the collar that held it back was almost cutting its throat in two.

The innkeeper called for a stop-watch and also elected an umpire, quite a dandy of a man with a fat cigar.

'To see whether the rats are dead or alive when killed, as Paddy says!'

In the meantime the man who'd brought the cage into the pit was pulling rats out by their tails and jerking them into the arena. While he was doing this some of the rats scurrying about the painted floor, others were running up the man's trousers.

'Get out, you varmints!' he shouted, shaking them off.

Some of the ugly little animals sat up on their hind legs, cleaning their faces with their paws.

After the cage of rats was emptied the first dog was brought forward, stretching itself excitedly in its master's arms. It had thighs like a grasshopper and a mouth that opened back to its ears. The umpire patted it then looked round the room.

'Well, folks, time to begin the first match. Who'll bet on this little beauty killing a dozen in five minutes?'

Bets were busily taken and eventually the umpire said, 'Right, toss him in!'

In a second the rats were flying round the white floor as fast as black balls or trying to hide themselves in openings in the boards round the pit. But Luther could see that the dog was not much use as a killer. Its owner had to keep bullying it on by loudly beating the sides of the pit with his hands and bawling.

'Get them! Get them, you stupid bastard!'

Some of the rats, as the dog tentatively advanced towards them, sprang up into his face, making him jerk back in astonishment. Those he managed to bite curled round his nose and he was forced to carry them like a cat with a kitten.

Even the dead ones he didn't know what to do with and the owner had to shout:

'Drop it! Drop it, you fool.'

The match was lost, the dog only having killed five out of the dozen. Luther could tell by the furious look on the owner's face as he paid up that the dog was going to be kicked all the way home.

One thing was certain, Luther thought, if Drum lost he couldn't kick it back to the stables. It would have the leg off him first.

While the money was being squared up and bets taken on the next dog, it was allowed into the pit to amuse itself with the dead bodies. Much laughter was caused by the dog seizing hold of one as big as himself, shaking it furiously and thumping its head on the floor like a drumstick.

While the next few matches went on, Drum writhed about, mad with rage, scratching and struggling to get loose. Eventually Luther decided to move forward with it.

'Make way for the champion!' he shouted. 'Sixty in five minutes. Any takers?'

'Sixty?'

A ripple of excitement coursed round the room.

'Sixty, you say?'

'Sixty.'

Bets came pouring in and Luther, despite his iron calm, could not stop sweat from boiling up and pricking over his face as he held on like grim death to the demented terrier.

The floor was swept and another, larger rat cage brought in. When the animals had been flung into the pit they immediately gathered themselves into a barricade which reached a third up the side. They were all sewer or ditch rats and the smell that rose from them reminded Luther of a hot drain.

While the bets were still being taken, the umpire amused himself by flicking at the mound of rats with his pocket handkerchief and offering them the lighted end of his cigar. They tamely sniffed at it, then drew back as they singed their noses. He also blew on the mound, and the rats, obviously disliking this, fluttered about like feathers in the wind, only to form another wall as hastily as they could.

The moment the wildly barking Drum was let free he became quiet in a most businesslike manner and rushed at the rats to bury his nose in the mound and bring out one in his mouth. In no time a dozen rats with wetted necks were strewn around, reddening the white paint of the floor.

Luther closed his eyes. The suspense made him feel sick. If the dog lost, and the howling mob of men discovered he'd tricked them, they would batter him to death. He would fight like a madman to get out but against this crowd he knew he didn't stand a chance. They were after blood. He prayed it wouldn't be his.

'Blow on them! Blow on them!' the crowd were shouting and when Luther opened his eyes again he saw that the ugly little animals had again found a barricade and the umpire was puffing away at it as if trying to extinguish a fire and making the rats dart off like so many sparks.

Luther cursed to himself. For Drum to be forced to race about after his prey meant wasting precious seconds. But suddenly the inkeeper bawled:

'Time!'

Luther leapt into the ring and caught the dog and held it as it panted and stretched its neck out like a serpant's to stare intently at the rats which still kept crawling about.

In an agony of suspense Luther waited until the umpire counted the dead animals. Then the shout went up.

'Sixty-three! A champion indeed!'

He felt relief yet his sickness remained and he was hardly aware of collecting his winnings.

Another dog was in the ring now and a voice from the crowd was crying out: 'Any dog could kill quicker than him. I'll kill against him myself.'

Laughing and jeering and scoffing greeted this offer but the voice insisted: 'I'll kill against that dog for a sovereign.'

Eventually the wager was accepted. Then Luther saw a desperate skeleton in tattered clothing clamber into the ring. The man got down on all fours, his mouth twitching and trembling, his eyes enormous.

The appalling sight triggered Luther into pushing his way fiercely towards the stairs, vowing to himself that no matter what happened he would never become as degraded as that.

Chapter Seventeen

Augusta had flinched in distaste when Luther told her how he'd got the money. Her sensitivity angered him so much that he had grabbed her by the shoulders and said, 'Don't you look at me like that, you high and mighty little bitch. Just think yourself lucky you're going to be sure of something to eat for the next few weeks.'

She could see by his staring eyes and white face that he was genuinely distressed and this revelation of his feelings touched her and made her see him in a new light. It made her experience, too, a stab of resentment against fate that her husband should be reduced to such revolting ways to try to earn some money. He had been such a swell dragsman and everyone had admired his prowess on the box. It wasn't right that he should suffer such indignities. And he *was* suffering, she realized that now. She saw how he had lost his jaunty swagger. His ready smile and twinkling eyes had been replaced by dourness and flashes of temper like sporadic eruptions of a volcano.

She longed to help and comfort him, but faced with the violence of his anger she could only retreat into herself in confusion. She believed that by doing chores in the house it would please him and she kept stubbornly trying to learn to make porridge or bannocks or soup or to clean the fire grate or work the water pump. But she was thwarted at every turn by his mother. If in desperation she clutched at the water bucket, for example, and insisted on going for the water to make the tea, Mrs Gunnet would reply, 'My husband and I have never needed to depend on help from anyone and we're not starting now. This is my house and I'll fetch the water for my husband's tea.'

Once Luther had come in as Augusta was verbally battling to make his mother understand and crying out in frustration: 'You're mad! You're a madwoman!'

Once he had actually caught her physically struggling with Mrs Gunnet.

'You told me to help your mother,' she protested as he dragged her roughly into the room, 'and that's all I've been trying to do.'

'She certainly needs help.'

'I know she does.'

'And yet you abuse her.'

'I don't mean to but I just can't get her to understand. Luther, half the time she's away in a world of her own. She keeps talking as if your father's alive. She even sets a place at the table for him. Or she sits and reads that letter to the children and to herself as if she's just received it. And after all it's only an ordinary character testimonial. I've written one exactly like that when one of Mama's servants was leaving to be married – '

'If I ever catch you belittling that letter to her, I'll kill you.'

The intensity of his bitterness and the way it was twisting his face as well as his nature depressed her. She knew it stemmed from all he was suffering as well as from concern for his mother. She even realized when she thought back to the night of the blizzard that what had happened was as much her own fault as his, if it was anyone's fault. She could see no point in trying to apportion blame any more. The immediate problem of survival was too all-absorbing.

Every day she seemed to be getting heavier and clumsier. Her clothes no longer fitted her, they tilted grotesquely with front hem far higher than the back and showing an indecent amount of stocking. Her hair was dirty and tangled. Occasionally she washed it but it had become such a chore to struggle in with extra water and to get down on her knees at the tin bath, she could be bothered less and less as time went on. She had no desire to strip off in the cold and have a bath very often either. It seemed a miracle to her now how anyone living in circumstances like these could keep themselves in any way decent. Yet she knew that there were families living in even smaller, more over-crowded and far more dreadful hovels than this.

Only the other day when she was out at the pump she'd heard a woman in a panic of sobbing. She'd hurried over to enquire what was wrong and before she knew what was happening the woman was pulling her along a filthy passage swarming with vermin and into a room about eight feet square. Vile putrescence oozed through cracks in the boards overhead and ran down the walls. The window was stuffed with rags. Five young children crouched on the damp earthen floor. In the corner lay a lad of about fourteen. His clothes were as thin as paper and his appearance death-like. He was trembling with cold and writhing about in pain with cramp and diarrhoea. The stench and closeness of the room made Augusta cough and retch and grope away back along the corridor. The woman had hastened after her, frantic with grief.

'Tell us, missus. What's to be done?' she kept repeating. 'My poor laddie. What's to be done for him?'

Augusta gave her a blanket from her own bed to warm the boy. She had been tempted to try and soothe and comfort the woman by telling lies about believing that the boy was going to be all right, but she knew instinctively that lies were a luxury neither she nor the woman could afford.

'I'll give you some gruel,' she told her instead. 'It will warm and strengthen your other children. There's nothing either of us can do for the boy.'

She didn't tell Luther about the incident. There seemed no point in depressing him more than he already was. Instead she tried to get him to talk about what occured during his day, but since the rat-killing episode he had stubbornly refused to confide in her. She suspected that occasionally he found a menial task that earned him a

120

shilling or two. At least, sometimes he produced a few shillings.

At night in the blackness of the set-in-the-wall bed they sometimes made love. It was becoming more difficult because of her swollen belly but making love, in any position or in any manner at all, was the only pleasure in her life. She felt it must be for him too. As a result she became more and more daring, touching him, stroking, caressing him, and knowing by his little grunts and groans that it must be giving him pleasure too. It was the only time she experienced any real closeness with him. As each day followed another the bitterness formed a harder and harder shell around him.

She tried to preserve daily contact by talking with him but her attempts at conversation never got very far. She wept for him and the remnants of his pride that he hung on to so desperately. But she couldn't tell him why she wept, and he thought it was only because she was hungry and he couldn't give her enough money for food.

His face had set with the strength of bitterness. He had visibly drawn further away from her and hardened as if he were cast in a mould or iron that would never break.

She had tried to melt him with her hands but the feel of his big frame and how it had obviously lost much of its covering of flesh only served to make her tense herself. She could not sleep for worrying about him. Her mind sought ways in which she might help him. Could she find a job? A post as governess would be the only employment she might be qualified to do, but who would employ a governess from the Briggait? Who would give her any kind of work? Her soul quailed at the thought of the mill. Yet she resolved to ask Tibs if there would be any chance for her there. Of course, her baby was due any time now. It might be better to wait until the baby came. But then – what to do with the child? She supposed she would have to depend on Mrs Gunnet's looking after it. This gave a painful edge to her worry. But the more she thought of it, the more it became obvious that she had to find work. They were barely

121

surviving now. How could an addition to the family be supported?

Luther was doing his best. It was not his fault that they were all but destitute. He had taken her into his home and made her his wife. Many another man, she realized now, would have left her to fend for herself on the streets.

As soon as the baby came, she determined, she would seek employment. In the meantime she would do her best to cope with the work in the house and the search for scraps of food.

She insisted that she received the children's wages and any money that Luther managed to earn so that she could do the shopping. Their mother was no longer fit enough and needed more rest, she explained amidst Mrs Gunnet's protestations. She resolved to do better than her mother-in-law in squeezing the most from the shopkeepers.

She learned where to go by simply wandering round all the shops in the poorest areas until she found her bearings, and soon she knew not only the best places to go but the best times. If she went last thing on a Saturday night to a shop that sold perishable good and pointed out to the shopkeeper that his merchandise would be stinking rotten by the time he opened again on Monday, the chances were he could be talked into giving her a bit of fish or a jug of milk for next to nothing.

It was on one of these shopping expeditions that Augusta took a sudden longing to stroll along Argyle Street and gaze at the windows of establishments in which she had once been able to buy without ever bothering about cost. It was a balmy September evening and the gas lamps were strung along the street like a diamond necklace. The shop windows too shone jewel-bright through the velvety dusk. Carriages with lanterns swinging clattered cheerfully over the cobbles. Augusta allowed herself to be jostled along as she gazed this way and that with interest. The din of the streets had just about reached its climax, with vendors lining the whole length of the causeway shouting their wares, when despite the racket she picked out a familiar voice:

'Do be careful, girls. Keep behind McKenzie. He will clear a path.'

Dumpling-faced Mrs Binny was shepherding her two daughters across a pavement towards a waiting coach. Halfway there, she stopped abruptly and cried,

'Mary, Fay, look! It's Augusta Cameron!'

The sisters put gloved palms to mouths in shocked dismay and fluttered back as Augusta stepped forward to greet them. 'Oh, Mama!' they twittered in unison, like two tropical birds in their pink coats and their yellow and white feathered bonnets.

Augusta was suddenly aware that no bonnet covered her grubby hair; it had long before been sold. The coat she wore was shabby and so tight she could not fasten it across her enormous belly. Her slippers as well as her stockings were dirt-splashed and torn.

'Oh, my dear,' wailed Mrs Binny, 'what has that dreadful man been doing to you?'

'You mean my husband?' Augusta tilted her head in a defiant show of pride. 'He has been trying to keep me from starvation. And it has not been easy since my father has banned him from decent employment.'

Now Mrs Binny stepped back and brought out her handkerchief to waft about as if to dispense an unpleasant smell. 'But, my dear, at best he was only a common servant.'

'My husband was never common, Mrs Binny.' She turned to the Misses Binny and eyeing their ringless fingers said, 'Still not able to get a man of any kind, I see.'

Leaving them fluttering behind their mother in dismay, Augusta continued her promenade along Argyle Street. But the pleasure had gone. The glare of gaslit shop windows, the stentorian-voiced hucksters, the push and pull of the crowd exhausted instead of excited her. Homesickness for Cameron House and for her own mother was swelling in her chest like a dangerous balloon.

Chapter Eighteen

'There you are, squire!' Luther's eyes creased with a hard mockery of his old laughter. 'I was in the area so I thought I'd meet you and walk you home.'

Neither Billy nor Rose answered and his gaze sharpened and probed at them to discover why they looked so apprehensive as well as tired. He hoisted Rose into his arms, but instead of flopping immediately into sleep as she'd done on previous occasions, this time she nervously picked at his jacket. Billy's shoulders hunched against the cold but there was an aura of misery about him that went beyond physical suffering. The child's distress sent rage bludgeoning about inside Luther.

'Where's Tibs?' he asked the boy.

'I don't know.'

'What do you mean, you don't know?' He stopped in his tracks. 'She comes home with you every night, doesn't she?'

Rose began to moan and weep until Luther gave her a shake.

'What's happened?'

'She's run away,' Billy said.

'Run home, you mean?'

'I don't think so.'

'Where, then?'

'She wouldn't tell us. She was crying at dinner time. She said she'd never see us again. Afterwards the overlooker came searching for her. He beat us to try and make us tell where she'd gone. He wouldn't believe we didn't know. We don't know, Luther, I swear it.'

Luther stared down at the strained face topped with the tufty stubble of hair.

'It's all right, Billy,' he managed. 'I'm not blaming you. Maybe she's at home. Let's hurry and see. If she's not there I'll come back out and search the town.'

He lengthened his stride for the rest of the way and Billy had to run to keep up. The child was palpitating with breathlessness by the time they reached the house. His mother, rigid-backed and tight-mouthed, was dishing potatoes on to plates set around the table.

'Has Tibs been in yet?'

She threw him a wary look. 'Tibs? Isn't she with you?'

'Where's Augusta?'

His mother made no reply and putting Rose on one of the chairs he strode through to the room where Augusta was tugging a brush through her hair.

'Have you seen Tibs today?'

'Not since last night. Why?'

'She's disappeared. Run away, Billy says. God knows where. I'm going back out to search for her. You see that Mother stays here.'

Mrs Gunnet was already marching across the room for her shawl but he stopped her. 'No, Mother. I don't want to be worried about you as well. Leave this to me. I'll find her even if it takes all night.'

Augusta hastened heavily towards him and blocked his path to the door.

'Luther, have your supper first. You've had nothing to eat since morning.'

'For God's sake!'

'You must eat something.'

'That's all I need. You to start nagging me.' Irritably he turned back to the table and began stuffing potatoes into his mouth without sitting down.

At his side again, Augusta held up a cup of milk. Without a word he drank it down.

'You'll feel better after that.' She touched his arm and had an almost overwhelming longing to have her caress returned. She needed him. The burden of herself had become too exhausting, and the mystery of birth a frightening reality around which her thoughts revolved more and more.

She had tried to talk to Mrs Gunnet about what giving

birth would actually mean, what she should do and who could help her. She knew of course that a doctor was out of the question. They could not even afford a midwife. But Mrs Gunnet had completely closed her mind against Augusta.

Suddenly Augusta didn't want Luther to go at all. It wasn't that she didn't care about Tibs. But she was frightened. What if the baby started while Luther was gone? She had not been feeling well all day.

'I wish you worried about me half as much.' She didn't meant to sound childish but somehow she couldn't help it. 'All I'm good for it seems is looking after your mother. It's your mother this and you mother that . . .'

'Can you never think of anyone but yourself?'

After he'd gone she wiped her face dry and dragged herself over to the table to eat her supper. No one spoke and the silence seemed to press down with the ceiling until she felt suffocated by it.

Mrs Gunnet was clearing away the plates when Billy at last said: 'I'd better go and look too.'

His mother gave him a brusque nod. 'You're a good clever lad. You'll find Tibs all right.'

Augusta thought it foolishness for him to go out trailing the streets when he was so tired but she said nothing. They would not listen to her anyway. To them she was nothing but the cause of all their misery and misfortunes.

She ached with restlessness. Despite her vague feelings of indisposition a fountain of energy leapt within her. Unable to bear sitting still a moment longer she went through to the room and began tugging the bedclothes straight, tidying drawers, rubbing at the furniture with a duster. Then unexpectedly her concentration switched back to herself. Pain crunched across her lower abdomen, making her gasp. It lasted for a few seconds and then it was gone. Her pulse quickened and loudened like the tick of a clock. The baby must be coming. She had to seek help without further delay. Forgetting to put on a coat she retraced her steps through the kitchen and then out to the yard. A full moon had draped a translucent veil inside the deep pit of the close, making shadowy mounds of the dunghills but covering the tall tenements in silvery scales. High in one of the buildings voices swirled in argument. From some low corner a cat growled. Augusta picked her way across the yard then steeled herself to pass along the dark corridor to the one-roomed hovel in which lived the woman with the children she'd once helped. The oldest boy had died, and at the time Augusta had done her best to try to console the woman, whose name she had discovered was Mrs Dinwoodie.

Mrs Dinwoodie's husband had been one of the few men employed by the mills to clean and sharpen the carding-frames but he was killed in an accident at work. She had not been able to find a job and had been recently forced to let out her home for a few hours each Friday and Saturday night for prostitution. On these nights she and the children slept huddled together on stairs or landings or shop door-ways. As the woman had explained to Augusta, to survive you had to get money somehow. They had become quite friendly. Meeting occasionally at the water-pump, they would stop to gossip for a few minutes. Sometimes they bumped into each other at the small groceries in High Street or Gallowgate Street where they both tried to haggle to get as much food as possible for the little money they possessed.

Mrs Dinwoodie was surprised to see her at such a late hour but immediately asked her in, apologizing for the lack of a chair.

'Tibs has run away,' Augusta explained. 'And Luther and Billy have gone out to search for her. They might be away most of the night for all I know and I'm worried in case the baby is on its way. You know what Mrs Gunnet is like and she gets worse every day. I will get no help from her.'

'Never mind.' Mrs Dinwoodie patted Augusta's arm. 'I'll do what I can. Pains started, have they?'

'I had one before I came across.'

'Was that the first?'

'Yes.'

'Well, I'd say there's not much fear of you delivering before morning.'

Augusta hesitated with a mixture of anxiety and embarrassment. Then lowering her voice to a whisper so that Mrs Dinwoodie's children shouldn't hear she asked, 'What . . . what happens exactly?'

'They'll start coming more often until it arrives. You'll manage. There's no need to look so feared.'

'You mean I could manage myself if the worst came to the worst?'

'I don't say that. There's the cord to cut and the mess to get rid of and you all cleaned up. The baby's eyes has to be wiped as well. But don't fret. I'll see to everything. Better than some midwives. Some aren't all that fussy.'

'When will you . . . oh!' Pain unexpectedly robbed her of breath and she grabbed at the older woman for support.

'Another already?' Mrs Dinwoodie remarked. 'You're going to be quick.'

Augusta ground out words: 'When will you come?'

'I wasn't thinking there'd be any call till morning. But I tell you what, I'll take a run over after I get the children to sleep.'

'You won't forget, will you?'

'Give me an hour. And see there's plenty hot water ready, and a pail or something for the afterbirth and scissors or a knife for the cord and something to tie round it.'

The moon kept flitting behind clouds as Augusta shuffled back across the yard. One moment a phosphorescent gleam lit her path. Then suddenly all was black and she had to edge forward with sensitive toes and hands protectively outstretched. Managing to avoid the dunghill, she scuffed her feet free of papers and other rubbish strewn about. The sound of argument from inside one of the tenements had soared into violence. The woman was screaming hysterically. The man made no sound.

In helpless harassment Augusta reached the rickety

wooden stairway with the familiar piece of wood trailing loose, then felt her way along to the corner under the stair where the Gunnet door was hidden. At the door she was startled by another grinding contraction. Clinging to the doorhandle she forced herself to take deep breaths until the pain went away. A resolution to be brave took possession of her mind. Mrs Gunnet, Mrs Dinwoodie, no one was going to see her go to pieces and behave in a cowardly or in any way reprehensible fashion. If Mrs Gunnet and Mrs Dinwoodie and innumerable other women could have their babies here, like this, so could she.

Already she regretted betraying a shaft of fear to Mrs Dinwoodie and, rallying all her concentration and courage, she prepared herself to cope with whatever was to come.

The kitchen table was cleared. Mrs Gunnet, eyes shut and face like a death-mask, filled the chair by the fire. Her feet were set apart but firmly on the floor. Her hands flatly gripped the arms of the chair. On her lap was the box that contained her letter and other remnants from the past.

The doors of the set-in-the-wall bed in which Rose was now sleeping were tightly shut. The dresser, the tables, the chairs were brooding black shapes beyond the faltering light of the candle.

With difficulty Augusta emptied the kettle into the big cauldron of a pot then trailed back out to the yard, praying that the pump had not been shut off. Fortunately it had not and she was able to fill the kettle and lug it back to the kitchen. Then it occurred to her that it would be better if the water was kept ready in the room so that Mrs Dinwoodie might be spared the ordeal of passing to and fro in front of Mrs Gunnet.

In between ever-increasing contractions she managed to carry a shovelful of coal through and set a fire burning in the room. Then she transferred some water into the tin bath which she struggled to carry through and clatter down in the fireplace. Next she crept slowly out to the yard to fill the kettle again. She had just managed to return and place the kettle on the room fire when she was brought to her knees with a pain that forced a scream from between clenched teeth.

The relief when the pain faded away was exquisite. But she hadn't time to savour the delicious release, she had too much to do. With increasing application of will and concentration she forced herself to fetch the coal pail from the kitchen, empty the few pieces it contained on to the fire then take it out to the yard to wash it at the pump. Pain drowned her again as she clung to the handle, and left her blindly fumbling and splashing at water and getting herself soaked. Somehow she found her way back to the house, past the stony Mrs Gunnet and into the room. Hardly knowing what she was doing any more, she set out scissors on the table, and thread and the gown she had made for the baby from one of her petticoats, and her face sponge and towel. She wondered if she would be able to climb into the high bed without Mrs Dinwoodie's help, and prayed that an hour had passed and that she would at any moment come.

The contractions were gripping more often now, hardly allowing her time to recover from one before another overwhelmed her. She longed for the comfort of the bed but she knew she could no longer reach it. She was marooned on her knees on the hard floor, tearing at the settee with broken fingernails. By the time she heard the faraway knocking on the outside door she was reduced to writhing on the floor like an animal, sometimes squealing, sometimes grunting, completely possessed. The persistent knocking grew louder and she heard herself cry out through a delirium of distress for the woman to enter.

Voices now. Mrs Gunnet's fury drowning out the pleading tones of her neighbour.

'How dare you have the effrontery to enter my house! This is a respectable place. My husband shall hear of this. If you don't get out of my house at once I'll run you out by the back of your neck.'

Sounds of protest, then urgent scufflings. A door banged. A bolt clanged. Then silence.

Augusta could not believe it. She opened her eyes and tried to see through a mist of sweat. She tried to heave herself towards the door, but she was helpless against the pain that kept dragging her back into herself. Thoughts of Mrs Dinwoodie swirled away and were forgotten. All her energies were needed to fight the battle with her body.

She was bathed in sweat and fainting with exhaustion by the time the pain stopped and she saw the tiny creature moving fitfully, blindly between her legs. It was still attached to her with what must be the cord Mrs Dinwoodie had spoken of. Reaching with difficulty for the scissors Augusta wept, partly from fatigue and partly because she was so unsure about cutting into the flesh in case it hurt or injured the baby. Then she remembered the neighbour had said something about tying the cord. Fumbling for the bobbin on the small table, she managed to unwind a piece of thread and somehow twist herself round to reach the cord and fasten a tight tourniquet round it. She had to move the baby in order to do this and it began to cry, its tiny hands stretching and curling in protest. She sobbed along with it in a distress of spirit far more harrowing than the physical pain she had just suffered. Then she fought with her weakness to lift the child and pull it into her arms. It stopped crying and she became aware of its sticky closed eyes and its naked, bloodied body, and the urgent necessity to wash it and put on its gown. The performing of these tasks was a nightmare of concentrated effort made all the more terrifying by the sudden rush of what she later realized was the afterbirth.

By what seemed a miracle she cleaned the child and somehow got it into the gown. Then she wrapped it in her shawl and laid it on the floor at her side while she struggled out of her petticoat, lifted it like a bag with the afterbirth inside and deposited it all in the pail. Finally she cleaned herself as best she could.

After that she must have slept, for the next thing she heard was the sound of dishes being put on the table and the early morning whine of Rose's voice. It took Augusta a long time to raise herself, lift the baby and make her way, with the help of the furniture, across to the bed. After tucking the child under the covers she returned to pick up the pail and to shuffle at a snail's pace through the kitchen and out to the dung heap to empty it. Similarly, taking the journey in slow, determined stages, she emptied the tin bath. She felt slightly mad. Her exertions had gone far beyond her capabilities. She was no longer aware of how she managed to complete each task.

Back in the kitchen again where Mrs Gunnet was sitting by the fire nursing yellowish brown paper curled up at the edges like leaves of a withered rose. Without warning, Augusta snatched the testimonial letter from her mother-in-law and tossed it into the flames.

Chapter Nineteen

During the night Luther had tramped through the streets and alleyways of the poorer districts. He had penetrated into every black cave of close, quickened his stride at the glimpse of every shawl-shrouded figure, the sound of every female voice.

Anger soured inside him as he returned to the Cross after having searched the High Street, Gallowgate and Saltmarket. As soon as he found the girl, he vowed, he would give her the thrashing of her life. He had enough to bother him without her making things worse.

Argyle Street stretched before him into the far distance, puddled with gaslight and washed every now and again with ripples of silver from the moon. The Tolbooth clock struck one against the silence. Not a living soul could be seen, although he knew that many a doorway would be hiding homeless men, women and children. It was his constant nightmare that one day there would not be enough money to pay his rent and his family would be flung out to survive as best they could in the open. Because of this it was a torment for him to walk along Argyle Street and view at close quarters the huddles of wretched humanity. Men leaned against doors, shoulders and heads sagging forward, hands pushed deep into trouser pockets or with arms hugged across chests as if trying to defend themselves against the pitiless onslaught of cold. Women clutched shawls over their heads or tried to shelter babies in their arms. One woman wore a limp bonnet, the flowers and ribbons that decorated it telling of better days past. She was keeping her face hidden down in a large handkerchief but he knew not only by the bonnet but by the black curls escaping from it that it was not his sister.

He quickened his pace. He could not believe that Tibs would venture into the streets of the better-class residential areas, with their large villas surrounded by iron railings. No shelter of any kind could be found there. Anyway, he was well aware of how timid and excitable his sister was. That also made it difficult to imagine that she would have struck out for the country in the dark. But where else could she be?

Gaslight faded out towards the end of Argyle Street and left only the moon to intermittently reveal a path through the blackness. He felt it useless to go any further yet at the same time he could not bring himself to return to the Briggait. The mere idea was like a desertion of Tibs when she needed him most.

He went on walking until it was as if he were the last man in the world. Only the rustle of some small animal in the hedgerows or the hollow hooting of an owl cut through the emptiness. He was just about to turn back when he caught sight of a larger shadow moving against a hedge. Then as he strode rapidly nearer he heard jerky moans of fear.

'Tibs,' he called, 'is that you?'

Suddenly the dark shape untangled itself from the bush and rushed at him.

'Oh, Luther, I've been so frightened. I was going to sleep here till morning but I was afraid I'd see ghosts or witches like in "Tam o'Shanter".'

'Don't be stupid.' His anger melted with the relief of finding her safe and sound. 'There's no such thing. That was just Robert Burns's imagination. Come on, I'll take you home.'

She kept a tight grip on his arm as they walked back along the road but a silence strained between them. He felt her tenseness as if she was continuously struggling on the verge of telling him something.

Eventually he burst out, 'The mill's no worse than a thousand other places. You were lucky to get in there.'

'Lucky!'

'Yes, lucky. And you haven't a chance of being taken back. I suppose you know that. You've probably lost Billy and Rose their jobs as well.'

'They hate it too.'

'I know they hate it. The crowd of you have been too bloody pampered, that's what's wrong. Well, any day now there's going to be no money to pay the rent and you'll all be out on your arses on the streets.'

She began to wail. 'Isn't there anything you can do, Luther?'

'Oh, yes,' he said bitterly. 'I'm just allowing my family to starve because I choose to.'

'I'm sorry, Luther. I didn't mean . . .'

'I've done all I can. I can do no more.'

He knew he was lying. He had not grovelled. He had not begged. He had not slunk cap in hand, whining to house doors. He had not stood in full view of the gutters with hands helplessly outstretched. The mere idea nauseated him. It wasn't his nature to do it.

Yet when he returned home to find Augusta lying like a ghost in the room bed and the child sleeping innocently beside her, he knew he no longer had any choice.

'It's a boy,' Augusta said.

'How do you feel?'

'I'll survive.'

'Mother managed to see to things all right, did she?'

She turned her face away from him. 'Don't talk to me about your mother.'

'All right.' He touched the child. 'He looks a fine lad. What shall we call him?'

She looked round at him again. 'I thought something from the Bible. Samuel perhaps?'

He nodded and she went on, 'Luther, what are we going to do? Will Tibs get her job back, do you think?'

'She's at the mill just now. We'll just have to wait and see.'

'How do you know she won't run away again?'

'She'd better not. Will I fetch you a cup of tea?'

'Thank you.'

Through in the kitchen his mother was repeating words to herself like some sort of litany.

'A woman of Christian character and smart appearance, a good efficient worker. A woman of Christian character and smart appearance, a good efficient worker . . .'

He was appalled at how much of a stranger she looked. Her big frame, once softly rounded, had become gaunt and angular. Her best black dress was crushed and food-stained. Her once handsome face, topped with a greasy bird's nest of hair, was dirt-ingrained and darkly lined like old leather.

'Would you like a cup of tea, Mother?'

'A woman of Christian character and smart appearance . . .'

'Mother . . .'

'A good efficient worker . . .'

He took the cup back to the room and gave it to Augusta before going over to the window to stare blankly out at Stockwell Street. Memories flickered across his mind. His mother had never been a demonstrative woman but there had been times when she had given some rough yet affectionate prodding, or a quick glance of pride that had betrayed the depth of her feelings and the high hopes she had in him. He had promised her a cottage in the country, fine clothes, a whole new life. He had meant to keep those promises. He could have kept them . . .

135

'Luther,' Augusta's voice forced its way through his thoughts. 'I'm worried about what's going to happen now that we've got the baby. I can't bear him to suffer.'

He made no reply.

'Luther!'

'I heard you.'

'Maybe I could find work. Luther?'

He kept his back towards her, not trusting himself to speak.

'I'll do anything, Luther. I don't care about myself any more. I just don't want my baby to suffer.'

He left the house with long rapid strides.

Around the hotels were favourite places for beggars. Often he'd whipped them out of the way to clear a path for ladies and gentlemen emerging from the Black Bull to board his coach. It was the same at the Tontine Hotel and that was where he made for now. On reaching the archways in front of the Tontine he found the Royal Mail was the centre of attraction. The usual bustle of humanity crushed about on all sides. Apart from the crowds of onlookers in the street, maidservants watched and giggled in the doorway of the hotel, aprons dancing in the breeze. In front of them, arms akimbo, beamed the landlord. Luggage spilled across the pavestones while the guard, with proud ritual, attended to his most important duty, the securing of the mail. Ladies and gentlemen ebbed and flowed, bidding their goodbyes. Or they swirled around like rainbows, checking that their boxes and bags were among those heaped on the ground.

A man in rags so thin and tattered they were barely decent pushed his hat in front of one of the gentleman travellers.

'Spare a penny, sir? For the sake of my children. A penny to help soothe their hunger pains. Please, sir?'

The gentleman was laughing at a joke told by one of his companions, a dandy of a fellow in a full-skirted coat with a fur collar.

'Please, sir,' the beggar persisted in his attempts to catch one or other of the gentlemen's attention. 'For my children.'

Luther was wearing an old black topper. He'd long since sold the smart white hat he'd worn in his coaching days. He removed the hat and for a few minutes stood crushing it against his waist, fiddling with the brim, agitating it round and round. The breeze frizzed out his hair and side whiskers, giving him a wild look. Suddenly he jammed the hat back on his head and pushed his way so violently through the crowd he caused yells of protest to erupt and fists to be raised.

Ignoring them, he automatically made for the Green, the nearest place where he felt he could breathe, where he could be free from crowds. Yet even in this country oasis in the middle of the city there was no escape. Here he found an even larger gathering. Indeed there was such an enormous multitude it stopped him in his tracks, until he remembered that this was the day that the famous Clem Doberman was taking on his latest challenger, Jack Kitson. Thousands were anxiously waiting for the fight to begin. Grassy lawns, stretching up from the river to daisy-spotted banks fringed on top by tall trees, were tightly packed with people.

Luther edged through them, rehearsing pleas for money and struggling to squeeze out the necessary words. But his mind kept paralysing his tongue with excuses. This wasn't the right time, or the right place, or everyone was spending too much money gambling on the pugilists. There would be nothing to spare for beggars here. Rain that had been sporadically whipping the town lashed across the scene without him noticing it, so intense were his secret arguements with himself. He almost blurted out a plea for money but recognized just in time a group of coachmen he had once known. There they posed, great swells in their white toppers and gloves and fancy waistcoats. Managing to avoid being seen by them he pushed forward again until he could go no further. He had reached the outer ring, the place cleared around the boxing ring for the umpires, the referee, the wealthy backer, their particular friends and other gentry of the town.

It was obvious from the tall polished hats and well-cut frock-coats, the cigars and heavy gold watch-chains, that there could be no evading the fact that he was faced with plenty of money now.

Taking off his hat he stood twisting its brim, at the same time fixing belligerent attention on a prosperous-looking man immediately in front of him. The man's companion was saying,

'Time's up, McLure. I claim the stakes.'

McLure fished a gold watch from his waistcoat pocket. 'There's another five minutes yet.'

'There's not a sign of your man. And I can't blame him. Clem Doberman is enough to frighten anybody off.' He gazed proudly at the ring on which three men restlessly roamed about.

It was easy to distinguish Clem Doberman from his seconds. The pugilist was bigger and burlier with legs like tree trunks and a shaved head to protect him against any other fighter's grip. That head had butted many an opponent insensible.

'You'll have to pay up. No challenger. No fight.'

McLure was obviously struggling to hide the keenness of his anger and disappointment. He kept his eyes down on his watch but a dark flush was creeping up from his neck. In a reckless impulse Luther caught hold of the man's arm.

'Can I have a word with you, Mr McLure?'

The man twisted round in surprise. 'What about?'

'You still have a chance of winning.'

'Come to the point.'

'I'll take up the challenge for the same purse as Kitson.'

'Who the hell are you?'

'Luther Gunnet.'

'What prize-winning experience have you had?'

'None.'

'And you can beat the champion?'

'I don't know but I'm desperate enough to make one hell of a try.'

McLure's hesitation only lasted a few seconds as he puffed at his cigar. Then he shrugged and said, 'What more can I lose? You're on!'

Chapter Twenty

The P.C. ring was raised about two feet from the ground, covered over with dry turf and a cartload of sawdust.

Colonel Bentley, the referee, had mounted the ring to bawl out that because Jack Kitson had failed to come to scratch there would now be a trial of manhood between the champion and one Luther Gunnet from the Briggait.

The colonel, a stiff-limbed man, then retreated through the ropes with some difficulty to the outer ring. The seconds tossed a coin. Doberman's won and, after testing the state of the wind, led their man to the corner of their choice.

The mark or scratch in the middle of the ring had already been made and Doberman had tied his colours (a black handkerchief which he took from his neck) to the stake in his corner. McLure passed a blue handkerchief to be secured to Luther's stake.

Laughter guffawed around the outer ring at the combination of colours and Josh Cribben, Doberman's kneeman, shouted:

'I'll take one hundred to one we'll see black and blue on their mugs before it's over.'

Lord Deerston, the umpire and timekeeper, took out his stop-watch. The combatants stripped to the waist and placed themselves in attitude at the scratch.

It was obvious to Luther as well as everyone else that Doberman, although of similar height, had a weight advantage of at least a stone. Luther was anatomically sound, with broad shoulders and hard knots of muscle bulging in his arms, but his belly and loins had a thin fragility by comparison.

They had only taken up the stance for a few seconds when the champion, legs planted like oaks and toes glued to the line, let fly right and left. Luther warded the blows off with a guardian arm. He was well aware that the normal practice of defensive boxing was 'never to shift' and to try to ward off blows with the arms without the aid of footwork. It occurred to him however that if he was to stand a chance of even surviving the fight he had to manoeuvre about and keep free of his adversary whenever possible. He had seen Doberman fight before, had seen him in fact kill two men in the ring. He had also witnessed the eye-gouging, the crippling kidney punches, the cross-buttock throws and the suit in chancery at which this pugilist was a master.

He tried though, as he kept retreating and Doberman slowly advanced, to jab at the heavier man's jaw. He landed several punches, one of which jarred Doberman's head back but didn't stop him. Then suddenly they were wrestling. Their sides had come together, Doberman's arm was over his neck, had grasped his loose arm with his other hand, had shifted to his front, had got his crutch on his hip and canted him over the gorilla-like shoulder.

His heels shot up in the air and he went down with tremendous violence. But he was quick-witted enough, in the second he had before Doberman fell on his abdomen, to tighten his muscles and jerk up his knees to break the full force of the other man's weight. Had he not done so he would, he realized, have been knocked insensible or been injured enough to lose the power of resisting future attacks. As it was he felt as if his abdomen had caved in and his spine had snapped. He rolled away, dodging most of the blows from the iron knuckles but catcing a few on the ear and neck before managing to struggle up. Doberman was slower to rise and Luther's foot caught him a crack like a horse's hoof on the face and knocked him off-balance. The fall marked the end of the first round and the beginning of the half-minute interval. During this interval each kneeman squatted down to provide a knee for his fighter to rest on, while the bottleman administered water or 'prime jackey' from his bottle. Brandy was kept for emergencies. The bottleman was also ready with the sponge and the orange.

Luther's bottleman had barely the chance to douse him with cold water when the umpire's cool aristocratic voice called:

'Time!'

Luther got to his feet and set himself at the mark. Doberman did the same and before Luther could harden his arm in defence he had received a couple of facers that covered him in blood. He shifted from side to side, blinking through a crimson haze. The yells of the crowd battered through his head as if the two rings had folded and the multitude had surged in.

His return blow all but fractured his knuckles against Doberman's ribs before he was nearly hit down by a vicious jab below the ear. He managed to stagger to one side then regain his balance, only to have Doberman run in sharply with his head and butt him in the stomach. His fingers tore at the man's face before he went down, vomiting on to the sawdust.

The seconds hauled him to his corner and stuck out a knee for him. Brandy spluttered into his mouth and at the same time water splashed away the blood and vomit.

Lord Deerston's voice rang out again.

The seconds hoisted Luther to his feet but in a sudden burst of anger he jerked them off. Walking to the centre he toed the line without their help. Pain was a monster devouring him but he strained to ignore it and concentrate only on the massive figure of Doberman posed in threatening attitude before him.

'Shift about,' he kept reminding himself, and despite the agony when he moved, he managed to avoid the pugilist's iron fist and to deliver a flurry of punches that succeeded in drawing blood from Doberman's eyes and nose.

Doberman's lunges became wilder as Luther continued to spring backwards and forwards and weave from side to side. Eventually the champion roared in frustration:

'Stand still and fight like a man!'

Determinedly Luther refused to stand still but exhaustion as well as pain slowed him down. Because of this, Doberman in one of his forward rushes managed to trip Luther then grab him by the hair and batter his head against a corner post.

The monster completely devoured him and he disintegrated into darkness. He only became aware of splintering light with the bawling of his seconds and the shock of ice cutting his skin.

He tried to widen his vision but the corner post had bludgeoned one eye until it had disappeared under a massive swelling. Through the slit of his other eye he pinpointed Doberman squatting at the opposite corner, grinning like a giant gargoyle at a shared joke with his seconds.

The shout of 'Time' went up and Luther was manhandled to his feet. He attempted to push himself free but stumbled on rubber legs, was grabbed and dragged across the ring to where Doberman had already taken up the stance. He was still grinning and his smugness and the deafening cheers of the crowd told of everyone's certainty that the champion had all but taken the purse. The thought of the money forced Luther to make the superhuman effort of standing on his own. The thought of the money lashed him to his feet again after his adversary had butted him down. The thought of the money put the kick of a mule into his fist when he caught Doberman a blow on the kidneys that sent a rush of urine spurting down the man's breeches. The champion staggered, dropped to his knees grunting with pain then rolled moaning and vomiting in the sawdust. The fall gave both men another thirty seconds' respite in their corners.

Luther's chest was heaving like giant bellows and blood kept spilling from his mouth. He stared intently round, willing his mind and vision to clear, but the outer ring was packed with stovepipes that merged into a blurred mass of colour on the hill. His eyes swivelled down again and found the opposite corner and Doberman's scarlet-splotched figure just as Lord Deerston's voice, excited now, exploded with,

'Time!'

Luther groped up, lurched drunkenly, then by sheer effort of will steadied himself and got his feet to the mark.

He could smell Doberman's hate now as well as the sour stench of his body. The kidney punch had given him a forward crouch and made him even more gorilla-like. Small blood-red eyes sought him out and before Luther could move away the other man's knuckles rocked into his face. Luther staggered but countered almost immediately with a left hook that caught Doberman in the throat and nearly felled him. The champion looked beside himself with rage and the thought penetrated Luther's dazed mind: 'He's going to kill me.' The will to survive dragged energy to his aid and hardened his muscles. He smashed a blow into Doberman's face that was immediately returned with such ferocity that Luther was hurled back and fell like a stone. His seconds bawled urgently at him as they half-carried him to his corner but their shouts, like the screaming and cheering of the crowd, were close yet very far away. He didn't remember being in the corner. He only knew that he was willing himself to stagger out again to toe the line. He swayed there, blindly, impotently thrashing the air with tightly closed fists. Doberman caught him by the hair and gouged at his eyes.

In a superhuman effort Luther brought his fist round and down. Like a sledgehammer it sunk deep into Doberman's kidney, making him scream and release his hold on Luther's head. As the champion staggered screeching and bent over like an old man, Luther made one last effort and brought his fist up to crack against Doberman's chin.

Doberman thumped down, shaking the ring to its foundations. His kneeman and bottleman dragged him unconscious to his corner. There they tried every method they could think of to force him back to life including biting through his ear until blood flowed down his neck. But the big man remained inert and they had no alternative but to throw in his colours.

Luther was vaguely aware of having the colours tied round his neck and then being hoisted from the ring and pushed into his shirt and coat. He heard a voice asking where exactly he lived. Then he was in a carriage and was beginning to recognize the owner of the voice. It was the man called McLure. Now he was counting out money and stuffing it into Luther's coat pocket.

'You deserve your winnings, Gunnet. It was a good fight. You're a man of courage and determination. I like that.'

'I needed the money,' said Luther.

'What do you work at?'

'That's the problem. I don't.'

'You need a job?' McClure shrugged. 'I can give you a job if you're that desperate.' With a wry smile he added, 'In fact you'd have to be desperate for this one.'

'I don't care what it is, I'll take it.'

Already the other man was writing something on the back of a calling card.

'Here,' he said, tucking the card into Luther's pocket. 'Give that to the ganger at the railway cutting. He'll start you as a navvy.' He lit up a cigar. 'You survived Doberman. Let's see what you can do with a horde of Irish savages.'

PART TWO

Chapter Twenty-one

The covered wagon waddled from side to side like a woman in a hooped skirt. The reins dangled loosely in Billy's hands as he whistled in tune to the song of the army of navvies who were crushing in front, behind and all around them.

'I am a navvy bold, that's tramped the country round, sir,
To get a job of work, where any can be found, sir.
I left my native home, my friends and my relations.
To ramble up and down and work in various stations . . .'

Samuel, now a sturdy five-year-old, sat between Billy and Augusta. Three-year-old Alexander was perched on her knee.

Augusta felt reasonably happy. Indeed, the only thing that hedged in her feelings and made her cautious of betraying them was the enigma of Luther. She glanced across to where, sitting astride his horse, he towered above the navvies.

After a minute or two she called out to him, 'What kind of place do you think it will be?'

'For working or living?' he asked without bothering to return her look.

'Living.'

'Huts with slated roofs, I've heard.'

'One or two rooms?'

'Two.'

Relief as sweet as wine trickled through her veins.

In the past five or six years they had been forced to live in a variety of hovels from windowless turf erections to huts that had wooden walls. Floorings and windows were without plaster and generally unfurnished.

She would never forget the first place she had to cope with. She could see it still in her mind's eye as the wagon

146

wobbled, and the horse peacefully plodded, and the men sang:

'Last Saturday night, I received my full pay;
On Monday morning, I ran away.
I buzzed up the Tommy shop and stopped the score,
And swore that I'd never go that road no more . . .'

Huts of all shapes and sizes were huddled together in bewildering confusion. Some shacks had windows, some had none. Some had tarred canvas roofs, and some had roofs of turf. Some were covered with rotten grass and when a fire was lit inside they looked like burning hayricks. Some doors faced south, some faced north and everything looked as if it had been tossed into the valley and just left as it fell.

Rats swarmed at the foot of the hill, feasting on the refuse that had been thrown there. Gulls swooped to squabble over crusts while pigs rooted about in the mud. They had been lucky to get a hut to themselves at that place. Few married men were numbered among the workforce and most of their wives had no alternative but to share one of the dormitories used by the rumbustious army of bachelors. Share these narrow bricklined huts not only with the men but with the dogs they kept chained under their beds during working hours.

For most of the first year, of course, she had stayed behind in the Briggait and no navvy hell could be worse than that festering sore of Glasgow, especially during the cholera epidemic. Both Rose and Mrs Gunnet had been among the thousands of cholera victims in the narrow closes and wynds that cluttered the heart of the town. Whole families had been wiped out and she had been terrified that baby Samuel would perish with the rest. But after his mother and sister's death Luther had packed their few pieces of furniture and possessions on to the wagon and taken them away from the Briggait.

He had shown no emotion at the time but she knew that the loss of his mother and sister had affected him deeply. She could understand how he felt bitter at fate depriving them of the chance of enjoying the fruits of his new-found earnings. She could not however see that he had any justification in blaming her – especially for his mother's death.

'You never looked after her,' he said. 'Never as much as gave her one drink of water.'

'Your mother never wanted me near her,' she protested. 'And Tibs managed very well. Anyway, I had more than enough to do nursing Rose and worrying about Samuel.'

'You were as much the cause of my mother's death as the cholera.'

It was unfair but nothing she said penetrated this bitterly held conviction of his.

Tibs had now a place at a farm and Augusta found some consolation in being the mistress of her own household with no other woman to worry about. She didn't mind the fact that her household was a nomadic one. Moving had added a sense of freedom, interest and even pleasure to her life that had been out of the question in the dark, congested Briggait.

There was excitement in visiting a new part of the country and facing new challenges. There were the hills and valleys and streams and trees and wild flowers to enjoy on the way.

As it turned out, there was even satisfaction to be gained from the navvies. Appalled at their ignorance she had made it her business to start a little school in the evenings to teach them to read and write; at least she had at the beginning visualized it as a little school. The eagerness of the men to learn, however, was both rewarding and overwhelming. She had been forced to co-opt Billy into helping with the hordes of giant creatures in clothes so stiff with earth that they cracked against their enormous tackety boots. Like overgrown awkward children they sucked their pencils and drew their letters until, painfully, they managed to copy the moral text she had given them. Some were even able to write a simple message home and were embarrassingly grateful to her for performing this miracle.

She believed that her school was the reason this gang of navvies had struck together for so long and were now moving en masse to the next job. Although of course Luther, who was now a ganger, also commanded respect and loyalty. A proud body of men they looked at the moment in their blue bonnets, scarlet neckerchiefs and waistcoats and moleskin jackets. Moleskin breeches were supported not by braces that might constrict the movement of burly shoulders but by a leather strap round the waist. Leather straps were also fastened under the knees to keep out mud. High-laced boots also served this purpose. Some of them sported coats, trousers and waistcoats all in white double canvas. The coats were large and stiff and each had four pockets.

She had been extremely apprehensive about living in close proximity with the navvies at first. They appeared such coarse creatures and she had kept herself as aloof as possible, at the same time developing a sharp edge to her tongue to cut any man down who had the temerity to address her. But she had quickly discovered that, when sober at least, they were artless, generous, good-natured men. But they could consume frightening amounts of liquor and under its influence could become brutal and absolutely ungovernable. Once they started fighting even the police and the soldiers couldn't control them. Their rowdiness didn't seem to bother Luther. They enjoyed a good fight, he told her. Especially the Irish.

Trying to cure the Irish of fighting was like Canute trying to stop the ocean, although if a fight broke out on the job he made a point of rapidly squashing it by the use of his own fists. She had been horrified to witness Luther doing this. Two giants in tackety boots were brawling over some grievance and battering each other to the cheers of the other navvies who had immediately downed tools to watch until Luther appeared and viciously felled one man after the other. With both navvies sitting dazedly in the mud he warned,

'Nobody wastes time on my job. Fight in your own time. Back to work, all of you!'

She supposed that incident, coupled with his reputation of having beaten the champion, was why Luther had been nicknamed 'Big Gun' although as often as not he was just addrressed as 'Ganger'. Of course all the navvies had nicknames. It never ceased to amaze her how singularly incurious they were about one another's real names or family or relatives. They would work, eat and sleep beside one another for months without referring to each other as anything except Curly, Ginger, Dry Dick, Tunnel Jim, Sulking Sam, Foxy and so on. She'd witnessed funerals at which hundreds of navvies had marched to the grave to pay their last respects to a comrade – a victim of a fatal accident – who had been buried under the name of Coppernob or Uncle Ned.

The children loved the men despite their rough ways and laughed in delight when tossed into the air or if confronted by one of them making either a comical or even a frightening face. There were times when she couldn't help laughing herself. If Samuel was crying and she was in a bad temper and scolding him and one of these uncouth creatures happened to be passing he would stop, hunker down and pull such a cross-eyed ridiculous face that both Samuel and she would burst out laughing.

She no longer feared them and could, at times, bully them unmercifully. Her small ladylike stature seemed somehow to disarm them and she felt convinced that they would never willingly do her any harm, though what they were capable of under the influence of alcohol was always an unknown quantity. She kept well away from the nearest town or village on pay day because the navvies were sure to be creating violence or turbulence then. Of course, sometimes it wasn't their fault; often everything would have been perfectly all right if only they had been left alone. But prejudice was so strong among the indigenous population that the locals felt impelled to interfere even when the navvies were enjoying themselves in a harmless fashion:

foot-races or feats of strength were condemned because a few pence was wagered on the outcome. The navvies' sprightly temper, natural vociferousness, variety of gesticulation and exuberance of argument never failed to shock the sober populace into voicing their disapproval.

It wasn't just the men who showed their sort of exuberance, either. It was exactly the same with Maureen, the only wife who had turned up at the school – at least Augusta had thought Maureen was married until the young woman shamelessly informed her that she was not. 'Ach, is a priest going to make Boozer and me any more married than we are?' she laughed. Maureen could be disturbingly wild at times, mostly when Boozer had spent too much money on the tommy-shop's 'knock-me-down', as one of the most potent whiskies was called. It was quite common to see Maureen, her long carotty hair flying loose, chasing a helplessly inebriated Boozer around the huts, bombarding him with stones or whatever she could lay hands on. Occasionally Boozer stood his ground, if somewhat unsteadily, and put up a fight. But no matter what he did, he always got the worst of it.

Maureen nursed a dream of becoming a lady and had total faith in Augusta bringing this much-desired transformation about. Not that Augusta entertained any hope of success. In her opinion, and she had made this quite clear to Maureen, a lady was born not made. But Maureen had brushed the information aside:

'If you can learn a drunken idiot like Boozer to write his name you can learn me that's got brains to be a lady.'

Augusta was glad that Luther didn't drink to the excess that men like Boozer did. She often thought that if the navvies were paid fornightly or even weekly it might reduce the severity of these drinking bouts. But most companies paid every four or five weeks. Some waited for as long as a quarter and even a whole year before paying out hard-earned wages. As a result the men had to exist on subs in the form of tommy tickets which had to be spent in the company store. Then when they did eventually receive a lump sum the temptation to celebrate overcame them, especially when they were actually paid in the tommy-shop which sold strong drink.

Occasionally Luther got drunk but only once had his drinking seriously affected her. He had burst into the hut and proceeded to behave in the most outrageous manner. A vicious kick had upturned the table. One sweep of a clenched fist had sent her precious brush and comb set flying from the dressing-table. She had not reacted at first, partly because his unexpected behaviour had so taken her aback. But as soon as she found breath she had indignantly accused him of being an uncouth drunken oaf, no better than the lowest of the navvies he had been consorting with. Then, even more unexpectedly, he had struck her. Over and over again until she was screaming in panic. The children had wakened and begun sobbing in distress. She often thought afterwards that it was only the children that had saved her, for immediately on hearing them, Luther stopped. Then his big hands had smoothed over her, not gently but with a carefully restrained violence, until her agony of body merged with ecstasy as he invaded deep inside her. Yet all the time she suspected that his hatred of her was so strong it made even his lovemaking a humiliation for her.

Disturbed by these thoughts she stole another glance at him. His thick blue-black hair and luxuriant sidewhiskers made a starling contrast against the white peaks of his collar that curved high round his sturdy jaw and the scarlet neckerchief wound round and knotted underneath it. His ramrod back was given a certain elegance by the cut and quality of the black velveteen jacket she had been so proud of finding for him in a second-hand clothes shop. Obviously it had once belonged to a gentleman and she was glad that it had proved such a good fit. His reddish brown breeches and high black boots completed the outfit and gave him as good an appearance as any gentleman. But a gentleman he was not. She averted her gaze. She had never forgiven him for striking her. To use violence on a lady was contemptible. Even worse was the humiliation, the fact that he was able to give her sensual pleasure that despite her hatred she could never resist. She felt shamed by this weakness. Other women could turn their duties as a wife into a very useful source of power with which to smooth their own paths and get their own way. Looking back, she realized now that her mother had been an excellent example of this.

Maureen of course used much less subtle and delicate means. With embarrassing and, as Augusta never failed to point out, unladylike frankness, Maureen often told her how she never allowed Boozer on top of her if he was drunk. Even for days after a severe drinking bout Boozer was repulsed with punches and kicks and bites unless he could promise a pair of shoes to replace her worn ones, or some small domestic article that was needed, or it they were in or close enough to town, a night's entertainment at a penny theatre. Sometimes nothing would soften Maureen and Boozer would have to do without. Augusta had lectured her on wifely duties and what it said in scriptures about a wife obeying a husband and other passages that were relevant to the occasion. Secretly, however, she envied Maureen's strength of character.

She was not without strength and courage herself, despite her petite and delicate appearance. Many times she had tried to get the better of Luther. Sometimes, in small ways, she succeeded. Nevertheless she was aware of a cruel, invisible line over which she dare not cross.

Suddenly she noticed him spur his horse and jerk it on ahead. Billy stopped whistling.

'We're nearly there,' he said.

Chapter Twenty-two

Luther said: 'I want you to help run the store, and that's all about it.'

'No, it is not all about it.' Augusta raised her chin defiantly. 'What about Samuel and Alexander?'

153

'Maureen can look after them.'

'But I don't see the point; why should you take over the tommy-shop as well as working as a ganger?'

'I would have thought the point was obvious. Money.'

'I can do without that kind of money,' she said disdainfully.

He shook his head. 'You're incredible.'

'What do you mean?'

'For years you lived in luxury. Did you ever question what kind of money you were enjoying then?'

'But that was Papa's money, honestly and decently come by.'

'Honestly and decently come by my arse!'

She averted her face. 'Must you be so coarse?'

'There was nothing you took pleasure in that didn't come as a result of someone's misery. The food you put in your mouth, the clothes you wore on your back, the fire you lazed in front of.'

'I knew nothing of that, nor could I do anything about it. But I do know what evil places tommy-shops are.'

'Evil?' he scoffed.

'Yes, evil. And it's against the law to deal in truck. The men are entitled to be paid all their wages in coin of the realm, not just a small per centage, and not in groceries, inferior and far too expensive ones at that.'

'You don't know what you're talking about, woman.'

'I should know. I've had to put up with the tommy-shops often enough when you were a navvy. I've walked for miles to the nearest village to shop there, rather than pay extortionate prices for truck, and was victimized for my trouble.'

'I was vicitmized, you mean. You lost me another job.'

'You were not without one for long.'

'That's hardly the point.'

'What I cannot understand, Luther, is why the companies force people into continuous debt. Surely if the wives or the men could save a little money they would have no need to ask for subs and – '

'It's the subs that keep the tommy-shops going.'

154

'Exactly. Because instead of being given coin and allowed to spent it wherever they wish the men are given tommy tickets that have to be spent on truck. It's not fair.'

'Fair? Of course it's not fair. Life isn't fair. Why should your precious mama and papa be kept warm and pampered and overfed in George Square while my mother and sister died of hunger and cold in the Briggait?'

Augusta sighed. 'Luther, destroying yourself with bitterness is not going to do any of us any good. There are some things in life that simply have to be accepted. Everyone has their allotted place. The poor will always be with us. That is not to say they should not be encouraged to be thrifty.'

'There are times,' he said, 'and this is one of them, when I could cheerfully strangle you.'

'And there are times,' she replied stiffly, 'when I simply do not understand you.'

'Don't try. Just do as you're told. That's our hut next to the store. Maureen and Boozer can take the one next again.'

'Luther, wait,' she called as he was about to ride off. 'Surely you don't expect me to sell strong drink?'

He erupted with laughter. 'The men would have something to say if you didn't. We'd have a riot on our hands. I've arranged for a storekeeper to work with you.'

He reined his horse away between the lines of huts. The chances were there would be a riot anyway if he wasn't careful. In his six years of navvying in various jobs, laying gas mains, underground pipes for sewers, working on the construction of reservoirs, bridges and harbours as well as laying wagonways, he had come across four categories of men: Irish, English, Lowland Scots and Highlanders. He soon learned the strengths and weaknesses of each group.

The Irish were warmhearted and generous, with a willingness to work that caused them to be hated by the other navvies. They would eagerly accept a job for any miserable pittance that was offered. They were fiery-tempered and reckless, especially when they had money to throw around. The English, on the other hand, would rarely pick a quarrel for the mere sake of it. They had a weakness for food, especially beef, and spent all their money on filling their bellies. The lowland Scots were less excitable than the Irish and could stand a much greater amount of provocation. They were also much more careful with their money. The highlanders were not dependable, being apt to disappear from time to time in order to cut their peats or sow their seeds back home. They were even more clannish than the men from across the water: stiff and reserved with strangers, they kept to themselves. They disliked their brother Scots from the lowlands and the English; the Irish they hated.

The only time in fact that Luther had seen the highlanders, the Lowlanders and the English unite was to drive away the Irish. It was the policy of most companies to keep the four groups apart but this was not always possible, and many a time he had witnessed bloody battles with shovels and pickaxes and rocks or whatever came to hand as weapons.

Already he'd discovered that highlanders were to be working on this section of the line so his first task was to seek out their ganger to organize them to work apart whenever possible, and to sleep in different huts. Ganger McAulay was a broad-chested man, not very tall but rugged as if gouged out of solid rock. Red muck had frozen deep into the lines of his face, neck and the ridges of his corduroy waistcoat. His moleskin jacket, breeches and kneestraps cracked with earth when he moved.

Luther dismounted and joined him. Immediately the slush rose over his boots. Mud was a continuous hazard at all the workings and most of the places where colonies of huts had been thrown up, but it was the midges that nearly drove the men frantic. One navvy complained, 'If you kill one midge a million comes to its funeral.'

Luther nodded at Ganger McAulay then gazed around at the tightly packed lines of shacks.

McAulay scraped off his bonnet and scratched his head. 'I am not liking this at all.'

'Keep them separate.'

'That is not so easy.'

'I've got the tommy-shop and the hut next to it. My men can fill the rest of the huts at that end. You start at the other.'

'That is not separate enough, and my men will be passing the huts of your men on the way to the tommy-shop.'

His lilting highland voice irritated Luther. 'You've a better suggestion?'

Another scrape at the closely shaven rock-like head. Another pause.

'Och, no, no, I have not.'

'Well, there's no point in wasting any more time.'

Immediately he began bawling orders at the men and tramping into every hut to make sure that it was filled. Most of them were long wooden erections with a fire at each end on which to cook food. Two glass windows, an unusual luxury, let in light. Along one wall were six beds that would accommodate twelve men. Already a couple of long-legged dogs were snarling in protest at being chained to the beds.

'You'll be in trouble yet with these bloody dogs,' he shouted above the boisterousness of the men and the clanging and clumping of boots. 'Keep them away from the locals and don't let anybody catch you poaching or the dog'll be shot and you along with it, if you're not careful.'

In each hut he organized the shifts. 'Dayshift – Digger, Tunnel Joe, Red Regan, Busher, Horse O'Conner, Mike the Moocher. Nights – Ginger, Paddy the Cards, Doolan . . .'

Back outside he could hear Ganger McAulay calling to his men in the Gaelic. It might have been Chinese for all Luther could understand of it.

Horses neighed and whinnied as they were led behind some of the huts where a cluster of trees and bushes made a convenient tethering place. The bushes, the trees and the hillocks of long grass around the clearing were convenient in more ways than one.

He returned to the end of the lines of huts to where his own place claimed a little privacy from the others, thanks to a broad-trunked oak tree. Across a patch of churned up earth and stones stood the longest and the only building made of brick. This was to accommodate not only the tommy-shop but the pay office and a public house.

The shop had already been opened by the storekeeper, a lowland Scot called Wylie Grant. Old Wylie, as he was now known as, had been forced to give up navvying because like most men over forty he was no longer strong enough or fit enough for the job. Navvying was a young man's occupation. Old Wylie and his family would have joined the scrapheap of starving unemployed if Luther had not offered him the job as storekeeper.

'Aye, Wylie,' Luther greeted him now. 'What do you think?'

'A fine place, Ganger. A fine place . . .' Ceaselessly he stumped about, lifting goods on to counter and shelves as if determined to belie his frail appearance. 'The wife and lad are helping unload the stores wagon. We'll have the shelves packed up and everything ready in no time. You won't regret giving me the chance, Ganger, by God you won't.' He had taken off his moleskin jacket and the bony elbows jutted from under rolled up sleeves. But his blue bonnet was still cocked at a jaunty angle over his sandy-coloured hair.

Luther said, 'Mrs Gunnett will be in later.'

'It'll be a pleasure for my wife and me to work with her, Ganger.'

Luther smiled wryly to himself as he strolled behind the counter and through the door that connected the store with where he planned to have the public house or bar-room. The counter continued along the whole length of this apartment. Wooden benches lined the walls and a few round tables and stools furnished the place. The bar-room had two doors for the use of the men: one for direct entry from the front of the building and another from the pay office which was the third apartment in the building. There was no entry in or out of the pay office except through the bar-room.

Well satisfied with his inspection Luther returned through the store.

'There's a heap of clothes in my wagon. I'll send Billy over with them. Mrs Gunnett will price them for you.'

For some time now Augusta had proved very useful and successful in purchasing second-hand clothes which she resold to the navvies and their wives. They had saved a tidy sum as a result.

Later in their hut she worriedly asked, 'I hope it was not my little project of buying and selling second-hand garments that gave you this tommy-shop notion?'

He shook his head in reply but wasn't sure if that had not been partly responsible. Mostly, however, it was his recognition of the profit to be made in a tommy-shop that gave him the resolve to acquire one.

He went to unload the last of their possessions from the wagon under Augusta's anxious eyes.

'Be careful with that table now, Luther. I do not want it scratched.'

'Out of my way, woman,' he said but she paid no heed, fluttering about with her loose clusters of ringlets bouncing forward over her brow and her skirts swishing. In no time, he knew, she would have the hut looking like home with a picture she'd acquired from some junk shop and a clock and some crockery. He had become fairly proficient at woodcarving and she always proudly displayed his work on the dresser or table or mantlepiece – if there was one.This hut did have a mantlepiece and she was excited about it. Her emotion was not quite so childish and unrestrained as it had once been. Yet there was something about her delicate-boned structure and the way soft wisps of hair escaped from where she'd pinned it up at the back that gave her a childlike appearance.

'What do you think, Luther?' she gazed up at him and then back at their new home with ill-concealed pride. 'A lady with spirit as well as good taste,' she had once told him, 'can make any dwelling pleasing and comfortable'.

She possessed, he realized, now, more spirit and intelligence than he had at first given her credit for.

'You've made a good job of it,' he said of the hut. 'If you can put as much enthusiasm into the tommy-shop we'll do well. I'll keep the accounts and supervise the ordering of the stores at first, but I'm sure in time you'll be perfectly capable of taking on the responsibility of ordering most of the goods. You can also keep your eye on old Wylie and Mrs Grant. I think they'll be honest employees. You make sure that they are.'

She sighed and her eyes became vague.

'Yes, life's hard,' he said guessing at her thoughts. 'And we've little choice in it. It's a case of sink or swim. Don't forget the Briggait.'

'I'm not likely to.'

'No, nor am I. I had a damn sight more of it than you. I'll tell you something. I'll never be hungry again. I'll never be like dirt under men's feet again. It doesn't matter what must be done to prevent it, I'll do it. And you'll do it, Augusta. For the sake of the children if not for me.'

He saw her face tighten warily and he knew he'd struck the right note. There was nothing she would not do to save Samuel and Alexander from starving.

Chapter Twenty-three

They sold everything but coffins at the store. Luther contracted with the farmers in the district for all his supply of dairy produce and potatoes. Each workman had a credit book which was continually scrutinized by both Luther and Old Wylie. Any attempt to slope the store or spend cash elsewhere put an abrupt end to a navvy's chance of further subs. It could mean his dismissal.

Augusta did what she could to ensure that a decent standard of quality was maintained to compensate for the fact that the prices they charged were often more than double the prices in Paisley or Glasgow. She also tried when she could to help customers in urgent need by giving some change instead of goods to the total of their money. How else could these people pay for their shoes to be mended or meet other contingencies for which the store did not provide? It was very difficult for her to do this if Old Wylie or his wife was around. Luther had chosen them well. They carried out his instructions to the letter and were completely insensitive and ruthless as far as the customers were concerned. The only time Augusta could help the occasional customer with cash change was when Old Wylie and his wife were busy in the bar-room. She had insisted that they serve the drink and not she, and fortunately Luther had been agreeable to this arrangement.

It was no use her pointing out that they were making a great deal of money very fast indeed and could well afford to be more liberal. There was never enough money and it was never made fast enough to satisfy Luther. He could not rest content. Indeed he hardly took any rest at all.

'If I expect the men to work hard, then I've got to work hard,' he told her. 'They respect me for that. They know there isn't a job I ask them to do that I haven't bent my back to or turned a hand to myself, and still can if the need arises. They know they can depend on me, too. If I say they'll be paid every four weeks, they'll be paid every four weeks without fail. No contractor would dare run out on my section. I'd follow him to the ends of the earth and strangle the money out of him if need be.'

There was another reason for Luther's position of respect, despite the fact that he now owned the normally hated tommy-shop. Some of the men had given him a rough time at first. It was normal, of course, for absolute novices to the navvy brotherhood to be put through a gruelling initiation by the men on the job, although in most cases it was meant as a joke. Extra work would be piled on, pace quickened, taunts of weakness and inability to cope increased, everything done to push beyond endurance the strength and will of the newcomer. It had not been a joke in Luther's case. When he, a Scotsman, had arrived to start work among a gang of Irish navvies they had tried their damnedest to drive him out. But he had not been driven out and there were those who remembered his testing and who still spoke of it.

Now their attitude seemed to be that as a hard worker, a strong determined man, he deserved to get on. And so there was not the usual amount of hatred for Luther's tommy-shop. Certainly every customer was treated with civility. Augusta insisted on that and kept a sharp eye and tongue on Old Wylie and Mrs Grant until they learned that good manners were not something to be reserved for Luther and herself alone. She enquired politely as to each and every customer's needs and attended to them as smartly and as promptly as she could. She had known of other tommy-shops who kept long lines of customers waiting for hours in hail, rain or snow while the storekeeper dawdled over breakfast or for no reason at all. She made it the rule that while the shop was open someone had always to be on duty behind the counter, so meals were taken on a rota system.

Yet although she was civil to the customers she was never familiar. She knew her place and saw that they knew theirs. Apart from the fact that she was a lady, she was the ganger's wife and Luther was no ordinary ganger. He knew his worth as well as she knew hers.

Already he was talking scathingly of the contractors on the workings.

'One day I'm going to put in a tender for work on the line, Augusta. I could make a better contractor than most I've seen so far.'

'But I thought the whole line from Glasgow to Paisley had been contracted.'

'That's not the whole line, only the stretch we're working on. This line goes all the way to Ayr and there's the Greenock stretch too. And there'll be a lot more before it's done. There's already talk about one as far as Edinburgh. I'm telling you, there's going to be railways all over the land. No, don't look at me like that, Augusta. I'm not mad.'

'But who would want to travel on such dirty, noisy, dangerous contraptions? They may have limited possibilites for carrying heavy goods like coal. I remember Papa saying there've been railways at pits for some time. But can you imagine ladies and gentlemen travelling on that railway you worked on last year, for instance? What did those wagons carry? I can't remember.'

'Iron. But it's got to come, Augusta. It stands to reason.'

'I don't see how it is reasonable at all.'

'Think of how many people could travel at any one time on the railway compared with a coach. At the public opening of the Glasgow-Garnkirk line one steam engine, the "St Rollox", conveyed nearly two hundred people. The other, the "George Stephenson", drew a train of thirty-two wagons loaded with freestone lime, grain and iron to the amount of twenty times its own weight. Think of that. Think of the power there.'

'It must have been horrid for the passengers. I'm sure no one would wish to repeat the experience.'

'Take a look at this.'

The piece of paper he pushed into her hand was an advertisement stating that 'Railway Pleasure Trips' would be run, with a steam engine and train of coaches leaving the Railway Depot, Townhead, at one o'clock for Gartsherrie without stopping at intermediate stations and returning at half-past two, to reach Glasgow at three. 'Genteel Parties', it said, 'will find the trip an agreeable and healthful mode of spending part of the day.'

'You see,' Luther said, 'it's not just a matter of having to be transported from one point to another and suffering all sorts of discomforts and dangers on the way. It can even be a pleasure.'

She laughed. 'Oh, Luther!'

'You don't believe it?'

'Of course not.'

'Well, we're due to go to Glasgow to pick up stores. There's no reason why we shouldn't find out for ourselves.'

Her smile merged into apprehension. 'You mean ride in a railway train?'

'It seems ridiculous that I'm building railways yet have never travelled on one.'

'Oh please don't, Luther. It's dangerous.'

'Coaching was dangerous.'

'Yes, but surely steam engines are very much more so.'

'There's no real evidence of that. To hell with the danger, anyway, I'm going to try it. If you're too much of a coward . . .' He shrugged. 'Suit yourself.'

She bristled with offence. 'You know perfectly well that I am not a coward.'

'Well?'

Recklessly she agreed. Luther wanted to take the boys too but to this she vehemently objected, and eventually they were left behind with Maureen.

They set out in the wagon for Glasgow, Luther in shirt sleeves and hatless at first and Augusta with a protective shawl over her curls. Dust from the horses' hooves made them grubby-faced by the time they reached the outskirts of the city and she reminded Luther to stop for a wash and to don his velvet jacket and top hat. She briskly cleaned her face and hands and gave her hair a rub with a silk scarf before fastening on her coat, tying on her bonnet and pulling on her gloves.

'Now we can proceed,' she said, perched back up on the wagon with her hands clasped primly on her lap.

He grinned and shook his head but said nothing, and the wagon rolled into the town. They attended to the ordering of the stores first then left the wagon to be packed with goods and collected on their return from the railway.

Augusta did not speak as she strolled along Argyle Street by Luther's side, her arm linked in his. The turmoil in her mind belied her appearance of calm dignity. Not for anything would she have betrayed the fact that she was quaking with terror, although if the new young Queen Victoria had appeared before her in the street Augusta would have been incapable of a curtsy. She would have

164

been far too obsessed by monstrous steam engines to recognize even such an important personage. She certainly did not see any of Argyle Street or High Street as they passed along or Castle Street before arriving at the canal side of Glebe Street, Townhead, where the railway depot was situated.

There, at the sight of the metal charger snorting steam and fire, she felt quite faint. Third-class carriages, roofless and seatless, were already packed with people. Second-class carriages with the advantage of roofs were also crammed with noisy passengers. Luther guided Augusta firmly into one of the train of first-class carriages. Here there were seats and the other ladies and gentlemen squeezed along to give them enough room. The air quivered with nervous excitement.

'The engineer is opening the valves!'

The hissing of steam was suppressed and the engine moved and panted, not from exhaustion but from impatience and restraint. Blazing cinders flew past and the train of carriages was suddenly dragged along like the tail of a comet.

Luther grinned round at her. 'Are you all right?'

He was obviously enjoying the experience and she had to admit that despite her fear she was beginning to feel elated.

'Yes,' she admitted. 'Only it seems so strange to be journeying like this without any visible cause of progress.'

'There's nothing magic about it. But if it'll help you to understand, think of it as a fire horse and the reins, bit and bridle is a small steel handle which applies or withdraws the steam from the legs or pistons. The more steam that's applied to the upper extremities – hip joints, if you like – of these pistons the faster they move the wheels. Are you listening?'

'Oh, yes. I find it fascinating.'

'When the speed has to be diminished the steam is allowed to evaporate through a safety valve into the air. And there's a small glass tube fixed to the boiler which shows when more water is needed.' He grinned again and kept grinning until she had to laugh at him.

'Come on, be honest,' he said. 'Admit it – you're enjoying it too.'

'I do believe I am.'

She sounded so surprised he laughed loudly and grasped her hand in his. It was the first time as far as she knew that he had ever held her without lust. There was nothing in his eyes but affection and happiness. Never before had she felt pure joy as in that shared experience as they flew along together in the railroad train. When she closed her eyes the sensation of flying was delightful and strange beyond words.

All too soon the short journey to and from Garsherrie was completed, they were back in Glasgow and Luther was helping her from the train. They both took a last lingering gaze of admiration at the snorting little animal.

'Oh, Luther, it was like being part of a fairy tale,' she told him as they returned to the street and made their way back to the wagon.

'Now do you understand why I saw it's the coming thing? Do you see the potential in it?'

'Yes, you were quite right. And it was foolish of me to be so afraid.' She flushed at her unintentional slip. 'Well, not afraid exactly, perhaps a trifle apprehensive.'

'Most people are afraid of the unknown. There's still a lot of opposition to the railways. Apart from potential passengers like yourself who just haven't realized what it's like, there are the landowners: They're the very devil of obstruction. They squeeze thousands out of the rail companies in compensation for the so-called inconvenience of a railway going through their land.'

'They should be thrilled,' she said, her enthusiasm running away with her again. 'And to think that you are actually building these wonderful railroads. You should be proud, Luther.'

'There's no money to be made out of pride.'

'Luther, money isn't everything. I know you are ambitious, but . . .'

'It's time we were on our way back. Get up on the wagon.'

His voice now made her feel shut out and far away from him once more. Barely giving her enough time to climb up and settle herself beside him, he snapped the reins and gave a coarse shout at the horses. She stared straight ahead and said no more. The wagon jerked and jolted and they were away.

Chapter Twenty-four

'I'm sorry, ladies and gentlemen,' Luther called, spurring his horse towards the group of coaches that had stopped in the deep bowl of the workings. 'You must keep up on the hill or much further back.'

The liveried dragsman perched high on the box, flicked him a disdainful glance. Ignoring him completely, the footmen continued to help the ladies and gentlemen from their coaches. Hordes of men, women and children were already covering the hill. Luther could not blame crowds of people flocking to watch a railway line in the course of construction. It was, after all, a new and absorbing spectacle full of movement and excitement. Hillsides were being scooped out, rocks blasted away. Armies of navvies in their flamboyant clothes coloured the landscape, their shovels and pickaxes glinting in the sun.

'How dare you,' said one of the gentlemen, 'tell us what or what not to do.'

'It's for your own safety,' Luther said. 'But, of course, if you are not concerned about either your own safety or that of the ladies in your care . . .' He shrugged, 'You are free to come as close as you wish. Now there is an operation that should interest and impress you. That wall of rock has got to be broken up so that it can be shovelled into the wagons and taken away. Because the wagons are on rails, of course, each horse can draw a much heavier load than normal.' He pointed to where a couple of navvies were alternately swinging hammers at a wedge held by another navvy squatting on the ground. 'You see the military precision of these men?'

The hammers kept up their vicious donging rhythm and the ladies and gentlemen murmured not only in appreciation but concern.

'Yes, it is dangerous,' said Luther. 'One slip and that man underneath the hammers is dead. But after they get the gunpowder in it's dangerous for all of us. Gunpowder is not dependable. But you'll know soon enough when it goes off. There's a growl and roar that echoes all round the hills and masses of rocks are hurled high into the air. There's more skulls cracked that way than any other.'

The ladies squealed in alarm and their gentlemen escorts were forced to turn their attention to reassuring them, helping them back inside the coaches and ordering the coachmen away to a safer distance.

Luther chuckled to himself as he watched their hasty retreat, although he had told no lies about the dangers. Before every explosion, however, any passersby or onlookers were warned by the blowing of horns and bugles.

It never worried the navvies whether there was rock or earth at the diggings. A good navvy and his mate could fill fourteen or sixteen wagons every day. That meant shovelling more than twenty tons of material and swinging it higher than six feet with his shovel to reach the wagon. During the night the work continued by candlelight or by the smoky flare of torches.

Luther guided his horse along to where an excavation of earth was being worked to a vertical face. The usual method was to undercut the bottom to produce a large fall of earth. This broke up the compact ground into loose masses that would be easier to shovel into the wagons.

'Where the hell's the look-out?' he shouted at the men busy undermining the face. 'Do you stupid bastards want to get buried under there? Donovan, get on top and shout down the minute you feel movement.'

A bluster of rain suddenly swept over the countryside

and made Luther curse to himself. The greatest enemy at the diggings was mud, and when rain fell the freshly broken ground was soon worked into a knee-deep quagmire by man and horse. Walls of earth towering on either side of the cutting slipped out at the bottom and subsided at the top. Temporary rails which had been laid down for the haulage of earth and rock, and the wagon-wheels became clogged with mud and made movement doubly difficult and hazardous on the already insecure foundation.

Easing his horse round, Luther returned along between the high earth walls with their steep planks up which navvies, showing immense strength, were 'running the barrow' to where they could tip the muck. This was the last Saturday of the month and the men's pay day. He had to meet Campbell the contractor and go over the timesheets with him to calculate the amount of money to be laid out for wages.

Campbell was already in the pay office when Luther arrived. Augusta was there too, looking very neat and ladylike in the blue cotton dress she had made herself; the blue was the same shade as her eyes and complemented her golden-coloured hair. Campbell was usually quite enamoured with her and made no secret of how he enjoyed calling at the store office because it means 'feasting my eyes on your beautiful wife, Gunnet.'

This time, however, Luther detected a distraught look about the man. He seemed barely to be listening to Augusta's conversation while he sipped the cup of tea she had brought him. They both rose when he entered.

'Ah, there you are, Luther,' Augusta said. 'I have been doing my best to entertain Mr Campbell until you arrived but I have not been very successful. I am sure he has not heard one word I have said.'

'Do forgive me, dear lady,' Campbell murmured. 'My mind is distracted with problems.'

'What problems?' Luther asked abruptly.

'Would you like a cup of tea, Luther?' Augusta enquired.

'No. Just leave us now, if you please.'

169

'Certainly.' She swished away, closing the door behind her.

'What problems?' Luther repeated.

'It's about the men's wages.'

'What about them?'

'Look, Gunnet, I'll be honest with you. I'm having to back out. I'm giving you the chance to get out as well.'

'The men's wages,' Luther said in an almost bored monotone.

'Can't you understand? I haven't got the money. I've bitten off more than I can chew. That's what it comes down to. I didn't realize how many difficulties we'd come up against and how costs would soar. My tender was too low. I see that now. Much too low.'

'Campbell, I've told my men they'll be paid this afternoon. That means they'll get paid this afternoon.'

'It's hopeless, I tell you. I've bills to pay. I can't get any more credit. I've tried everywhere. We won't even be able to get feed for the horses, let alone plant like rails or sleepers. So what's the use of paying the men? They won't be able to work for much longer.'

'The men have got to be paid.'

'You're as stubborn as a mule, Gunnet. There's no use talking to you.'

'I may be stubborn but I'm not a fool. In fact, Campbell, it's been perfectly obvious to me from the beginning that I've a better business head on my shoulders than you. Not only that, I know the practicalities of the job. I've worked on railroads before. You haven't.'

'I blame the engineer,' Campbell's voice turned bitter. 'There's far more rock on this stretch than I was led to believe. And look at this cutting we're on now. It's having to be much deeper than was reckoned, and that's meant more men and more working hours.'

'Blaming the engineer or anybody else won't save your skin or pay the men's wages.'

'Oh, to hell with the men, Gunnet,' he said rising in a

170

flurry of harassment. 'You can suit yourself what you do. I'm getting out with what money I've left.'

'No, you're not, Campbell.'

'Are you threatening me?'

'Yes.'

'How . . . how dare you, sir!'

Luther riveted him with an unblinking stare. 'I could hammer you into the ground. Or I could throw you to the men. Either way you could get killed.'

The other man sat down again, a nervous twitch fluttering across his face like a persistent fly.

'How much is it you need to become solvent?' Luther asked.

'Two thousand pounds.'

'I could get that.'

For a minute Campbell's face went blank with surprise. Eventually he repeated: 'Two thousand!'

'Two thousand.'

Relief melted over Campbell. 'You mean you'd be willing to give me a loan?'

'Not a loan.'

'What do you mean then?'

'An investment. I would want a controlling interest in the business. I would want to make all the decisions.'

'You're a cool one. You sit there and talk about controlling my business . . .'

'If you don't agree, you're out of business.'

'But if you loaned me the money I could soon – '

'Fritter it away.' Luther cut in. 'You're no use, Campbell. If my money goes in, I control it. If any mistakes are made I'll take full responsibility.'

Campbell still looked poised on the verge of flight. But only his nervous twitch moved.

'You're not giving me much choice.'

'No.'

'I suppose it might work.'

'It'll work very well, Campbell, you have my word for that. From now on we'll make money.'

Campbell gave a short laugh. 'One thing I'll say for you, Gunnet, you do inspire confidence.' He nodded as if convincing himself. 'Yes, yes, why not? Here's my hand on it.'

'Right. We'll meet at the solicitor's in Glasgow on Monday, fix up the details and make it legal.' Suddenly Luther spread out the time sheets on the desk. 'But before we arrange that, we've this job to see to. I should have enough in the store to cover my own men. The highlanders will have to wait until we go to the bank on Monday.'

Campbell laughed again. 'You never give up, do you?'

'No.'

'You've quite a reputation for it.'

'As good a recipe for success as any, I'd say.'

'Yes, maybe you're right, Gunnet. You certainly have the look of a man who's going to push his way on.'

Ignoring this, Luther studied the time sheets. But his mind was also pleasantly savouring what his conversation with the contractor meant. This was his chance to push on, although it had come sooner than he had expected. Still, he had not let it pass him by. That was the important thing. He was well aware, of course, that the first hazardous result would explode like a barrel of black gunpowder as soon as the highlanders heard that they were not to get paid. But surely Ganger McAulay would be able to control his men, especially when he could assure them they would get their money on Monday. And they could always get as much drink as they liked on credit from the bar-room. Nevertheless, to be on the safe side, Luther arranged for the Irishmen to be paid early and put the hint around that it would be wise for them to get the hell out of the camp and away to Glasgow. This they did without even waiting to ask questions. Later Ganger McAulay and his men learned of the delay in their wages, but they did not discover about the Irishmen having been paid until after Mr Campbell was safely away to Glasgow. It was Old Wylie who unintentionally let slip the fact, and Luther heartily cursed him for it.

'I'm sorry, Ganger. I could have bit my tongue out the

172

minute I said it. I was a bit harassed at the time, you see. The bar was packed and . . .'

'Never mind the bloody excuses. Where the hell are they now?'

'They've rampaged off like madmen after the barneys.'

'Why the hell didn't you tell me all this earlier?' Luther demanded.

'I couldn't find you, Ganger.'

'Don't lie to me. You knew I was down at the workings.'

'They were thirsting for blood, Ganger. I didn't want it to be yours.'

'The stupid bastards! They were told they'd get their money on Monday. And they didn't need to be short of anything until then.'

'But it's the fair, you see. That's what done it.'

Luther gave the man a puzzled look, then understanding dawned. 'Oh, Christ, I forgot about the Glasgow fair.'

'It's the one thing they look forward to all year, Ganger.'

Luther suddenly strode away. Once inside the store he went straight to his hut and took his pistol from the dresser drawer.

Seeing him, Augusta cried out in alarm. 'Luther, what's wrong? What are you going to do?'

'There's going to be a massacre in Glasgow tonight if I don't get there and try to stop it.'

'Oh, no, please, Luther. Your duty is here with us. If the men are foolish enough to fight, let them fight. It is not your responsibility.'

'I've got a stake in this business now and the men are my responsibility.'

She ran after him, calling his name with a sharpness that failed to disguise her fear. Paying no attention to her, he mounted his horse and galloped away towards the town.

Chapter Twenty-five

'Hear, hear! what a discordant din
With trumpets, cymbals, drums!
The warning cry of "Just begin,"
From every showman comes,
Haste, tumble in – no time to lose –
Fun riding upon fun –
See and believe, without excuse –
Such feats were never done
Before this day . . .'

The man with the drum hanging round his neck stumped around the streets, head flung back, words bellowing out, drum banging. Everywhere men advertised to the world that the fair was in town. Some dressed as clowns did somersaults along the road, narrowly missing death under horses' hooves or carriage wheels. Others held up placards on which a coloured drawing of a lion or tiger or a grotesquely fat lady was embossed. Others again clashed cymbals and simply bawled:

'The fair! The fair!'

Luther pushed through the lively bustle of the streets. He had stabled his horse so that he would be free to search in closes and houses if need be to find the highlanders. It might make them think twice about causing any trouble if he told them it could cost them their jobs. Pinning down any man in Glasgow was no easy task, however. In Edinburgh the whole pace of the city was slower; there, people walked the streets with dignity. In Glasgow busy crowds of men moved compulsively and continuously at a half-run.

He found the spectacle of such an immense town lying before his view, enveloped in thick clouds of smoke from so many factories, and the energetic movement of it exhilarating and exciting. Here was wealth, opportunity and success for the man forceful enough to grasp it.

The fair was held in the stretch of street alongside the river from the foot of Stockwell to the area in front of Glasgow Green and the jail. It was at this spot – facing the entrance to the Green – that public hangings now took place. As Luther made his way down Stockwell Street bitter memories hacked through him, especially when he passed the Briggait. Despite his efforts to harden his mind away from the past he could still see the ghost of himself on his way to school with Tibs. He could see his father arm in arm with his mother as they returned from church with the children skipping around them. He could see his mother's straight back and hear her prim, proud voice: 'Behave yourself now. Remember who you are!'

The crowd became so dense he could hardly move. The whole stretch of East Clyde Street was packed with huge caravans from London with their wild beasts, and other caravans and circuses with attractions like the man of the wild beasts, the freaks of the Punch and Judy, a giant and giantess, a dwarf, a fat woman, living skeletons, swings and roundabouts.

The stench from the dung depot which occupied the bank of the river filled the nostrils, clung to the clothes, tainted meat pies, soured lollipops, pungently flavoured milk. But the weight of the dung smell did nothing to repress the enjoyment of the revellers in being free from drudgery and to sample instead the excitement and novelties of the fair.

Every time a fight erupted among the crowd Luther struggled towards it but so far he had seen no sign of any of the navvies. It was to be expected of course that at least a few of the fights at the fair would involve some Irishmen – 'hunting the Barneys' as it was called was a common sport of a hooligan element. Indeed this was regarded by many as the *pièce de résistance* of the annual fair. No Irishman who came near it was safe. Suspects were seized by gangs and forced to pronounce words like 'peas' and 'tea'. If the words came out as 'paze' and 'tay' the unfortunate man was belaboured with bludgeons. Sometimes the fair hooligans would hustle their victims into the quadrangle formed by the booths so that the kicking and clubbing of the 'Barneys' could prove an added diversion for everybody. When sport lagged for lack of victims the hooligan element rooted among the warrens of the Saltmarket and the Briggait, broke windows and doors, clubbed Irishmen out of their homes and ducked them in the stream of the Molendiner which at that point flowed into the River Clyde.

Luther doubted however that this annual demonstration would be allowed free flow today because the number of Irishmen in and around Glasgow – including his own men – would have shortened the odds for their attackers.

Of course if a fight started between the highlanders and the Irish navvies there was a risk of the indigenous population joining in. Not that Glaswegians had any particular fondness for highlanders. They had helped massacre quite a few of them at Culloden. Against an Irish Catholic, however, there was always the danger that they would unite.

He reached the Glasgow Green end of the fair without having seen a single familiar face. The only conclusion he could come to was that the Irishmen were at the moment enjoying themselves in the taverns of the town and would not emerge to sample the pleasures of the fair until they had drunk their fill.

Luther bought a couple of pies from a pieman and while biting into them he squeezed his way from the crowd and into the comparative quietness and emptiness of the Green. He needed a few minutes to himself to mull over his own concerns. The men concerned him, of course. He wanted a full efficient work force at the diggings on Monday, not the crippled remains of a bloody battle. Yet the men and their problems could not consume his mind with the urgency and cordiality that his other thoughts afforded. They could not quench the keen sense of achievement he felt at having manoeuvred Campbell into a partnership. The money that the contractor still had would just be enough, along with his own capital, to see them through to the end of the job.

He would make sure it did. He would organize the men into butty gangs and pay them by the lump. He had seen men united in this way, by qualities of strength and endurance and a desperation to earn as much as possible, attack a job with feverish activity and complete it in an amazingly short time. This was important because the contract was let on a time clause and as was usual in such cases there would be penalties for exceeding it, penalties that neither he nor Campbell could afford. On the other hand the company had let it be known that any contractor would be paid an extra sum multiplied by the number of weeks that the finished job fell short of the date set down in the contract.

He had reached a hilly part of the Green and had just finished off his pies with considerable relish when on gazing back over the panorama of the fair his eye was taken by the rapid silvery flashing of the sun over the heads of one part of the crowd. He watched this phenomenon for a minute or two while noise bounced and rolled in the distance like a giant ball. Then suddenly it dawned on him that he had seen the silvery glitter before. It was the sun reflecting on navvies' pickaxes and shovels.

He ran swiftly along the grassy banks and through the gate but once outside the Green he was slowed to snail's pace by a solid wall of hilarious humanity. No amount of cursing or rough pushing or shouldering could extinguish the obstinate good humour or create a path between the tightly packed revellers. By the time he did manage to squeeze his way through and reach the other end, the navvies were milling up the Stockwell. Dodging in and out of closes and wynds he managed to get to Argyle Street before them. There, from the corner close, he saw strung across the street a line of policemen with batons drawn standing at the ready.

'We've a cart here,' the sergeant was bawling. 'Either you leave your pickaxes and shovels on it and allow them to be taken back to the diggings, or you all get out of the town. We're not allowing a mob to ge stravaiging about the place brandishing dangerous weapons. And if you refuse to do either of these things then we'll arrest as many as we're able at the moment and seek out the rest later, at diggings if necessary. We'll have the lot of you transported before we're done.'

The men hesitated, shuffling about and muttering in the Gaelic between themselves. Eventually Ganger McAulay shouted out to them in the same tongue.

'What are you telling them?' the police sergeant wanted to know.

'I am telling them to do as you say and put their pickaxes and shovels on the cart. They were taken in anger. We do not need them. We can match fist to fist with any Irishman.'

'We want no trouble,' said the sergeant. 'No trouble at all.'

'Och, aye. Aye. That is true. There you are now.' Ganger McAulay's polite lilting voice did not in the least match the compact earthy box of a man who clumped forward to where horse and cart stood waiting. There he gesticulated and shouted encouragement at his men unenthusiastic to part with their pickaxes and shovels.

The policemen gave an order to the carter and the car trundled away. Then he turned to Ganger McAulay.

'Now where are you off to?'

'Och, I think we are just having a wee wander along to the High Street.'

'Right, move along then and no trouble, remember.'

Luther decided for the moment it was best not to interfere. The police had handled the situation very well and would not take kindly to him making what could be constructed as threatening remarks to the men just when they had more or less calmed them down. At least now if there was a fight it would be a fair one. No weapons would be involved.

As the ponderous clatter of highlanders' boots faded along Argyle Street towards the Cross and round into High Street Luther strolled after them. Both thoroughfares were comparatively quiet, most of the populace thronging the streets by the river.

A few cabmen fronting the Tontine Hotel were sitting fast asleep on the doorsteps of their vehicles, their hands sunk deep in their pockets. Their equally tired-looking horses drooped their drowsy heads almost down to their knees and even the chiming of the Tolbooth clock did nothing to rouse either man or beast.

Then suddenly a commotion erupted from the Havanah, one of the closes in the High Street, and Luther recognized two or three of his Irish navvies protesting in loud voices at the same time as giving punch for punch with their highland attackers that to 'the bist of their knulledge' the highlanders had been paid as well and that they were as blameless as the Virgin Mary herself. It was doubtful, judging by the abusive screeches in Gaelic, that the highlanders understood these protestations of innocence. This was confirmed by the fist that smashed into Luther's face as he waded in to the centre of the mêlée. The sight of their ganger being given such summary treatment brought roars of indigation from the Irishmen and a host of their colleagues stampeding from, it seemed, every public house and tavern in the district.

The battle rolled backwards and forwards between thousands of cheering spectators who had deserted the fair to watch this new excitement. The police also arrived but were kept on the outside for most of the time. When they did struggle through, some Irish navvies paused in their battle with highland adversaries to thump the police over the head with their own batons. Other Irishmen, finding themselves temporarily squeezed out of reach of a highlander, gave vent to their exuberance by executing step-dances on the edge of the battlefield until seeing an opening and plunging once more into the fray.

Several times Luther tried to make himself heard but every time he opened his mouth he got a highland fist in it. This never failed to spur him into violent retaliation. Eventually, however, he fired his pistol into the air and the surprise of this explosion was successful in halting the proceedings.

Like the rest of the men, his clothes were torn and bloodied and he could only make a lurching effort to stand but the effort he made as he shouted at the highlanders:

'You'll be paid on Monday, damn you! You have my word on it. And the fair will still be here then. But I've enough in my saddle bags at the stables to give you half-a-crown each just now. And there's as much whisky as you can drink back at the store.'

One of the policemen who had been felled also lurched to his feet.

'Send for the troops,' he shouted. 'Arrest the lot of them. Send for reinforcements!'

'Come on,' Luther urged. 'Let's get out of here!'

The cobbled street clattered and clanged and echoed with tackety boots. The crowds hastily parted and before the policemen could find their batons the navvies had gone.

Chapter Twenty-six

Augusta's feet crunched over the snowy ground as she trudged from her hut to where she conducted the school. Usually when it was dark Billy accompanied her. He carried a torch that sliced a yellow path through the blackness between the tightly packed rows of huts. Tonight, however, a full moon beamed down and reflected on a crisp icing of snow. She needed neither Billy nor his torch. It was Billy's turn to work nights at the diggings and his job was to tend the horses and run them to the tip. She viewed this with considerable unease. Indeed she had mentioned her concern.

'Luther, I cannot bear to look when Billy is running with a horse and wagon to the tip. Surely it is very dangerous to leap aside like that at the very last moment before the wagon tips over.'

'The horse can get out of the way quick enough,' Luther said.

'It seems to me it is most hazardous for both man and beast.'

'Every job at the diggings is dangerous, Augusta. What do you want me to do with him? He's thin and agile but has little strength. But perhaps I should try and make a navvy of him.'

'No, I did not mean that. He is intelligent, Luther. He would make a good dominie.'

'There's little money in teaching.'

She sighed, remembering the conversation, and her uneasiness trickled from Billy and touched Samuel and Alexander. She wanted better things from them than Luther seemed to be able to appreciate, though she was not foolish enough even in her own mind to denigrate his propensity for making money. Tonight the highlanders were just clearing up their part of the diggings. Luther's section of the line had been finished in record time and he had been paid a handsome sum for his efforts. Now he had bid for and won the contract for another section, this time without Mr Campbell. She had been uncomfortable about that too, sensing that Luther had been very hard on poor Mr Campbell.

'Why should I carry him any longer than is necessary?' Luther said. 'It wouldn't make sense. Or good business.'

She supposed he was right but she would miss Mr Campbell's visits. He had quite gentlemanly ways and knew how to speak to a lady. She had enjoyed his little courtesies and their conversations about books. Not that Luther was ignorant about literature; he had been to college and could even read some texts in the original Latin – something she could not do. But he just did not seem interested in literature or literary discussions. The diggings and the making of money were his most urgent interest and concerns. He had very little time for anything else.

She wondered what this next section would be like. Starting the New Year in a new place seemed significant to

181

her, as if they were on the verge of a whole new life. In a way they were. For the first time Luther was a contractor in his own right. In view of his new status he had rented a cottage for her and the children. She had not seen it yet and was afraid to give way to the joy and excitement she felt in case somehow it would not materialize, or it would not be so very different from the huts. Her emotions, however, despite her trying to keep them firmly in order kept spilling over and straying out of control. When Luther had first told her about the cottage she had listened with dignified attention. Then later, for no apparent reason, she had burst into tears.

She had not really felt like taking her school this evening because she would have to be up very early next morning to organize everything on to the wagon before they moved away. But Maureen had pleaded with her so vehemently to come she was obliged to agree for the sake of peace.

A few of the other wives had joined and brought some children so that there were now pupils of all ages from four years up to forty. All of them were Irish.

The long dormitory hut was packed when she reached it and lit by many candles. Seats had been improvised by planks supported by bricks. Augusta loosened her shawl but did not take it off as she made her way to the front. Despite the glow of the fire the air had a frosty nip and draughts made the candle flames jig about.

Suddenly, to her astonishment the men roared out in song.

'For shay's a jolly good fella, for shay's a jolly good fella.' Boots clanged to a deafening crescendo with the voices. 'For shay's a jolly good fe-ella-a – and so say all of us!'

Riotous clapping and laughter filled the building to bursting point.

Standing before them in her blue cotton dress she somehow managed to look ladylike despite the shawl and the boots she'd been forced to wear to protect her from mud and snow.

'Come now!' she called out sharply in an effort to bring

order to the proceedings. 'This will not get any lessons done.'

Maureen, who was sitting in the front row next to Boozer, dug him in the ribs with her elbow and he shuffled to his feet grinning and pulling off his bonnet to reveal a knobbly shaven head.

'Mrs,' he said, 'we've been grateful, so we have.' Then he stood twisting his bonnet, laughter fading from his eyes and anguish replacing it as he struggled to remember the rest of what he was obviously expected to say.

Maureen bounced up. 'Jaysus, will ye sit down and let me do it.' Rummaging deep in his jacket pocket she came out with a box. This she immediately presented to Augusta. 'Here ye are, Mrs. It's from all of us and we thank ye.'

Speechless, Augusta opened the box. Inside was a beautiful gold watch engraved with the words: 'To Augusta Gunnet, February 1839. With gratitude and respect from the navigators of the G & A Railway.'

Augusta raised her head to its haughtiest tilt. Only a panic of desperation kept her dignity intact. Even so, tears filled her eyes, making them over-large and unnaturally bright. But her voice without being loud reached every corner of the room with its usual polite distinctness.

'How very kind! And what a beautiful gift. I shall always treasure it. And I shall always remember the kindness and thoughtfulness of every one of you. Thank you very much indeed.'

More clapping and stamping of feet and cheering followed and she had to put up a hand to quell the noise.

'But you must not think of this as the last evening of our school. Although I will no longer be living in the huts with the rest of you and it will not be convenient to hold classes so regularly or so often, nevertheless I will try my best to hold a class whenever possible.'

More cheers ensued. This time she waited patiently for silence and then continued:

'Meantime I suggest that this evening, instead of lessons, we might have a little soirée. I know some of you have excellent singing voices. Perhaps one or two can entertain with recitations and, Lump Regan, you have a flute, have you not? Who shall be first? Come now, you cannot pretend that you are bashful.'

'I'll give you a song, Mrs.' Up jumped Digger Donovan to immediately explode into a lusty bellow:

'To view the railroad, away they did go,
It's a great undertaking, you very well know,
It surpasses all others, believe me it's true,
There's tunnels for miles that you have to go through.'

The rest of the men began to thunder the words along with him.

'The cobbler left all the old shoes in the shop,
Old women on crutches were seen for to hop,
And the tailor his customers would not obey,
But rode on his goose for to see the railway.'

Augusta smiled approval and encouragement.

'Come, all you young fellows, and let us be free,
Again fill the glasses, now merry we'll be,
Success to all trades in the reign of our Queen,
And the boiling hot water that travels by steam.'

No encouragement was needed. One song and singer followed hard on the heels of the other. Even Augusta took her turn with a rendering of 'Where e'er you walk'. Horse O'Hoolahan gave a comic recitation and was rewarded with tumultuous laughter and applause which delighted him so much he gave an encore.

Lump Regan obliged with a tune to which Maureen danced with mounting abandon, fiery hair streaming loose and skirts lifting and swirling higher and higher. Augusta tried to catch her eye to indicate that this was not ladylike behaviour. She did not succeed but once the dance was over she firmly announced that the soirée had come to an end and reminded everyone that they had an early start next morning and a long march to the new section. Then after thanking them once more for the gift of the watch she bid them goodnight.

Outside it was very cold and quiet. Not too far away there were sounds of the men working at the diggings. Yet they seemed to come from another world. The rhythmic beat of pick and shovel, the sudden trundle of barrow and wagon wheels, the gathering speed of horses' hooves, the sudden stop then the beginning again, reached her along beams of moonlight with ghostly unreality.

Her emotions were so stirred by recent events she could not settle her mind to return to her hut and bed. Sleep would be impossible. She stopped and looked around. This would be the last time she would live in a colony of huts. She wondered at the regret she felt. Why should she feel an attachment to any of these squalid places? Yet as she stood in the deep brown shade of the walls, around which the children had so often played hide and seek, she recognized the close community and the comradeship they contained which was completely misunderstood by the world outside.

This sense of comradeship extended even after death and if a navvy died on the line hundreds would march with the coffin to the graveside even though the deceased was a newcomer and unknown to most of the mourners. In fact, a man who had just come from across the water and was a stranger in a strange land could be sure of the biggest turn-out of all. Every navvy for miles would arrive to keep him company on his last journey. Augusta had always thought this to be wonderfully kind. There was never any question of burial by the parish. The rough brotherhood of the navvies always ensured that enough money would be collected for the interment and something over for the man's widow and family if he had one.

She had gone in the wagon and on foot to many funerals, so had Billy and Luther. She had read in the newspaper afterwards of how the local population had been shocked to witness these processions at which most of the deceased's fellow labourers had been wearing their usual working clothes. It had never occurred to the writers of such articles that the navvies not only might not possess a suit of blacks in their wardrobe but might not even possess a wardrobe.

But what really horrified outsiders was witnessing the navvies smoking their pipes on such occasions especially while they took their turn at bearing the coffin. This each one of them always did, moving up two by two to carry it upon their shoulders. The people in towns and villages or the newspapers that reflected their opinions obviously did not appreciate or understand the fellow-feeling and the kindness involved.

Surprised at how sad she felt, Augusta took several deep stimulating breaths of icy air before continuing her walk to her hut.

Luther was sitting at the table reading a newspaper. He glanced up when she entered. Yet he did not seem to see her. He was smiling but it was an inward secret kind of smile that shut her out.

'What are you reading?' she asked for his eyes had returned to the paper. 'Is it good news?'

Luther leaned back, tipping the wooden chair on to two legs and hooking his thumbs into his belt. 'Yes, it's good news.'

'Well?' Augusta said after a minute. 'Are you not going to share it with me?'

'I told you railways were the coming thing. Now they've passed the bill for the line from Glasgow to Edinburgh.'

'But we already knew about that.'

'The stage-coach proprietors have begun to see the writing on the wall. But now they're too late.'

Augusta's heart gave a flutter of concern. 'What do you mean?'

Luther stared at her long and straight and for no apparent reason she felt afraid of him. Breaking away from his stare she fussed with her shawl, taking it off, folding it neatly over the back of one of the chairs, then sitting herself down.

'I mean,' Luther said, 'that coachbuilders and proprietors like your father and his friends are going to be ruined.'

'Surely not,' she managed faintly.

'Why not?'

'But . . . there will always be coaches. Railways cannot *replace* coaches.'

'They already are.'

'What does the newspaper article say?'

'It's a report of a coach proprietors' meeting. It's one long whine about road taxation and trying to blame that.' Flicking out the paper he read: '. . . is yearly increasing and hastening the destruction of the most respectable establishment in the country, no remedial measures have been introduced into Parliament, nor any means taken to avert the certain loss and ruin which await all those who are interested in Land Carriages moved by animal power . . .' He flung the paper down again. 'Road Tax or no, they can't compete. They're finished.'

Augusta's mind could not take in the implications of such a sweeping statement.

'Not finished, surely. They could balance their losses by joining forces with the railway companies. They could buy shares in the railways.'

'They haven't had enough sense or foresight for that. They've ruined themselves by trying to compete. They've cut their prices down to nothing until they've no business and no capital left.'

'My papa has always been a good sensible businessman.'

'He thought he was God Almighty.'

'He would see . . .'

'No, he wouldn't, Augusta . . .'

She turned away to prepare for bed. Her uneasiness had increased a thousandfold. So many changes and thoughts of changes were milling about that she felt helpless and confused.

And there was something, it seemed to her, very disturbing and frightening about Luther at times.

Chapter Twenty-seven

'Cream and sugar?' Augusta reigned like a queen in her new parlour. A tray on the japanned table was set with china cups, gilt-edged and hand-painted with roses, and also a matching teapot, sugar dish and cream jug. On lace doilies on a tiered cakestand were arranged crustless sandwiches no bigger than a thumb, buttered scones and a Victoria sponge cake.

Maureen perched on the edge of her chair at the opposite side of the fire. Her face shone like a russet apple. Her hair had been tamed with much water although there seemed a danger of it springing back to unruly life the moment it was dry. Her best green dress was hitched up to show that her boots had been scraped and polished and her legs properly clad in stockings, although the amount of bosom showing above her dress was anything but proper.

'Wouldn't that be a fine treat? But Holy Mother of God, them cups are so thin, amn't I frightened to touch them. You could spit peas through them cups. They're that bloody thin.'

Augusta winced. She was careful however not to let Maureen see that she was causing any embarrassment or disapproval. After all, Maureen was her guest.

'Oh, isn't it the miraculous thing that Father Mathews has done, God bless him for the holy man that he is.' Maureen had a habit of bursting out with vigorous and unexpected pronouncements.

'You don't mean Boozer has taken the pledge?'

'Hasn't him and every man in the gang become as teetotal as the Holy One himself? Oh, and it's doing my Boozer a power of good, so it is. He was always a big strong fella but half the time he didn't know it himself with him being under the influence. Now isn't he home from work and having his supper and fit and ready to get on top of me right away. Why, last night . . .'

188

'His name,' Augusta hastily interrupted, 'is no longer relevant, it would appear. Boozer is hardly a suitable name for a teetotaller.'

'Jaysus, and there isn't one of us that's thought of that.' Maureen laughed loudly and long, making Augusta wince again.

'So what will you call him?'

'Ach, Boozer he's always been and Boozer he'll stay.'

'May I help you to a sandwich?'

'You've a heart as big as a bucket, so you have.' Maureen popped the whole sandwich into her mouth.

Augusta watched her with growing discomfort. It was not of course the first time that the other woman had been in the cottage. In the first few months since she and Luther had moved in, Maureen had called several times to help with the papering and painting, the scrubbing of the floors and the washing of the windows. It had been a great thrill for both women when they had seen the cottage and found that as well as two rooms and a scullery downstairs it had three tiny attic rooms upstairs. Right away Maureen had volunteered to help and had set with joyful enthusiasm, singing all the time. She could not have been more elated if the good fortune of acquiring such a dwelling place actually had been hers. Together they had sighed happily over the finished work. Into the stone-flagged kitchen with its whitewashed walls and brown woodwork they had arranged the brown painted dresser, table, stools, rocking-chair and the antimacassared easy chair. The warm dark brown was nicely set off by two green shelves stretching the whole length of one wall. The bottom one held pots and basins and a brass jelly pan and other utensils. The top shelf displayed china dogs, one at each end, and in between a water jug and bowl and a giant cheese dish and two soup tureens. A scullery led off the kitchen and it boasted a sink, some shelves and cupboards all painted green. A back door led into a drying area and a patch of vegetable garden. The stretch of garden was overgrown and neglected but this did nothing to dampen Augusta's enthusiasm.

'Imagine, just imagine!' She clasped her hands under her chin in a rapture of delight. 'A back door as well as a front door!'

Luther had grinned with amusement at her reaction to the first sight of the house. 'You like it?'

'Like it? Like it? I adore it. I simply adore it, Luther. You and Billy will be able to take your boots off and leave them in the scullery.'

He had laughed but as soon as his laughter died down he said:

'Augusta, I'll tramp all over this bloody house with my boots on if I feel like it.'

'I was only thinking of the mud.'

'You're duty's to think of your husband. Remember that.'

'Jaysus!' Maureen who had been with them at the time burst out indignantly. 'If my man spoke to me like that I'd belabour him senseless with his own shillelah.'

'I know what you're needing,' Luther told her.

'Oh, do ye now? And what might that be?'

She had looked up at him in such a flirtatious manner that Augusta had felt it necessary to put an immediate stop to such impertinent familiarity.

'It is time you went to the huts and got yourself and Boozer settled in, Maureen. You may come back tomorrow if you wish – when my husband is at the diggings.'

It was the next day Maureen had helped with the attic bedrooms and the parlour. The bedrooms, one for Samuel and Alexander, one for Billy and one for Luther and herself, were so small they could accommodate little more than a bed, a bedside locker and a stool. The parlour, however, was a great joy. Not that it was very big but it was a room that could be kept for entertaining, and for displaying nice things. The more ornaments, needlework and *objets d'art* one could display the better. This after all was proof to the world of success. Luther obviously agreed because he was pleased when she kept herself busy with embroidery and *petit point* as well as dress-making and he helped her scour

190

the shops for household goods and took her to sales of household effects every time they visited Paisley which was now the nearest town of any size. Already she had acquired a framed picture, several china ornaments, a brass fender, an oil lamp and a potted plant in a pumpkin-shaped bowl made of brass. Then, to her great joy, Luther had bought her the beautiful china tea-set.

Unfortunately as far as entertaining was concerned he was not so obliging. She knew he was meeting important people in his job as contractor but he did not seem interested in developing any social life with them.

'I've no time to waste,' was all he would say when she tried to persuade him to invite someone to tea. Once she had suggested the engineer and his wife and Luther said, 'When I own a mansion like the engineer, I'll offer him hospitality.'

'Oh, but, Luther,' she protested, 'I know our cottage is small and we have no drawing-room but we need not be ashamed of our parlour and, after all, I do know how to behave. If one behaves with good breeding that is the main thing.'

But as usual he brushed her aside with, 'I've no time to waste.'

So in the end, desperate for the little formalities and refinements of social intercourse, she had invited Maureen to come for tea in the parlour. Maureen had always been given a cup of tea in the kitchen on the various occasions she had come to help with the housework but this, they both knew, was to be very different. Ostensibly it was to give Maureen some extra practice and tuition in becoming a lady but Augusta had never been more depressed about the success of this project than she felt now. It was not so much Maureen's appearance, although that was hopeless enough. But at least there an improvement was clearly visible. When the two women had first met, Maureen had been a shocking sight. Her hair was so thick and tousled it looked as if it had never seen either a comb or water. Her clothes were torn, encrusted with mud and indecently short. She wore no boots or shoes or stockings. But right from the start she had disarmed Augusta as well as embarrassed her by her enthusiastic eulogies.

'You're a right lady, so you are, Mrs. We all thought by the looks of you you'd be too haughty to have anything to do with the likes of us. But, Jaysus, haven't you a heart as big as a bucket!'

She had turned up at the school and showed a quick intelligent mind at picking up reading and writing. Her derisory and noisy displays of impatience with the slowest of the men, however, had proved a difficulty that nearly led to violence on more than one occasion. Augusta had to reprimand her severely.

'No lady,' she had pointed out, 'would ever behave in such an undisciplined and outrageous manner.'

Maureen's immediate reaction was, 'Teach me to be a lady, Mrs.'

'I'm sorry, I do not believe that is possible,' she had answered truthfully, but Maureen was an irrepressible optimist.

'Didn't I learn my letters no bother at all? Isn't all I'm needing somebody to tell me how?'

She had certainly taken quickly enough to keeping herself clean and she was seldom seen now without boots and stockings. Her broad Irish accent was not quite so pronounced but her wild nature, along with her enormous sea of social ignorance, had defeated Augusta and left her stranded on a very lonely shore. She realized now, too late, that the tea party in the parlour was the height of folly. It increased her feeling of social isolation a hundredfold.

As Augusta passed Maureen another sandwich she had never been nearer to dissolving into tears. She kept thinking of her mother and the friends they used to entertain at Cameron House. Most of them had been the wives and daughters of her father's business colleagues, coachbuilders and coach proprietors like himself. All had been successful people, ladies and gentlemen of good breeding, education and social refinement. Maureen would never acquire the polish of these things. She was a servant, good-hearted and hardworking but a servant nevertheless. Augusta felt ashamed to have subjected both Maureen and herself to the ordeal of this formalized visit. She had no doubt that Maureen was as relieved as she was when it came to an end. But Maureen would fling off the embarrassment very quickly and go racing down to the huts to boast of the tea party as a stupendous success. She was capable of great flights of imagination.

Augusta on the other hand was left with a niggling nostalgia that she could not shake off. Never since her marriage had she longed more for her parents and their elegant and articulate friends.

She also worried about them, though she did not really believe Luther's gloomy forecasts of how the railway would affect them. The streets were full of private vehicles and there must be many towns all over Scotland to which stage-coaches were still travelling and not at a loss as he claimed.

She had more time for brooding now that she no longer worked in the tommy-shop since she had trained two men to assist Old Wylie and Mrs Grant. Sometimes she even tentatively wondered how her parents might receive a visit from her now. If they saw how respectable she looked in her new yellow batiste dress and shoes and white bonnet and pretty white parasol surely they would be favourably impressed. Luther looked very presentable too in his walking costume of blue waisted coat, grey trousers, yellow waistcoat and blue-grey top hat. But the faint flutter of hope soon died. She did not really believe her mother or father would ever forgive her for associating with Luther and his being connected with the railway now would certainly not improve their opinion of him.

There was a coarse streak in him that she often suspected he indulged and even at times exaggerated, for some perverse reason, to shock or annoy her. Whenever she told him of her disapproval her rebuke only incited him to worse behaviour. He would pursue her lustfully about the room, crashing furniture out of his way and breaking dishes and, despite her indignant protests, tearing at her clothes.

'You still look down your snooty little nose at me,' he said on one occasion, grabbing her close. 'Yet you like it, don't you? And the coarser the better.'

Hating him, she had tried to struggle away, to beat him with her fists, but weeping she had eventually succumbed. Afterwards she felt ashamed of her weakness and despised him for tormenting her. At times she observed his coarseness at a distance. Looking down at the diggings she would see him, hat tipped back on his frizzy head, thumbs hooked in waistcoat, sharing a joke with the men or bawling some obscenity at them in reprimand. Then she would hasten away as if from a stranger she did not wish to know.

There were times, however, when he could be both generous and kind, and she believed it to be one of those times when he suggested she and the children went with him to Glasgow to see the new work that was underway in the Glasgow to Endinburgh line.

They caught the early morning stage coach. Samuel and Alexander were very excited and determined to see out of the window all the time. They refused to keep still, one minute kneeling up on the seat, the next minute standing holding on to the leather strap. Once the jolting movement of the coach was too much for them and they were thrown to the floor. Augusta scolded them but could not really feel angry when she looked at the two little boys so handsome in their wide-skirted coats and their caps with puffy crowns and stiff shiny peaks. Samuel was dark-haired like his father, Alexander had her fair colouring. Both children were bright-eyed and bouncing with health.

'Once the Glasgow-Ayr line opens they won't need to worry about being thrown around in a coach any more,' Luther said.

They alighted at Argyle Street and strolled along for a time admiring the shops. Then, before she realized it, they were in Queen Street.

'The new station is being built up here,' Luther said.

'In George Square?'

'They've bought Crow Ewing's place. But the entrance has to be in Dundas Street round the side of the Wardlaw Church. Dundas Street Station, I hear it's to be called.'

The Crawford mansion had been a most imposing edifice set well back from the square and fronted by lawns. Trees had clustered on either side of it and it had been famous for its rookery, which was why its owner was nicknamed Crow Ewing. She had often awakened in the morning in Cameron House to the sounds of the birds.

Now she approached the square with mounting horror. The beautiful Crawford mansion lay in ruins, and in front of it plunged a deep black pit like hell itself. Mountains of earth and clay reared high on all sides, planks of wood crisscrossed, barrows and wagons trundled noisily about and a vast army of navvies hammered and dug and boomed off explosions.

In disbelief Augusta gazed at Cameron House which not only faced this dreadful upheaval but was completely engulfed by it. Stocks of iron rails lay waiting along Queen Street in front of the Cameron door. Carts heaped with muck or bricks jammed together in West George Street outside the Cameron drawing-room. Muddy pools slushed about, covering the back stairs with slime and gathering deep and stagnant outside the kitchen. The front door was fouled by muddy splashes. So were the walls and all the windows.

Augusta was too shocked for tears. Luther, who had been busy explaining the workings to Samuel and Alexander, eventually turned his attention to her.

'They're selling up and leaving, I hear. Not that they'll get much for the house now. I told you they were finished.'

It seemed only by some miracle her legs continued to support her.

'What will happen to them? Where can they go?'

'There's plenty of room in the Briggait,' he said.

'I couldn't let them go there!'

'They let you go.'

195

'They must have some money. Surely what they get for the house will be enough to secure them a smaller but comfortable dwelling somewhere.'

'I hope not. It would deny me a great source of pleasure and satisfaction.'

'How can you be so cruel, Luther?'

But his attention had returned to the children and Augusta was left alone in her pain and distress to stare at the ruin of what had once been her home.

Chapter Twenty-eight

Augusta found herself in the hotel with food on the table before her without any clear recollection of how she had reached the place. Her mind seemed to have taken on the chaos of the unfinished railroad station in George Square. Surely there was something dreadfully wrong with what she had just witnessed. She felt threatened. For the first time she realized that the old order of things was changing and would never be the same again. Certainly Luther had always maintained that the railway would be a great leveller.

'The gentry were always well apart from the common herd,' he said. 'They stepped into their private carriages at their doors and were closeted inside them until they reached the house of whoever they were going to visit. Now they jostle elbow to elbow with bricklayers and farmers' wives in railway stations and travel in carriages with complete strangers.'

But above and beyond Augusta's personal feelings of confusion and social insecurity there was an overwhelming pity for her father and mother. She did not dare to think how they must be suffering.

She picked at her food, her throat contracting against it, while the children and Luther ate heartily, and he conversed with another two men at the table. Occasionally their words drifted across the pain of her thoughts. The men were telling Luther about a sale which included horses but she paid no more than surface attention. Even afterwards when Luther announced that he was going to the sale she followed, still completely obsessed by her thoughts. It was not until they were actually entering the crowded yard of the Black Bull with its long lines of stables that she realized what was happening.

'Luther!' She caught him by the arm. 'You are not going to buy Papa's horses. You cannot cause him such a terrible humiliation. He has suffered enough.'

Luther brushed away her detaining hand. 'This is business.'

'I think it is revenge.'

He shrugged. 'Think what you like.'

'Oh, Luther!' She felt distracted and when she suddenly caught sight of her father she hastened towards him, although at the same time hardly able to believe it was him. Gone was the proud bearing and the immaculately cared-for clothes. Even his brassy hair and sidewhiskers had dulled into grey. His stoop gave him a shrunken appearance as if he was trying to disappear inside his mudstained suit. He was a shadow of a man.

'Papa!' She tried to embrace him but he swerved away and disappeared into the crowd. Returning to Luther she made up her mind and was able to lie with comparative calm.

'I beg you to spare me the ordeal of this, Luther. If you will keep the children with you and allow me to spend some time shopping I would be most obliged.'

'If you wish.'

'I shall see you later at the coach, then.'

He nodded, his attention already riveted on the sale which had now begun. A concentrated rapier-like pleasure glinted from his eyes, making her wince and look away. After leaving the yard of the Black Bull she made straight for Cameron House.

The door was eventually opened by Nessie the cook, who had lost a great deal of weight and had the trembly frailness of a very old woman. On seeing Augusta, tears spilled from her eyes and wet her white tufts of whiskers. Shuffling aside, she allowed her to enter.

'What is happening, Cook?' Augusta asked. 'How is everyone?'

It took Nessie some moments before she could speak. 'Fiona McPherson has left. So have the footmen. Everyone's gone except Sid and me. We've done our best, but it takes me all my time to do a bit of cooking. I just can't manage the housework. There's your mama's hair and toilet, you see. Sid sees to the fires – '

'I am sure you both have been of great help and comfort and I thank you most sincerely. Where is Mama just now?'

'In the parlour, Miss Augusta.'

'Thank you. I shall come down to the kitchen to speak to you again before I go.'

Augusta took a deep breath before entering the parlour. Inside, the filthy neglected state of the room shocked her beyond words. In silence she stood like a beautiful doll in her frilled gown and pristine white bonnet and gloves. Suddenly she heard her mother's voice cry out:

'Oh, my dear girl! My dear, Dear Augusta!' Felicity Cameron had changed little in appearance. Nessie obviously did a good job on her ringlets and had helped her dress in her usual elegant style.

They embraced warmly before sitting down beside each other on the sofa.

'Mama, it is so good to see you again. I am so sorry for the obvious misfortunes that have befallen you and poor Papa.'

'Poor Papa?' Felicity rolled her eyes and flicked a lace-edged handkerchief as if to rid herself of the annoyance of him. 'Poor Papa indeed! It is all his fault, the stupid man. He and his useless friends, they are all the same. All they can do is whine about how the railway is ruining them. Mr Binny, Mr Harington, old Mr Fotheringham, even Mr Laidlaw-Smythe.'

'But surely, Mama, you can see for yourself how the railway is spreading . . .'

'I've told Mr Cameron. A thousand times I've told him. Why don't you do something about it? But has he done anything about it? Not a thing.'

'Oh, I'm sure Papa has done his best.'

'So he said, my dear. But I said, "Well, I may be a simple soul, Mr Cameron, but it does seem to me that your best is not good enough."' She patted her ringlets. 'He is to blame for everything, Augusta. I told him that what happened to you was his fault too.'

'No, no, Mama. You mustn't say that.'

'Yes, dear, it has to be said. I remember exactly what your papa did that dreadful night of the blizzard when we had our accident. He gave the order – I remember it perfectly well and I have reminded him. "Take my daughter," he said. Those were his very words – "Take my daughter."'

'There's no point in dragging up what happened years ago and blaming Papa or anybody else. What we have to think of now is –'

'How is your dear husband, Augusta? Doing very well I hear. I am told he has already amassed quite a fortune although he keeps only a very modest residence in the country. You must speak to him about that, my dear. Men have to be made aware of a woman's needs. You must insist on an establishment more in keeping with his fortune.'

'Mama, I will have to go shortly. I don't want to waste time talking about myself and my needs. It's you and Papa I'm worried about. What are you going to do? This house will have to be sold eventually. Then where will you go?'

Felicity fluttered her handkerchief again.

'That is Mr Cameron's problem. He has got us into this dreadful situation. He will now have to get us out of it. But I have warned him, Augusta, that I must have an establishment in keeping with a lady's needs. And I insist, absolutely insist on two things. One, a personal maid. It is quite ridiculous having Cook look after me. She is not trained as a lady's maid and anyway she is far too old. She cannot even fulfil her duties as cook any more. Two – a parlour maid. Just look at the dreadful state of this room, Augusta.'

'If I could just speak to Papa and find out what plans he has made then I would know better how I might help. But I have not time today. I have to meet my husband at the stage and I want to go down to the kitchen for a few words with Cook before I go.'

'Oh, my dear, must you go?'

'I will try to come back again soon, Mama. But it will depend when my husband has business in Glasgow. He will not allow me to travel up on my own. But I will keep in touch by letter until I can visit you again.'

Felicity kissed her with much affection. 'I am so glad we have found each other again. I'm sure everything will be all right now. We were always so happy together, were we not?'

'Yes, Mama.'

'Oh, my dear Augusta, how beautiful you look and how elegant. I do like your gown.'

'Thank you, Mama. Now I must hurry.'

They kissed again before Augusta made her way across the hall and downstairs to the kitchen. Despite her distress over the dreadful happenings to her mother and father, at the same time she felt quite elated. It was most peculiar. She realized of course that her gladness had been stimulated by her reconciliation with her mother. And she was confident that the next time she saw her father she would be reconciled to him too.

The kitchen was a sad place in comparison with what it had once been.

The fire was a poor imitation of its former glory, a feeble smoky affair unable, it seemed, to produce either a glimmer of heat or light.

Cook hirpled shakily up from her chair.

'No, sit down, Cook,' Augusta said.

'I'm sorry about the fire, Miss Augusta. We've so little coal these days, you see.'

'Where is your husband?'

'He's at the Black Bull, Miss Augusta. He was worried about your papa. This is the day of the sale, you see.'

'Yes, I know. Have either of you been paid any wages recently?'

The old woman's face worked about in distress and she avoided Augusta's eyes. 'As long as we get a bite to eat and a roof over our heads . . .'

'Take this.' Augusta placed some money on the table. 'It is all I have with me. I will do my best to send you something else as soon as I can. I must hurry away now. No, there is no need to see me out. I can manage perfectly well by myself. Enjoy your rest. You deserve it.'

Once outside and away from the upheaval of the square she began to feel optimistic as well as happy. After her parents were settled in another, smaller house they would be all right. Her mother, with persuasion and help, would adapt eventually to a more modest standard of living.

By the time she was approaching the waiting stage-coach Augusta had a spring in her step and a smile on her lips. Then she remembered Luther and caution tempered her newfound joy.

Chapter Twenty-nine

'You've come a long way since that first navvy job I put you on to, Gunnet.'

'And I've a long way still to go, McLure,' Luther grinned. 'I look forward to it. I've always been a travelling man.'

The Railway Company director and Luther were enjoying a drink together in the Tontine. The last section of the line had now been completed and Luther had negotiated with the directors of the company a contract for the maintenance of the complete railway for a period of seven years. That contract had now been signed.

'You must be making money hand over fist,' said McLure.

'Don't forget that in the course of my work I've acquired enormous stocks of plant and material. My capital's so tied up with that I've got to keep looking for new opportunities for using it.'

'You don't need to tell me what the next opportunity is. The Glasgow to Edinburgh. Right?'

'Right. Then after that it's all the way to London.'

McLure laughed. 'Come now . . .'

'There's already been a meeting – chaired by the Most Noble Marquis of Queensberry, no less – to discuss the possibility of having a Parliamentary survey.'

'Yes, I know but . . .'

'But first it's got to be the Glasgow to Edinburgh.'

'I take it you're putting in a tender for one of the contracts that has been advertised.'

'For both of them.'

McLure slid him a sceptical look as he lit up a cigar.

'You'd have to put up ten per cent for each tender. That would work out at a very large sum of money.'

'True.'

After a minute or two, McLure shook his head. 'You're biting off more than you can chew here, Gunnet. Quite apart from the ten per cent, think of the plant needed, think of the labour involved. And this is going to prove a more difficult line than any of the others. Edinburgh's sited at a higher altitude than Glasgow, that's the main problem. But the damned proprietors of the Forth and Clyde Canal have really messed us about by refusing to allow a bridge across the Glasgow branch of the canal.'

'I'm well aware of the difficulties, including a hell of a long tunnel and a drop from Cowlairs.'

'Too steep for any locomotive to master. They just don't have the power or the brakes.'

'I've worked out a method to overcome that. A simple and inexpensive method.'

'Maybe so. But the tunnel . . .'

'I've built tunnels before.'

'But the complications . . .'

202

'Every railway has difficulties and complications.'

'Not with complications like this.'

'McLure, I thrive on challenges.'

'It goes without saying you want me to put my weight behind your tender.'

'More than that.'

McLure raised a brow and Luther said, 'That ten per cent . . .'

'Ah! You want me to put money into it.'

'Well, you're a gambling man and you've gambled on me before. You know I won't let you down.'

McLure savoured his cigar for a few seconds. 'What's your proposition?'

'I can raise the money for the one section. If you stake me for the other section I'll guarantee you a good return for your money.'

'What sort of return?'

'I'll double your stake when the job's finished.'

'What if you don't finish the job?'

'That's the gamble.'

'You think you can do it?'

'You asked me that once before. And the answer's the same. I don't know but I'm desperate enough to make one hell of a try.'

McLure laughed. 'That's good enough for me. But before we get down to exact figures, what's this idea of yours for the drop of Cowlairs to George Square?'

Luther brought a piece of paper from his pocket and spread it on the table between them.

'This is Cowlairs here. We build an engine house and install a winding engine and haul the train up with a continuous rope.'

'How would you attach the rope to the locomotive?'

'By attaching a messenger rope to an inverted hook on the locomotive. This would drop off once the speed of the locomotive exceeded that of the rope.'

'Yes, that sounds feasible. How about descending the slope? The brakes wouldn't hold.'

'At Cowlairs the locomotive would be taken off the front and put at the back. Specially constructed brake wagons could be attached to the front with expert brakesmen in charge.'

'Have you considered the cost of this and included it in your tender?'

'Of course.'

'Well, if I back you with cash no one must know.'

Luther gave a small smile. 'Oh, I realize that.'

'How much do you need?'

Luther scribbled a figure in the paper. McLure read it and nodded. Then he said:

'There's no guarantee, of course, that they'll all accept it but with my weight behind it you've got the advantage.'

'That's all I want.'

McLure laughed. 'When you build your London line, Gunnet, I hope you'll remember to include me in on it.'

'Let's drink to that,' Luther said.

He knew that he was taking a risk with this new venture. He was stretching his resources to their limits. If his tenders were accepted – and he was as confident as he could be that they would be accepted – the resulting contracts would be a tough challenge in more ways than one. McLure was right in his concern about the particular difficulties of the Glasgow to Edinburgh line. It was these very difficulties, however, that gave zest to the whole idea as far as Luther was concerned. He needed something against which to continuously test his wits and harden his muscles.

He could hardly contain his jubilation when the tenders proved successful. The enormity of what he had taken on afforded a thrill with which not even the most passionate lovemaking could ever compete.

The first thing he did was to organize a base in Glasgow. This meant finding a house and an office in the town. He settled for an office in George Square which was handy for the workings. Then he proceeded to train Billy in the administration side of the business and did him the honour of giving him an office room of his own. From Luther's window he could see not only the diggings but Cameron House – now a veritable slum of a place. The satisfaction it gave him to stare out of that window was well worth a lifetime of difficulties and hard work.

The fashionable part of the city was now on Blythswood Hill and there he secured a handsome three-storied terrace house in Blythswood Square, overlooking the leafy private gardens to which each householder had a key. But most of his time was spent at his office or inspecting the diggings.

At all times, however, he made sure that he was expensively and fashionably dressed. In his coaching days he had revelled in being a dandy and he had never lost his taste for clothes. Now he could afford to indulge it and was fast gaining the reputation of being the smartest man in Glasgow, and in more ways than one.

He tried to encourage Augusta to match his enthusiasm and panache.

'Order furs. Keep up with the very latest fashion. Money is no object. I don't care what it costs,' he would tell her grandly.

But with that lady-like gentility that he always found infuriating she would politely decline. Not that he could ever fault her in elegance. But there was always this reticence, this subtle holding back. It was as if every time she were silently accusing him of vulgarity.

The only time he could cut her down to size was when he had her in bed without any clothes on at all. And not always in bed. Sometimes he really scattered her wits and her sense of propriety by taking her in the drawing-room on the elegant new sofa or rolling about on the floor on their expensive Axminster carpet.

On these occasions she came near to disintegrating into complete hysteria. She babbled on about how Billy might come in, or the maid, or a caller might discover them, or how it was shocking, wicked, in bad taste, not the done thing, of how she loathed and despised and hated him, of how he was worse than any animal. But gradually her outraged babblings merged into equally uncontrolled and uncontrollable sounds of passion. Sometimes he thought that lust was a more appropriate word because she gave few other signs of being a passionate-natured woman. He often wondered how she felt about the depths to which her dear father had sunk. Only the other day while standing near the diggings smoking a cigar and talking to the engineer and one of the Railway Company directors he had noticed from the corner of his eye Cameron coming shuffling along. The man looked no better than a tramp, unshaven, with grubby linen and stooping figure almost lost in a suit two sizes too big for him. Suddenly Luther realized Cameron was faced with a dilemma. He and his friends were blocking the entrance to Cameron House. Ignoring his father-in-law Luther continued to puff nonchalantly at his cigar. Cameron hesitated for a moment then hastened furtively round the corner on to West George Street, obviously to enter the house by the back door.

Luther reckoned that it would probably be the first time Cameron had ever used his own back door. The Cameron back door had always been strictly for the lower orders. Luther also reckoned that this was one of the most deliriously happy moments of his life. Revenge was sweet all right. Nobody would ever convince him that it was anything different.

And success was sweet. He began to really enjoy it. He even told Augusta that she could organize a small dinner party as part of the celebrations for Queen Victoria's marriage to Prince Albert.

The engineer and his wife were invited and McLure and his wife and Drummond the banker and Mrs Drummond. The evening proved a great success. He had to give credit to Augusta. She was a superb hostess, dignified, attentive, correct. Yet her delicate-boned face and blue eyes, the creamy curve at the nape of her neck revealed by her pinned-up hair, the cluster of ringlets dangling over her temples gave her a vulnerable look. She had also been successful at entertaining Miss Hester, the young lady Billy was courting, and Miss Hester's wealthy parents.

206

The only social occasion which had been a failure, although there was nothing specific that he could level at Augusta, was when Tibs had married the farmer's son. It had been a quiet affair – both Tibs and Geordy Geddes had wanted it that way. However he had insisted that Augusta should give a reception in Blythswood Square for the newly-weds. A luncheon had been arranged and the bridegroom's father and mother and sister had attended and of course Billy was there.

The food had been excellent and Augusta's manners impeccable. Yet somehow Augusta cast a blight on the whole proceedings and he was sure that Tibs and her new family of broadspoken farmer-folk were much relieved to escape back to their farm kitchen. They had been completely overwhelmed by Augusta and there was a horrible moment while they were bidding their goodbyes when Mrs Geddes actually bobbed a curtsy to her.

'They are family. Family!' he angrily reminded Augusta afterwards. 'And in future I wish them treated as such.'

'I treated them with the utmost politeness,' she protested indignantly.

'You snooty little bitch. At best you were bloody patronizing.'

He was tempted to put the knife in by comparing the rough and ready but respectable and well-doing farmer Geddes to her own seedy, down-at-heel failure of a father. But as long as she never mentioned her family he refrained from doing so. He never even thought of them unless something forced them upon this attention, like the other day when he had met Sid Cruickshanks in Argyle Street. The old man had been tottering feebly along leaning on a stick.

'How's Nessie, Sid?' Luther asked over a drink in the Tontine. Sid's hands trembled so much he could hardly lift the glass of whisky Luther had treated him to. Eventually he managed to tip the liquid down his throat and when Luther filled his glass again he gratefully drank. Then taking his time he answered,

'You wouldn't know her, Luther. No, you wouldn't know her.'

'Has she been ill? Is there anything I can do?'

Sid shook his head and stared morosely at his empty glass until Luther took the hint and gave him yet another refill.

'I'll have to send you home in a carriage, old man. Then what'll Nessie say?'

'She'll be too distracted trying to keep up with all the work to even notice me. Nessie's a good cook, Luther. I say, my Nessie's a good cook.' His voice had begun to slur and this time he reached for the bottle himself and refilled his glass, spilling some and nearly crashing it over in the process. Luther rescued both glass and bottle.

'Your Nessie's a good cook,' he agreed.

'That's what she was trained for.'

'True.'

'I may be wrong, Luther, but I don't think I am.'

'About what?'

'Nessie shouldn't be carrying up water for baths, and struggling to tie the mistress's corsets and put on her clothes and do her hair and run up and downstairs and in my lady's parlour doing a thousand jobs a day she's not been trained for.'

'Christ,' Luther said in disgust.

'Nessie weeps all the time now. The mistress keeps saying she can't do anything right. But I tell Nessie it's just that she hasn't been trained for these jobs. You can't learn an old dog new tricks. Nessie's as old as me, Luther. I think that woman's a marvel for her age. I see to the fires and do what I can but I'm not able to run about the way she does even though I haven't got her bad legs.'

He slid his empty glass across the table. 'My wife's the best cook in Glasgow, and don't you forget it!'

'You'll have to get out of there, Sid, before that selfish parasite's the death of the pair of you.'

'No, no. I won't have that and neither will Nessie. You mustn't speak disrespectfully of the mistress. She is our mistress and there is such a thing as loyalty. You can't change that.'

'Balls!'

'You don't understand, Luther. Anyway where would Nessie and I go?'

'I'll soon get you a place. And there's no need to worry. I'll see that you don't starve.'

Sid shook his head. 'The master and mistress have given us a home for all these years. We owe them –'

'You owe them fuck all!'

The very next day he sent a cart and four Irish navvies to the Cameron back door with the order to lift the old couple's belongings and the old couple if necessary and take them to a cosy room and kitchen he'd rented for them up near the college gardens. He warned the men to listen to no objections.

'Just go in,' he said, 'and get the poor old sods out of there.'

And there wasn't an Irish navvy in Scotland who would disobey his orders.

Chapter Thirty

It had been a long time before Augusta next found an opportunity to visit her mother. It was not in fact until Luther went to Glasgow on business in connection with the Glasgow to Edinburgh line. Again her father had avoided her but she had discovered from her mother that he had not been able to sell Cameron House. She was not surprised. It had become overwhelmed by the diggings. It was only one of the pieces of wreckage among the conglomeration of flotsam in a vast sea of mud.

As far as her mother was concerned, though, the fact that they were marooned in Cameron House was simply another example of Mr Cameron's bumbling incompetence. She absolutely refused to listen to any excuses on his behalf.

Augusta had taken some little comforts that Felicity

209

much appreciated, a bottle of eau-de-cologne, a herb cushion, a box of chocolates. She had also purloined – not without some secret palpitations – a few of Luther's cigars and a bottle of whisky for her father. She had kept in touch by letter as she had promised but it was not until some time after Luther acquired the house in Blythswood Square that she was able to contemplate another visit. The main reason of course was that she had been pregnant and for much of the time indisposed. The other reason was the difficulty of discreet entry to Cameron House. Its front door was in full view of Luther's office. Both back and front were visible from the diggings, around which Luther so often rode his big black stallion. Luther had forbidden her to have any contact with her parents. She could understand his inability to forgive them but what dismayed her was the fact that he found pleasure in seeing them suffer. She was sure he would pile more agonies on them if he was given the chance.

After the birth of her daughter Mary Jane she did brave the visit by setting off on foot from Blythswood Square dressed in a new hooded cape that Luther would not recognize. Keeping the hood well forward over her face she had risked the front door. The stairs leading down to the back entrance had been so covered in slippery slime she had been unable to descend them. In an agony of suspense she stood in full view of Luther's office. It seemed as if the door was never going to be opened and once more she rattled at the knocker. To her surprise it was her father who eventually peered round a narrow crack. Quickly recovering she pushed the door open wider and entered the house.

'Papa!' she embraced him before he could escape from her. To her horror he burst into tears.

'I am so ashamed, Augusta. I have failed your poor mama. Failed her completely.'

'You mustn't get so upset, Papa. Things will work out all right yet, you will see. Let us have a nice cup of tea and a chat in the parlour. There might be some way in which I can help.'

Cameron shuffled and wiped at his face with a grubby handkerchief. 'I'll go down and make it. Then I'll tell your mother you're here. She's upstairs.'

'*You* will make the tea? Why can Nessie not make it? Is she ill?'

'Gone. Everybody's gone now. One of the carts from the railway came and a crowd of Irish navvies. They took the cook and my last coachman away. The railway has ruined me, Augusta. It's taken everything. Everything.'

Fury against Luther gave Augusta a blinding headache. How could he be so wickedly vindictive. Forgetting about the tea and even about her father she went through to the parlour and sat down. The filthy, mud-splattered windows made the room funeral dark although it was daylight outside. The whole place shook with the continual clank, clank of a thousand hammers, and the endless cluck, cluck, cluck of the handworked jumpers. The house reverberated with the blast of explosions, fired in seemingly endless succession that brought the acrid smell of the gunpowder in with the cold draught.

She was still sitting, white-faced and stiff, staring ahead, when Cameron shuffled into the room carrying a tray. The china rattled precariously as he put it down on the table beside her.

'I hope it's all right,' he said.

'What?'

'The tea.'

'Where is Mama?'

'Confined to bed.'

'What's wrong, is she ill?'

Wretchedly, he wrung his hands. 'She has no one to help her to dress and do her hair. I cannot afford a maid. This house and its contents are all I have left, apart from a few pounds – barely sufficient to keep us in food.'

'What are you going to do?'

He began to weep again. 'There's nothing I can do. Absolutely nothing.'

'Oh, Papa! Surely things can't be that bad.'

'They are. They are. The railway has ruined me.'

'Then you must sell this house and purchase a much smaller place. Somewhere in a pretty rural setting. It should fetch a good price, and leave you with sufficient to live quietly on. Then you and Mama can be happy again. You must not give up hope.'

'Who would want to buy this place now? Unless,' he added bitterly, 'the railway.'

Augusta stared at him. She wondered if there might be just a chance of that. She could speak to Luther. Although the only chance of him even considering the idea would be if he could make money on the deal.

'I will speak to my husband, Papa. He might be able to help in that respect.'

'Gunnet, help me? He would see me in hell first, Augusta.' The tears welled up again. 'No, I'm finished, there's nothing I can do. It's no use, I'm done for!'

'Papa, try and pull yourself together. Drink a cup of tea.'

'I made it for you and Mama but she didn't want any.'

'I have drunk mine and it was most refreshing. Now I must go upstairs and see Mama.'

Felicity lay in the four-poster bed with her hair streaming across the pillows. Her cheeks were flushed as if she had a temperature, although the bedroom was icy cold.

'Oh, Augusta!' she wailed and stretched out her arms as soon as Augusta entered. 'Oh, my dear, what is going to become of me?'

Augusta kissed her. 'You must try to be brave, Mama. You must learn to help yourself.'

'I do not know what you mean.'

'First we must get you into a house small enough for you to cope with. This place is quite impossible without servants.'

'I told Mr Cameron that, Augusta. I told him it was

212

impossible to live without servants. No one can live without servants. It is quite impossible. I told him.'

'Try not to get excited, Mama. Look, I have brought you some novels and some sugar biscuits – your favourites.'

'Oh, thank you, dear. You are most kind to your poor mama. I do not know what I would do without you. I am being treated with frightful cruelty by Mr Cameron.'

Like a child she rummaged among the biscuits and after selecting one, nibbled at it with eyes closed in ecstasy of enjoyment. 'Now do tell me about your house in Blythswood Square. I know you have told me before but, oh, it sounds so elegant. I keep imagining myself calling on you, dear. I would have come before but I do not know what has happened to our carriage. Mr Cameron has become so parsimonious he has even denied me a maid to help me to dress and do my hair. And of course my clothes are shockingly neglected. I am ashamed to be seen in them. I am so out of touch with what is fashionable too. Do tell me about your lovely house, my dear.'

'We have converted one of the upper rooms into a schoolroom for Samuel and Alexander and I have engaged a governess for them. I have also a new under-nursery maid to help Nurse with Mary Jane. Mary Jane is a beautiful child, Mama.'

'Oh, I can imagine, my dear. And Samuel and Alexander must be quite the little gentlemen. What are the latest modes of furnishing? I am so out of touch.'

'We have a very nice square piano in the parlour. And we have another prettier one upstairs in the drawing-room. And of course stuffed birds, and animals, and wax fruit under glass domes are very fashionable now. We have quite an impressive display.'

Felicity took another biscuit. 'Oh, how lucky you are, Augusta. Your dear husband obviously – and quite rightly – indulges your every whim. I am most cruelly treated, you know. Most cruelly treated.'

'No, I do not have whims, Mama. As a rule it is I who have to go along with my husband's wishes and surely this is more correct, difficult though it may be at times. Already he is talking about building a villa in the West End.'

'Oh, my dear, how exciting. You mean along the banks of the River Kelvin – that lovely wooded area? I have been for a drive there – oh, a long time ago – I have not set foot out of this dreadful place for an age. But I do remember how peaceful it was. The sun was shining and the birds were singing. Oh, it was quite delightful. What a lucky girl you are.'

'Oh, it is not even at the planning stage. I expect we will be in the house in Blythswood Square for a long time yet. And that will suit me perfectly well. It is a very charming house. The rooms are commodious . . .'

'But a villa would be even more spacious, Augusta.' Felicity sighed with pleasure. 'You will have reached the very apex of society then. Oh, I am so proud of you, my dear, so very proud of you. And I would be happy, too, I would be able to lift my head high again if only I could get away from this dreadful place.'

'You will, Mama. I will help you all I can.'

'If I could just get established in another residence. I am completely overwhelmed by all this noise and all these coarse work-people milling about.' Her voice trembled pathetically and Augusta put her arms around her.

'I know, Mama. Try not to think about it. Read your novels. I shall come back as soon as I can.'

'Are you leaving already? Oh, Augusta!'

Her mother clung to her like a child and it was only with great difficulty that Augusta managed to quit the bedroom and return downstairs. Her father was nowhere to be seen.

'Papa? Papa, I must go now.' She glanced absently round the hall as she pulled on her cloak and gloves, the ordeal of going outside distracting her attention.

She called again. 'Papa?' Then, deciding he must have gone out, she put up her hood, eased cautiously from the front door and hurried away.

She felt harrowed by the shambles of Cameron House and the lives of her parents. This distress was intensified when she entered her own home at Blythswood Square. The comparison in comfort and success was too outrageously sharp. She let the neatly uniformed maid take her things and open the parlour door for her.

'Shall I bring the tea now, ma'am?' the maid asked.

'Yes. Have the children had theirs?'

'In the nursery, ma'am.'

'I do not wish them to come downstairs just now. I have a headache and must rest. Tell Nurse she may bring them down to say goodnight before they go to bed.'

'Yes, ma'am.' The maid curtsied and left.

The parlour was spotlessly clean and made colourful not only by the green of the trees flickering through the net curtains but by Augusta's own needlework, bead- and shellwork. Interest too was afforded by the indoor plants that she carefully tended herself.

She tried to think of how she might influence Luther to help her parents in their dreadful predicament. He talked of Tib's husband and mother-in-law and father-in-law as being 'family' – well, her parents were 'family' too and she wanted them treated as such. The thought of how Luther, far from helping them, had actually deprived them of their last and most loyal servants made Augusta's head throb until she thought it was going to burst. The realization of the complete impasse she had reached paralysed her thought. She knew that Luther would do nothing; yet equally she knew that something had to be done. She began to feel sick and was unable even to look at the cucumber sandwiches and seed cake that the maid had brought in.

Eventually she was forced to retreat upstairs to lie down. She remained in bed after Luther arrived home, still unable to formulate what she ought to say to him. It was several days before she could bring herself to broach the subject of Cameron House.

'It is so handy for the railway now, Luther,' she pointed out. 'Would it not be most suitable for their offices? Do you not think the railway directors might be interested in acquiring the property if it was brought to their attention?'

'No,' he replied abruptly. 'They're going to convert the Wardlaw Church into offices.'

'But do you not think they might need – '

'No,' he repeated, this time piercing her with a look that left no doubt in her head.

There was no hope at all of eliciting her husband's help or advice in this matter.

Chapter Thirty-one

Augusta occupied herself with her household duties as though nothing was amiss. She arranged the flowers with her usual delicate artistry. She discussed menus with the cook. Her fingertips searched along window ledges and furniture tops for any sign of dust. She issued necessary instructions to the servants, praised or lectured them, as the occasion required. She visited the children in the nursery to listen, with a fond smile, to their chatter. She even entertained some lady visitors to afternoon tea. All without betraying her deep distraction.

It seemed impossible that she could chat over the teacups about such trivialities as Miss Wallace, Marchande de Corset à la mode de Paris, the inventor of the improved French stays, who was coming to Glasgow.

The discussion regarding when one should leave a card at A & J Black, Silk Mercers of Argyle Street, to intimate that one wished Miss Wallace's attention was, to all outward appearances, of absorbing interest and importance. Yet at the same time Augusta's mind revolved obsessively around her mama and papa's problems. It seemed truly shocking that she and Luther should be living in luxury and do nothing for her parents who were in such dire need.

Luther had even deprived them of the services of Nessie and Sid. It was monstrously cruel of him. Unable to contain her outrage she had eventually confronted him with this but he had brushed her accusations aside with:

'It's time somebody gave a thought about Nessie and Sid.'

'But what about Mama and Papa? They have no one to look after them now.'

'Fine! They can start doing something for themselves for a change.'

'Luther, you are inhuman! You cannot allow this situation to continue. They are my family after all. You cannot just stand aside and let them suffer.'

'As far as I am concerned the Camerons don't exist.'

'If you do not do something to help them I will never be able to forgive you.'

'Did you help my mother, Augusta?'

'But your mother . . .'

'That's enough, don't say another word.' He interrupted her with such menace that she was afraid to continue. Nor did she dare to broach the subject again.

She continued with the daily routine outwardly calm and collected, but inwardly tense with pain. She longed to visit her parents again, but did not know how she could face her father. She dreaded having to admit to him that it was exactly as he feared. There was no hope of Luther coming to his assistance. Thoughts of her father's broken, weeping figure tormented her and made her grudge against Luther grow to such proportions that she could hardly look at him. When she did her eyes sent icicles of hate stabbing out at him. He did not seem to notice. When he wasn't at the diggings or at the office, he was engaged in conversation with Billy. This added another twist to her resentment. Luther spent more time talking to Billy than he did talking to her. More often than not, when he was alone with her, he preferred to read his newspaper. He was engrossed in doing so now, when suddenly he suprised her by putting it down and staring across at her. For a while he said nothing, just looked at her. Then abruptly, and without feeling, he said:

'Cameron has hanged himself.'

She froze at his words and stared back at him without moving a muscle.

'Here, read it for yourself.' He held the paper out but she ignored it. 'Will I pour you a drink?' he said.

'No, thank you,' she replied.

'Well, there's no use looking at me like that, Augusta. He brought his troubles on himself.'

'You could have helped him.'

'No, I could not.'

'You mean you would not.'

'We've been all over this before, and I've no intention of repeating myself. Either get on with your embroidery, or leave the room.'

She tried to stare him out but failed. Picking up her embroidery she stitched with trembling fingers for a minute or two. Then she said:

'I will have to go into mourning.'

'Indeed?'

'I shall have to buy new clothes.'

'Very well, but not black. I forbid it.'

'This is monstrous. You cannot forbid me to wear mourning for my own father.'

'How many more time must I repeat, he's not your father. He disowned you when he flung you out on the street.'

She went cold with hatred. 'You always found the greatest pleasure in Mama and Papa's misfortunes. You are completely wicked.'

'Did they grieve over my misfortunes?'

'That is not the point.'

'No, the point is that they caused my misfortunes. They caused not only me and my family to suffer but you too, Augusta. They had no thought for you, my mother, brother and sisters or our children. It was no thanks to them that Samuel didn't die in the Briggait. We nearly all bloody well starved to death there. You've conveniently forgotten that but I never will.'

She did not know what to say. Her lip trembled, but she kept her chin high as she rose.

Luther sighed. 'Come here.'

Ignoring him she swept across the room and out into the hall. She kept thinking, 'Poor Papa.' She kept seeing him in the last stages of his misery. The vision was too dreadful to bear and as soon as she was safely locked in the privacy of her own bedroom, she wept until she was empty with exhaustion. Then thoughts of her mother began to fill the void. Such an urgency of concern overcame her, it was almost more than she could do to prevent herself from flying from the room to go and comfort and assist her. She was forced, however, to wait until the next day, when Luther had left the house, before venturing out herself.

She found Mrs Cameron prostrate in bed in a deep sleep. A nurse in attendance told her that the doctor had left instructions that laudanum should be administered until Mrs Cameron recovered from the initial shock. Augusta paid the woman a week's wages to ensure that her mama would be properly taken care of for at least that length of time. Then she developed a headache with the worry of how to successfully cover up such a sum from Luther in her housekeeping accounts. Despite her headache, however, she called on her father's solicitor and discussed with him the arrangements for putting Cameron House along with most of the contents up for auction. A small cottage could then be purchased with the proceeds. Having done this, she returned to Blythswood Square, glad that she had managed to get something organized, yet wound up to a pitch of restlessness that made her sharp-tongued and impatient, even with the children. So much could go wrong, and the thought that Luther might discover what she was doing made the strain on her nerves almost unendurable. Yet she felt the necessity of helping her mother so strongly that she even went so far as to risk paying another week's wages to the nurse.

It was a great relief as well as a sadness when Cameron

House went under the auctioneer's hammer. The money it raised was a pathetic sum for the house that had once been not only elegant and impressive but also a happy home. However, it was enough to pay off the debts and purchase a cottage with an apple tree and a small vegetable patch at the back, plus a few chickens. At least her mother would have a roof over her head and with a little tuition and application would be able to keep herself with something to eat. Of course, it would not be easy for a lady to adjust to such circumstances but the adjustment would have to be made none the less. Augusta dreaded the day when she would have to introduce Mrs Camerson to her new spartan way of life and she nursed a grievance against Luther that such a nerve-racking ordeal was necessary.

Every time he mentioned his ideas for the building of a grand new mansion in the West End she froze with disapproval. She refused to contemplate living in luxury in a mansion when her mother had to face penury in a workman's cottage.

Chapter Thirty-two

'What heinous crime have I committed?' Billy asked Luther.

'What do you mean?'

'I've just passed Augusta on the stairs and she not only ignored my greeting but just about shrivelled me in my tracks with the look she gave me.'

'It's nothing to do with you.'

'Thank God for that. I thought perhaps my cravat was in poor taste or I had forgotten to genuflect.'

'Watch your tongue.'

Billy shrugged. 'Sorry.'

Luther lit a cigar. 'You took on some men today.'

'Yes, they applied and I knew we needed more navvies. Did you read the particulars when you got back? What do you think?'

'I think you're good with figures, Billy-boy, but I'm not so sure about men.'

'What's wrong with the men I took on? They've all had plenty of experience.'

Luther grinned. 'No need to get all hot and bothered. I just wondered how the men would take to the English ganger. English and Irish don't mix all that well as a rule.'

'Scots and Irish aren't supposed to get on all that well either and look how you've got on!'

'Touché. Have a cigar.'

They both laughed and after they lit their cigars and relaxed back in their chairs on opposite sides of the fire Luther said,

'Right, me Billy-boy, to what do we owe the honour of your company tonight?'

'I wanted to speak to you, Luther.'

'About something that couldn't be said at the office.'

'Yes.'

'Well?'

'You know that I've been courting Miss Hester for some time now.'

'Yes.'

'Well, we love each other and would like to become officially engaged in the hope that we could be married quite soon.'

Luther's lips pursed in doubt. 'Not too soon I hope, Billy. You're a bit young, don't you think?'

'I'm twenty and as much of a man as I'll ever be.'

Luther regarded the tall gangly lad with affection. 'You have my blessing.'

Billy's earnest face lit up. 'Thanks, Luther. A lot depends on you, you see.'

'Oh?' Luther's eyes twinkled. 'In what way?'

'Well, I know Hester's papa is wealthy and she will have a sizeable dowry and that's all very well but I want to be able to feel I can support my wife by my own efforts too.'

'You want a rise in your salary.'

'Only if you think I'm worth it, Luther.'

'Of course, you're worth it. You're my right-hand man, the most conscientious employee in that office. I've never known you even to be one minute late. You always give of your best. You're a trier, Billy-boy. I like triers. How does an extra twenty pounds a month sound for the moment?'

'Oh, Luther, most generous. That'll make all the difference. Thank you very much indeed.'

They drank a toast to Miss Hester and to her betrothal to Billy, and Luther basked in his young brother's joy.

He had meant what he said about Billy's conscientiousness. The lad had still a lot to learn but he was a hard and eager worker. Too eager perhaps. And too excitable, but he was young and had plenty of time to get to grips with himself and his job. To keep a firm grip on the navvies was important. Disturbances were apt to erupt for no reason at all after a few drinks or even without the stimulus of drink. At the moment the small village of Springburn on the outskirts of Glasgow housed a large number of navvies and it was such a hotbed of trouble that twelve special constables had been appointed and each supplied with a baton and a copy of instructions for police. This had proved a complete waste of time. The navvies paid not the slightest attention to the constables who if they did manage to arrest one navvy were overwhelmed by hundreds of them and forced to relinquish their prisoner, long before they reached a Glasgow police station.

Luther decided to ride out to Springburn the following day and size up the situation but was prevented from doing so by a meeting with some of the directors in Edinburgh. He was given notice of the meeting in a letter that came into his hands first thing in the morning.

After reading it he said, 'Bugger it!'

'Something wrong?' Billy looked up from his desk.

'I don't know. Some bloody meeting in Edinburgh. Would you let Augusta know? I probably won't manage back tonight.'

'Maybe there's more sections coming up for contracting?'

'There's been nothing advertised.'

222

'Maybe they won't advertise for tenders for the rest of the line. We've been doing such a good job so far maybe they'll . . .'

Luther's broad chest jerked with laughter.

'Nobody serves anything up on a plate, Billy-boy. It has to be fought for every inch of the way. Anyway, I'm leaving you in charge but I suggest you ride out to Springburn today. Have a look around the Bishopbriggs section as well. There's been too many disturbances there recently. We'll have to do something to keep a tighter control.'

The words were hardly out of his mouth before Billy was struggling into his coat and eagerly hastening away to comply with his orders.

Smiling to himself and shaking his head Luther set off for Edinburgh. The meeting turned out to be a dull routine affair. He gave his usual progress report and afterwards could quite easily have had time to return to Glasgow but McLure who had also been at the meeting suggested they sample the delights of the Edinburgh taverns.

Luther readily agreed and thoroughly enjoyed the carousal. Next day he had not felt so fit and full of fun and was in no hurry to arise from his hotel bed.

The pale December sun had disappeared and darkness muffled Edinburgh before he left the city and made tracks for home.

Later over dinner in the dining-room at Blythswood Square he asked Billy how he had got on at Springburn and Bishopbriggs.

Billy hesitated. 'You did say we must keep a firm grip on things, Luther.'

Luther nodded.

'And I take it you would agree that in order to do that one must uphold authority.'

'What are you getting at, Billy?' Luther asked but in a good-humoured tone.

'That English ganger . . .'

'A spot of bother, eh?'

'Not exactly. But he came to me and complained about

one of the navvies, a man called Doolan who had apparently worked under him in Cheshire. Green, that's the Englishman, said that Doolan was useless at his job. And apparently when he reprimanded Doolan and some of the other men, Doolan was impertinent.'

'I know Doolan. I've always found him a good worker. He's spirited, though. He could have been impertinent. What happened?'

'Green asked for Doolan's dismissal. So I paid Doolan off.'

Luther selected a bunch of grapes and proceeded to eat them in silence.

'Well?'

'Well, what?'

'Did I do the right thing?'

'That remains to be seen, sport.'

'Wouldn't you have taken the ganger's side?'

'I might.'

'You've taken the ganger's side often enough before.'

Luther grinned. 'Take it easy, Billy-boy. I'm not criticizing you. If you get all worked up like this every time you've to sack a man you're going to wear yourself out before you're thirty.'

Billy nodded ruefully. 'I wish I could be more like you.'

'You should be so lucky!'

Billy grinned then. 'Will you be going to the diggings tomorrow?'

'Bishopbriggs, you mean? Tomorrow or the next day I expect.'

'I'd like you to have a word with Green. See what you think of him yourself. He seems a really strong character to me. If he can't keep order there, no one can.'

'All right, I'll look him over.' He glanced across at Augusta who was daintly sipping a cup of coffee. 'I've some plans you might be interested in having a look at.'

She raised an eyebrow. 'Plans?'

'Remember I mentioned the idea of a villa out west?'

'Yes.'

'You might be able to come up with some useful suggestions at this stage.'

'You have made up your mind then?' She neatly folded her napkin and placed it on the table.

'If you're finished I've laid them out in the parlour.'

They all rose and the maid hastened to open the door for them.

Through in the other room Augusta dutifully examined the drawings that Luther had spread on the escritoire.

'Well?' Luther asked. 'What do you think?'

'I think that building railways has accustomed you to visualize everything on a very large scale.'

'You don't need to worry about running a place as big as that. We can afford to employ plenty of servants.'

Her small hand rested lightly on the paper.

Billy, who was standing at the other side of her, burst out enthusiastically:

'What a place, Luther! This surpasses everything.'

'Augusta?' Luther looked round at her enquiringly.

'A ballroom?' she said.

'Why not?'

She gave the tiniest of shrugs but the barely perceptible movement of her shoulders irritated him.

'Don't you think it's impressive?'

'Oh, if it's designed to impress,' she said, delicately separating herself from the word as if it was contagious, 'obviously it will be successful.'

Chapter Thirty-three

It had started snowing during the night and the blackness of the early morning was softly speckled with white. The sound of his horse's hooves clanged on the High Street cobbles then faded into a muffled crunch as he passed through Cathedral Square. Gas lamps dwindled away as he left the town. Occasionally an isolated cottage blinked with candlelight. Then darkness completely enfolded both man and horse.

Luther hunched into the fur collar of his coat and dreamed of the mansion that one day would be his. The pleasure in knowing that it would far excel Cameron House in size and grandeur penetrated to his very soul. His gratification was only spoiled by the fact that Cameron had not lived to witness its completion. Gunnet House he would call it. He savoured the name, saw the place in his mind's eye, conjured it up in all its virility, animation and enthusiasm. No companion could have kept him better entertained or so successfully riveted his attention.

He hardly noticed when the village of Springburn appeared with cottages huddling like ghosts on either side of the splashing stream. Many of the navvies had lodging in these cottages and also at the villages of Bishopbriggs and Auchinairn. The day shift would have started now. This fact was confirmed by the red glow illuminating the sky in the distance and as he neared Bishopbriggs the fires and flares blazing in every direction reflected various groups of workmen in ruddy light. Yet he could detect no busy rattling of wagons or rhythmic clanking of hammers. Wrenching Gunnet House from his mind he became immediately alert. He spurred his horse into a gallop and, on reaching the first group of men, quickly dismounted and strode among them.

'What the hell's wrong here?'

'It wasn't any of us, sur,' one of the men said. 'Although there's few of us who wouldn't say he deserved a good batin'.'

'Who's "he"?'

'Green the English ganger.'

Another man ventured, 'Some of us worked under him in Chester, sur, and a worse bullying divil never was born, praise be to God.'

'Where is he?' Luther asked.

'Ganger O'Hara took him on a cart to the hospital in Glasgow, sur.'

Luther was about to ask if they were still there when O'Hara pushed his way to the front.'

'He's dead, Mr Gunnet.'

'Christ!'

'They tried to keep me at the hospital while they sent for the police, could you believe it, sur, and me just trying to do my duty. I had to knock two of them unconscious before I got away.'

Luther groaned. 'You fucking fools, what did you have to kill him for? A lot of bloody good that's going to do you. You're not Scotland's favourite folk at the best of times. And, by God, the authorities are really going to be after your blood for this one.'

'He wouldn't get off our backs, sur. A divil he was. Then he gets Doolan paid off. For no reason, sur, we swear it. Doolan's a good navvy and like the rest of the gang niver a drop of liquor passed his lips. We're all wearing Father Mathews's teetotal medals, sur.'

'All right. All right,' Luther said. 'But what happened? Was it Doolan who killed him?'

The gang of navvies shuffled about in silence for a minute before one of them eventually said,

'They just meant to give him a batin' and teach him a lesson, sur.'

'Who did?'

'Doolan and two of his mates – Redding and Hickie. They set on Green as he was crossing the line.' The man jerked a head towards the temporary wooden bridge.

'Boozer Redding?' Luther asked.

'It's said Doolan felled him with an iron weapon. But if that's so then he was driven to it, sur, and niver meant to kill him. You know Doolan, sur. And we know Doolan. We've known him from Chester. He's a good navvy.'

'That's not going to save him from the Glasgow magistrates. Where is he now?'

Silence again.

'Boozer and Hickie?'

Still no reply.

'They won't get far. I'm surprised the police haven't been here already.'

O'Hara said, 'Holy Mother of God, is this them now? Are they meaning to take the lot of us in?'

From a watery grey horizon several large omnibuses, each drawn by four galloping horses, came careering towards them. No sooner had they reached the workings when out poured not only the sherrif substitute, the procurator fiscal, and a posse of police but a full company of the 58th Foot with pistols at the ready.

As they began rounding up the men and pushing them into one of the vehicles Luther addressed the sherrif substitute.

'The men you want aren't here. These navvies had nothing to do with the crime.'

'I've no doubt that's what they told you, Mr Gunnet, but that doesn't make it the truth.'

'It does for me.'

'Very loyal of you, Mr Gunnet. Very loyal. But the court's the place to decide what's true and what isn't.'

Afterwards Luther reckoned that twenty-eight men who worked in the neighbourhood of the bridge had been taken away. It was some time before he managed to re-allocate the work and get the diggings back to as near normality as possible. On his return to the office he discovered that Billy had already heard the news.

'Oh, God, Luther, I'm sorry. It's all my fault.'

'Nonsense!'

'I engaged that ganger.'

'How were you to know?'

'I shouldn't have put an Englishman among so many Irish.'

'This wasn't a racial thing. Forget it, Billy. You've got to be able to take the rough with the smooth.'

'How can I forget it? They've got twenty-eight of our navvies in the jail, including Ganger O'Hara.'

'I'm going to have a word with the sherrif and the procurator fiscal.'

The number in fact was whittled down to six detainees. The authorities offered £100 award for any information leading to the capture of Doolan but by Christmas neither Doolan, Boozer or Hickie had been found.

He had told Augusta about Boozer and she had been shocked and concerned.

'Has Maureen run off with him?'

'No, she's still at Auchinairn. Boozer didn't want to put her in any danger, he said. But she believes he's going to send for her when he finds a safe place. She's convinced he had nothing to do with the killing. Although she says Green was a sadistic bastard and had been tormenting Boozer's friend Doolan.'

'Poor woman. She must be suffering dreadfully. Despite the very rough and insulting way she has of speaking to Boozer I'm sure she is very fond of him.'

'She's looking for employment,' Luther said. 'could you use an extra maid?'

She hesitated. 'The kitchen or the scullery would be the only places she might fit in.'

'I'll tell her to come and see you.'

'Very well.'

He saw her hesitate again.

'Luther.'

'Yes.'

'Christmas is supposed to be a time of love and of the family.'

'So?'

'Can you not find it in your heart to forgive my mama and have her here . . .?'

'Have her here?' He could not believe his ears. 'That spoiled selfish emptyheaded – '

'There is no need to be nasty,' Augusta interrupted stiffly. 'It was a perfectly reasonable request at this season of the year.'

'No need? A perfectly reasonable request?' For a minute words failed him and so intense was his anger he could only see Augusta through a blood-red veil. He had never been nearer to killing her.

'You actually have the fucking nerve to expect me . . .'

'How dare you use such foul language in my presence.'

'The fucking nerve to expect me to provide for her? To have her enjoy every comfort of my home. To have my household dance continuous attendance on her. To have that useless selfish bitch reap the fruits of my labours. When my mother who worked hard all her life . . .' Words choked in his throat. 'Don't you mention that woman's name in this house again.'

The unexpected sound of children singing outside the drawing-room door made them both struggle to banish their tight, angry expressions before calling:

'Enter!'

Samuel and Alexander came in first, lustily singing,

'God rest you merry gentlemen, let nothing you dismay . . .'

Nurse Slater was carrying Mary Jane and Governess MacKenzie was following on behind and joining in the chorus with the rest.

'Remember Christ our Saviour was born on Christmas day
To save us all from Satan's power when we were gone astray.
O tidings of comfort and joy, comfort and joy,
O tidings of comfort and joy.'

Both Luther and Augusta applauded with conscientious enthusiasm.

'How delightful!' Augusta said. 'Come and look at the tree before you go to bed.'

'Have you hung your stocking up at the end of your bed ready for Santa Claus?' Luther asked.

'Not yet, Papa,' said Alexander.

'Well, don't forget, otherwise he might not come. What do you think of the tree? Do you know who thought of such a splendid idea?'

'No, Papa.'

'Prince Albert. They had them in Germany.'

'Did our tree come from Germany, Papa?' Samuel asked.

Luther laughed. 'No, this one came from the woods not very far from here.'

Suddenly the colourful scene in the warm and luxurious room made regret gnaw at him. If only his mother and Rose had been spared to know and to share in this comfort. When he remembered other Christmases . . .

'Listen,' he said, slamming the door on this thoughts. 'There's carol-singers outside too.'

They all went over to the window and after Governess MacKenzie swished open the plush curtains they peered down at the street.

'It's a ballad-monger and his family,' Luther said.

'What's a ballad-monger, Papa?' Samuel wanted to know.

'A man who walks the streets before Christmas singing and selling Christmas carols.'

'Is the baby singing too, Mama?' Alexander asked.

'I do not think so, do you, MacKenzie?'

'No, ma'am. It's younger than Mary Jane and not nearly so clever, I'm sure.'

'Come now, children,' said Augusta. 'One more look at the tree then you must say goodnight. You have a busy and exciting day tomorrow.'

This time Luther did not join the group around the tall fir with its branches laden with presents and shimmering decorations. He hovered near the window for a minute or two.

The moon shone down with cold brilliance on the group outside. There were four other children as well as the baby and all miserably shivering in too thin and insufficient clothing.

Gazing beyond them far into the night he had a vision of Maureen alone in the hovel at Auchinairn.

Then slowly he closed the curtains.

Chapter Thirty-four

'Oh, Augusta!' Felicity looked genuinely shocked. Face sagging and drained of all colour she stared at what was to be her new home. 'You cannot expect me to live here. I . . . I do not believe it. Two apartments no bigger than cupboards? And the other people who live here are farm labourers. You told me so yourself.'

'I was very fortunate to be able to get one of the cottages for you. It was only because I offered to buy the place . . .'

'I am only a simple soul, Augusta, but this is not what I have always understood a cottage to be like. Surely a cottage is a sweet little place standing on its own and surrounded by a garden filled with flowers. I have seen such pretty pictures in books.'

'Books are different from real life, Mama.'

'But these are hovels and they are attached to one another and there is nothing at the front except a rough track road to a farm.'

'There is a little vegetable patch at the back.'

'Oh, Augusta!'

'I am sorry, Mama. Truly I am. But there is no money left. You have no money. Not one penny. You will have your own eggs and vegetables but I will have to bring you a regular supply of other foods and it will not be easy. Cash will be even more awkward. I have accounts at various establishments for food and other necessities and Luther settles these bills every few months. We are in the habit of both checking over the bills and the receipts for any cash I have spent. Luther is an astute businessman and it will be very difficult for me to deceive him with household accounts.'

'But why did you not buy me a respectable establishment? I do not understand.'

'You must try to understand, Mama. There was only enough money to buy a small place, like this. The only alternative was a hovel in town and, Mama, believe me that would have been a thousand times worse. I have lived in the Briggait and I know what it it like. I have tried my best to spare you that.'

Felicity turned a tragic, pleading gaze on her daughter. 'But, Augusta, can I not live with you?'

'There is nothing would please me more, Mama, but,' she hesitated miserably, 'my husband has never forgiven Papa for what he did to him.'

'But Mr Cameron is dead.' Felicity shaded her eyes with a gloved hand. 'Oh, Augusta, how could your papa be so cruel to me? He knew I would be the one to find him . . . How could he do it to me? I have not yet recovered from the shock.'

'Sit down, Mama. See, there is your own comfortable chair from the parlour in Cameron House and your pretty little footstool.'

Tears filled her mother's eyes. 'I want to come and live with you.'

'Oh, Mama, I am sorry but it is impossible.'

'But why is it impossible?'

'My husband . . .'

'A most admirable man. Haven't I said so before? Every time you have visited me at Cameron House, haven't I enquired after the dear man with great affection and interest?'

'Mama, believe me, it is not possible. You have no alternative but to accept this as your home and from now on learn to look after yourself. I will come as often as I can and I will send Maureen when I can.'

'Maureen?'

'One of my maids. I think I can trust her but I wouldn't dare risk any of the others. But when either Maureen or I come, Mama, it will be to help you to help yourself – to teach you how to do your own hair, make your own meals, light your own fires.'

'Augusta,' the older woman shook her head and her handkerchief, 'this is all too too ridiculous.'

'Today the fire has been lit for you. The kettle is full and simmering on the hob. There is more coal in that bucket. Look, Mama! Pay attention,' Augusta said firmly. 'When the fire gets low you must put on more coal from that bucket. When you wish tea you must take some from the caddy on the mantleshelf. Up there, look. Put two spoonfuls in the teapot and fill it with the boiling water from the kettle. Are you listening to me, Mama?'

'Put coal on the fire?' Felicity said in bewilderment. 'But my hands would get dirty.'

'Then you must wash them. I have filled the jug on the washstand in the bedroom. When that is empty you must fill it again at the pump outside. It is at the front. You will see it when you go outside. Just watch what other people do to get their water. You will soon learn. Now about your hair. There is no use trying to keep it in ringlets.'

'But it is pretty that way. Why should I wear it in any other fashion?'

'Because it will be too difficult for you to manage on your own.'

'But the maid you are sending me . . .'

'Mama, Mama, Maureen will only be able to come very occasionally and only for an hour or two. And she will come to show you how to do such things as light a fire. You must learn to do everything yourself. As for your hair – Maureen could not do it for you. She cannot do her own hair properly. Her hair is about as wild and unruly as her nature. But she is a kind-hearted and generous young woman for all her rough ways. She will help you the best she can, I am sure. Now I must go, Mama.'

'Oh, Augusta!' Fear pushed her mother's voice into hysteria. 'You cannot leave me alone in this place. Augusta, don't go!'

In a flurry of panic Felicity clung to her daughter and kept clinging to her as Augusta struggled to make her way towards the door.

'Mama, please,' Augusta's voice was near breaking point. 'This is not easy for me either.'

234

'Augusta, I am frightened, please don't leave me.'

'When it begins to get dark,' Augusta caught her mother's clutching hands and held them for a moment. 'You must light the candles. There is also an oil-lamp but that might prove too difficult for you. Just light the candles. Goodbye, Mama.'

Ignoring her mother's screams of hysteria, Augusta hurried to where her carriage was waiting at the end of the lane. All the way home she felt harrowed beyond tears. Thoughts of her mama stumbling and fumbling about trying and failing to do the simplest tasks continued to haunt her. At night, lying in the big canopy bed beside Luther, she was tormented by visions of her mother alone and terrified in the darkness outside the city.

Subsequent visits did nothing to comfort her. Her mama became more hysterical each time. Eventually Maureen said,

'Jaysus, Mrs, we can't go on like this. Your nerves are shredded to bits, so they are, and won't I be on the run like that big ape Boozer soon for I'll be committing bloody murder myself.'

'I will not have you talk like that, Maureen. Mrs Cameron needs help and we must persevere in giving that help. It is our duty.'

'Holy Mother of God, isn't she supposed to be helping herself?'

'Yes, but it is more difficult to learn when one is older. We must try to be patient with her.'

'And wouldn't she try the patience of a saint?'

An extra strain was put on Maureen shortly after this by news that Doolan had been arrested in Liverpool and brought back to be lodged in the Glasgow jail. A month afterwards at the end of February the *Glasgow Herald* announced that Redding had been picked up in the north of England and brought to Glasgow jail where Hickie, the third man implicated, was already being held.

Maureen became so distracted that her work in the kitchen suffered. Cook and the rest of the staff complained bitterly of pans not properly cleaned, floors not properly dried, vegetables not properly peeled.

'And the shocking displays of temper, ma'am, if anyone dares to scold her,' Cook told Augusta, 'have to be seen to believed. I don't want to speak out of turn, ma'am, but she's quite unsuitable and I think you would be well advised to get rid of her.'

'I will decide if and when I dismiss a member of staff,' Augusta said. 'But thank you for keeping me informed, Cook.'

She agreed with Cook, of course. Maureen was most unsuitable. She was a disruptive influence that was gradually affecting the whole house. When she wasn't neglecting her work and inconveniencing everyone downstairs and upstairs, she was distressing the staff with her violent outbursts, and this affected their work. Maureen's tirades of outrageous insults against Boozer alternating with her weeping and wailing in sympathy with him did nothing to add to the harmony and smooth running of the house either.

Augusta was sorely tempted to dismiss her, but apart from the fact that she was so dependent on the Irishwoman for help with her mother, she still had a soft spot for Maureen from their old nomadic days.

The trial of Boozer and the other two navvies was set for the 23rd April and Maureen said all the navvies at the workings were subscribing as much as they could afford every week to fee counsel for the defence.

This cheered and comforted Maureen.

'Haven't they the hearts as big as buckets, Mrs? They'd give the shirt off their backs to help a mate, so they would. Do you think that big idiot of mine is going to be all right after all?'

'I hope so, Maureen.'

'He didn't touch the ganger, so help me God. Doolan didn't mean no harm either. He told me, Mrs. I didn't mean to kill him, he says, I just meant to bait him so's he'd remember.'

'What about Hickie?'

'Ach, God help him! Isn't he as simple as a baby? He just sits there all the time with a big grin on his face and him not even understanding where he is.'

The trial lasted twelve hours and Luther who had attended it was dark with anger when he returned home.

'What happened? How did it go?' Augusta asked him as soon as he entered the parlour.

'It was a bloody disgrace,' he said. 'That so-called counsel for the defence ought to be shot. Would you believe it – after half the navvies in Scotland had feed him he monstrously declined to offer any defence.'

'But surely it was his duty . . .'

'Of course it was his duty and it was an appalling abrogation of it to say as he did that he had come to the resolution of leaving the case in the hands of the judge and jury. No questions. No analysis of the evidence. Nothing.'

'That is shocking, Luther.'

'What a field day it gave for the prosecution and the prejudiced. My God, Augusta, I feel sick.'

He went over and helped himself to a large whisky.

'The jury returned a unanimous verdict of murder against Doolan and Boozer.'

'Oh, Luther!'

'They found Hickie guilty by a majority, not as an active participant but as an accessory, and recommended mercy for him. He'll probably be transported.'

'What has to happen to Boozer?'

'Oh, he and Doolan have to hang. There was no mention of mercy for them.'

Augusta closed her eyes, willing herself not to be overcome by horror. 'Poor Maureen,' she kept thinking.

'You look as if you need a drink as well,' Luther said, handing her a glass.

'Thank you. I do feel a bit faint.' She sipped at the whisky and Luther went on.

'As if it wasn't bad enough, the bastard of a judge

ordered them to be hanged where the murder was committed. I'll lodge an objection to that and the railway directors are going to do the same. As McLure said, it'll tarnish that section of the line with an unfortunate association, to put it mildly.'

'Does Maureen know?'

'She nearly caused a riot in the court. I had to practically knock her unconscious to get her out of there,' Luther said.

'Oh, this is really too much! The scandal. The wild and undisciplined behaviour. You being with her in court like that. I am sorry for Boozer. I am sorry for Maureen. But I must think of my family and the other members of my staff. The entire household is in a state of chaos because of Maureen.'

'Her husband is going to be hanged.'

'He is not her husband.'

'Common-law husband. What does it matter?'

'It matters a great deal in respectable society.'

'To hell with respectable society!'

'That is a ridiculous thing to say, Luther, and I know you don't mean it. I have done my best at all times for both Maureen and Boozer. And so have you. But there has to be a limit.'

'You've never really changed, have you?' Luther said. 'You're still a selfish, hard-hearted little bitch.'

'You have no right to say that. I have been very patient with Maureen. And good to her.'

'Well, you'll have to be patient with her for a bit longer. The execution's not until the 14th May.'

'I wonder, Luther, if you would be so very attentive and concerned if she were neither young nor pretty.'

He looked at her in disgust. 'Is that your level?'

'I am afraid that it is yours.'

Chapter Thirty-five

Terror lapped around the town behind a heady froth of excitement. Many times in the past when an Irish navvy had been arrested his comrades had stormed the police office and freed him. The fact that there were thousands of navvies in the vicinity of Glasgow made the authorities fear that Doolan and Redding would never reach the gallows. Enormous precautions were taken beforehand to ensure that no riot would explode in the streets and no rescue of the two men take place en route to Bishopbriggs.

A procession surpassing anything that had taken place in Glasgow for years was planned.

The railway company had protested in vain. The judge was adamant. Doolan and Redding had not to be hanged in the customary place of execution, the public square outside the jail; despite the dangers of riot or rescue they had to be taken in an open carriage through the streets until they reached that part of the railway where the murder had been committed. In the north field facing the temporary bridge over the line a scaffold had been erected the night before and a troup of cavalry stationed there to protect it.

Doolan's brother was on his way from Ireland to Glasgow to be with him but Doolan had informed Luther when he and Maureen had visited the two condemned men, 'His reverence told me to withhold him back.'

Bishop Murdoch had been with the men for a few hours on the night before the execution date.

'I'll be there,' Luther assured them. 'If it's of any comfort to you.'

'Indeed it is, sur. Indeed it is.' Both men shook his hand in gratitude.

Boozer turned to Maureen. 'I wouldn't be wanting you there.'

'What do you mean, you big ape?' Maureen shouted. 'Haven't I always been with you?'

Luther said, 'Be quiet, woman. He's thinking of you.'

'Thinking of me indeed! Did he think of me when he went off with Doolan looking for a fight?'

Boozer lowered his knobbly shaven head and Doolan said,

'You're a terrible woman, Maureen. I heard you say you'd like to bate the man yourself.'

'Bate him, not kill him, you pair of idiots!'

But before they left the cell Maureen had flung herself round Boozer's neck and was showering him with kisses and tears. It took Luther all his strength to drag her away. All along the corridors she fought him like a crazy woman, punching, scratching, biting, screaming abuse. In his private coach too the struggle continued until nearing Blythswood Square she lapsed into tears of exhaustion. Once at the house she automatically dragged herself downstairs to the servants' entrance which was below street level behind the iron railings. He climbed the few outside steps to the imposing front door. Not as imposing as the entrance to his mansion was going to be, though. Thoughts of the new house fast taking splendid shape on the western outskirts of the city were never far from his mind. They even suffused him with pleasure now at this sombre time.

In the parlour, Augusta eyed him in shocked disapproval. A glance in the mirror told him why. The black silk scarf tied round his standup collar had come loose. His frizz of hair was dishevelled and some of his waistcoat buttons were undone. He did them up then deftly retied his neck-piece.

'The girl's demented with grief. I had one hell of a struggle to get her away from the prison.'

'Was it absolutely necessary for you to go to that awful place?'

'They're my men. The authorities have asked me to be in the procession to the scaffold tomorrow. Apparently it's to be led by cavalry, then the city marshal, the open coach with the condemned men, my coach, more cavalry, the executioner, the sheriff, the provost, the magistrates, then more cavalry coming up at the rear. And as if that's not enough there's to be cavalry and infantry and police along each side of the procession. They're even talking about having a couple of cannons.'

'Why should they expect you to go? It is too dreadful.'

'I told you. They're my men. Not just Doolan and Boozer but the whole army of Irish around here. I suppose the magistrates think I could exert some influence if there was a riot.'

'Oh, Luther, you would be right in the middle of it. What could you do? Please don't go.'

'The provost says the men might listen to me because they respect me. But it would be one hell of a job to be heard if there's going to be the crowd that I suspect there will be.'

'Do not go, Luther, please.'

'I've promised Boozer and Doolan. What the devil's that?'

Wailing noises were floating up from the kitchen quarters, not getting louder yet pervading the whole house with an eerie melancholy.

'That's not just Maureen,' Luther said. 'It sounds like the whole staff.'

'Oh, dear,' Augusta wrung her hands in distress. 'What can one do?'

'I'll go downstairs and speak to them.'

'No, it is my duty to deal with the servants.' She hesitated in harassment. 'It is obvious that no one is going to have a wink of sleep tonight. We might as well resign ourselves to that.'

'Tell them to help themselves to some whisky, especially Maureen. She wants to come with me tomorrow, by the way.'

'Oh, no!' Augusta gasped. Her skirts rustled over to where she kept her bottle of eau-de-cologne, then after dabbing some of the cooling liquid on her forehead and temples she said, 'I must dissuade her.'

'I've already tried without success.'

The wailing was getting louder. It dragged at the air,

clung to the plush curtains, wound round the dark furniture, made the feeble gaslight feebler. It was like a place possessed. Suddenly Augusta swished from the room.

Only two small gas brackets flickered in the hall and were totally inadequate in dispelling the gloom. Candles were far more easily controlled and dependable and she always insisted that several candlelabras were kept lit around the house to supplement the fashionable but not very successful gas. Tonight the servants had forgotten to light the candles, as they had forgotten to build up the fire, and to bring her hot chocolate, and to turn down the beds.

At first Maureen had harassed the other servants and, although they had expressed pity and regret, nevertheless they made it clear they wanted to be free of her disrupting influence. Gradually, however, the anguish of Maureen's grief overwhelmed them. They had become part of it, despite themselves.

Descending the stairs to the staff quarters Augusta found the kitchen in chaos. The dishes from the evening meal had not been washed but instead flung in careless lopsided mountains on either side of the sink. The table was strewn with remnants of food and dirty mixing bowls and wooden spoons and ladles.

Around the table were crowded every member of staff, including even the nursery nurses. The only person not slumped at the table noisily weeping was MacKenzie the governess.

'Stop this noise at once!' Augusta snapped. 'Kennedy, run to the cellar and bring up a bottle of whisky.'

They had all groped to their feet when Augusta entered and now they stood wiping their swollen faces with aprons or handkerchiefs. Only Maureen remained on her seat like a rag doll, boneless, helpless.

'When Kennedy returns with the whisky,' Augusta continued, 'have a large glassful each. Then keep yourselves busy. Get all of these dishes washed and put away for a start. And this table is a disgrace. See that it is given a thorough scrubbing. Now, Maureen,' she turned to the still sobbing Irishwoman, 'what nonsense is this I hear about you going tomorrow? I forbid you to set foot out of this house. It is for your own sake, I will not allow you to subject yourself to such a dreadful experience.'

'I love him, Mrs,' Maureen said.

Augusta's eyes flickered away in embarrassment. 'Here is Kennedy. Have some whisky. It will make you feel better.'

'I love him.'

'Yes, yes.'

'The stupid big ape.'

'Drink the whisky. All of you. No, I shall have some upstairs with the master. Go on! Do as you are told!'

'I'm going to stay with him to the end, Mrs.' Maureen lifted a tragic face and immediately a new outburst of sobbing was let loose round the table.

'No, you are not!' Augusta raised her voice to make herself heard. 'He would not wish you to be there. You will only distress him and yourself to an intolerable degree. And I will not stand any more of this dreadful racket. Stop it at once! Get these dishes done. I will come back downstairs in one hour's time and if this kitchen is not clean and tidy by then I will by very angry indeed.'

Returning up the dark stairs she held up her skirts and moved slowly and exactly. Across the hall now and into the parlour.

'Well?' Luther was standing with his back to the fire, a whisky glass in his hand.

'At least I have got them to do something instead of just sitting there, all that is, except Maureen. She is in a state of complete collapse. She ought to be in bed. I shall tell her so when I go back down again.'

'I've poured you a drink.'

'Thank you.'

'She won't go to bed.'

Augusta sighed. 'I cannot see any of them going – or us for that matter.'

'It's late, drink your whisky and go upstairs.'

'What about you?'

243

'I feel restless.'

'Luther, there is no point in me going upstairs to lie in bed alone listening to those dreadful sounds.'

Intonations of anguish peppered the house erratically now like a ghost that had lost its way.

She and Luther sat opposite one another and after finishing her drink she attempted to while the time away with some embroidery. He lit a cigar and opened a book. The pendulum clock drummed ominously.

'I'd better go down again and at least try to get them to bed,' Augusta said after an hour had ticked away.

Out in the hall after opening the door to the servant's quarters she stood for a few minutes listening to the moaning. She had the impression of looking down into a pit full of lost souls.

'Kennedy!' she called. 'Bring a candle.'

In a few moments light quivered at the foot of the narrow stairway.

'Hold it high,' Augusta commanded as she carefully picked her way down.

The kitchen had been cleared up and the staff were now huddled around the fire with Maureen in the centre of the group as if they were trying to support her physically as well as spiritually by their closeness.

The Irishwoman gazed dumbly across at Augusta as if pleading with her to make everything all right.

'You should all be in bed,' Augusta said. 'Have you finished the bottle of whisky?'

'Yes, ma'am,' someone said.

'You have my permission to take another. Then go to bed.'

'We thought we could just doze in front of the fire here, if you don't mind, ma'am.'

Augusta's eyes clung to Maureen's. She longed to voice some words of comfort to the girl but did not know how. Eventually she managed to address the waiting parlour maid.

'Give me the candle and go back and sit with the others. Help them to look after Maureen.'

Then she left them to the long night.

Chapter Thirty-six

A festive air sizzled over the city. Everyone in Glasgow and the surrounding towns had a holiday from work. In house and hovel the populace were hurrying over breakfast, donning their Sunday clothes, sallying on to the streets. At five o'clock in the morning, crowds had collected in front of the jail. By seven o'clock they amounted to many thousands.

Waiting in the coach, Luther tried to divert Maureen's attention from the open carriage directly in front of them in which had been placed two coffins. The Irishwoman seemed dazed. The other members of staff said they'd had to dress her and do her hair. It had been pinned up, and its fiery colour and the thick red sweep of her lashes accentuated her unnatural paleness. She sat motionless beside him, hands clasped on the lap of her green dress.

Bewildered she gazed around when noisy clopping and jingling heralded the arrival of detachments of cavalry in scarlet trappings and glittering swords. Then the thunder of the horse-drawn cannon shook the ground, followed by the marching feet and the tartan uniforms of the infantrymen.

A square was formed by cavalry, infantry and police, and at precisely eight o'clock Doolan and Boozer were brought out respectably dressed in black suits as if they were going to someone else's funeral. They stared in astonishment and confusion at the spectacle before them, the gaudy uniforms, the magnificent robes of the magistrates, the provost's gold chain of office. But when Maureen suddenly galvanized to life and shouted his name, Boozer's craggy face lit up and he eagerly waved to her.

Luther tried to pull her back and shut the carriage

window, but kicking and wriggling free of him she leaned further out and shouted:

'You stupid big ape! Aren't you grinning there as if you were going to the fair? And, holy mother o' God, why are you wearing that suit and you with a perfectly good pair of white canvas trousers and the loveliest scarlet waistcoat that ever covered a man's chest?'

Luther jerked her back on to the seat. 'Shut your mouth.'

'Jaysus, what are they doing to the poor fellas now?'

The men, having descended the steps, were being taken back to the hall again.

Luther leaned out and called to the sheriff. 'What's happening?'

'The procession's not completely formed.'

'Christ!' Luther thumped back in disgust and five more minutes passed before the men appeared again. This time they were taken to sit on top of the coffins in the open carriage.

'And you without even your nice blue bonnet,' Maureen yelled.

'Sit down,' Luther said, trying to prevent her from seeing the men being handcuffed together and chained by the legs.

The Right Reverend Bishop Murdoch and two priests took their seats in the carriage with the condemned men and the exhortations which they had begun in the cell were continued in solemn chanting voice in the open air.

The procession slowly moved forward. The guard of six hundred cavalry men held their swords aloft. The guard of one thousand, two hundred infantry men marched with fixed bayonets. Doolan and Boozer, completely overwhelmed and out of place in the midst of all this grandeur, sat with bowed heads. They never raised them again despite Maureen's sporadic burst of shouting. Hers was the only voice to be heard above the clatter of horses' hooves on the cobbles, the trundle of carriage wheels and the shuffling of the infantrymen's feet. The crowd were silent. In the Saltmarket and High Street every window and even the tops of the houses were packed with onlookers but no one made a sound.

About half-past nine o'clock the procession approached the railway.

'My God!' Luther gasped when he saw the workings. Every part of them was covered with people. It was as if the diggings, the railroad, everything had been overrun by ants. Everythings except the temporary bridge and the platform on which stood the scaffold. It was surrounded by a guard of cavalry but pressing hard in on them on all sides was an enormous multitude as far as the eye could see.

At the sight of the gibbet Maureen let out a moan of panic. Luther pulled her into his arms.

'Hold on to me. Don't look.'

But as the scaffold drew nearer her panic increased. Wide-eyed she clawed at the door as Doolan and Boozer ascended the platform. The men, however, were told that the preparations were not complete and had to descend again. They were taken into a wooden shed.

'The divils!' Maureen shouted. 'They're tormenting these poor fellas.'

When the two Irishmen re-emerged, their arms had been secured behind their backs.

'Boozer!' Like a madwoman Maureen fought to get out of the coach, her hair tumbling wildly about her shoulders and her dress getting torn.

'Maureen, for Christ's sake!'

Luther struggled with her as they put the ropes around the necks of the two Irishmen. Her screams nearly drowned out the bishop's impressive prayer and the men's earnest response to it. The caps were then drawn over their eyes and at the moment the Bishop repeated the words, 'O Lord, receive their souls,' the bolt was withdrawn.

Neither man died immediately. Boozer's sufferings were so long-drawn out and severe that Luther felt caught up in a tornado of madness. The big Irishman's struggles became so convulsed that his knees were jerking up to his chest. And all the time Maureen's cries pitched higher and higher.

247

Only when the last quiver of Boozer's life had stilled did she allow herself to be gathered into Luther's arms and her cries muffled against his chest. One of his hands entwined in her thick hair, the other pressed her soft flesh against him so that she didn't see the bodies being cut down and placed in their coffins. Nor did she stir as the cavalcade made its way in the same order as before back to Glasgow jail.

Luther nursed her like a child, stroking her hair, smoothing his cheek against hers. Once back at Glasgow he waited until the bodies were carried into the prison and the military and all the dignitaries had dispersed before he ordered the coach to return to Blythswood Square. He carried her up the stairs and through the door opened by the parlour maid. Augusta was waiting white-faced in the hall.

'Where's her room,' he asked.

'I'll show you,' Augusta said. Then, turning to the maid, 'Go and fetch some brandy and bring it up to Maureen's room.'

In silence Luther followed Augusta up to the attic, still carrying the half-unconscious woman in his arms. There he laid her on the bed where Augusta began deftly untying her boots.

'There's no need for you to stay, Luther. I'll see to her.'

Reluctantly, he returned back downstairs and in the parlour he made straight for the whisky decanter. Some time later, Augusta joined him.

'I have given her something to make her sleep and told one of the other maids to stay with her. Are you all right, Luther? Was there any trouble?'

Pouring himself another drink he gave a humourless burst of laughter.

'Oh, it was no trouble. No trouble at all. It was a real Roman holiday. I reckon there must have been well over a hundred thousand sightseers lining the route and at least another fifty thousand swarming round the gallows. The Glasgow bailies put on a grand show. What a march of pomp and circumstance. What a triumphal, processional air the whole proceedings had.'

'Luther, you only do yourself harm by being bitter. You must try to put the whole thing out of your mind.'

'Just like that, eh?'

'It is over and done with now.'

'Over and done with?'

'Well, isn't it?'

'You're good at banishing things from your mind, Augusta. I must give you credit for that.'

'I have never evaded my duty.'

'Such perfection!'

'I know my own worth.'

'Indeed you do.'

'Luther, if you consume any more whisky you shall get drunk.'

'So I get fucking drunk.'

She winced in distaste. 'Will you never learn to behave like a gentleman? Think of your position. Think of the society we are mixing with now . . .'

'Augusta,' he interrupted. 'Piss off!'

She stood for a moment like a rosy-cheeked doll. In her sprigged patterned dress and with tiny flowers nestling in her ringlets she looked exquisite. He wanted to thrash her all round the exquisite room. He wanted to break something, everything.

'Get out of my sight, and quickly,' he said. 'Before I do something I'll be sorry for.'

Without a word she pattered from the room, closing the door behind her.

At first she did not know where to go or what to do. She was afraid of Luther when he was in this kind of mood. There was a volcanic menace about him that was impossible to cope with. The only safe thing for her to do was to keep as far away from him as possible until his mood had changed. The drawing-room, the bedroom, even the kitchen, she suspected, were not safe enough retreats on this occasion.

She decided it would be a good time to slip away and visit her mama. Today had been Maureen's turn to go and help but of course it had not been possible for Maureen to fulfil her normal duties these past few days.

Thankful that the parlour was at the back of the tall terrace house and Luther would not see the coach drawing up at the front, she tied on her bonnet, then after collecting a basket with a few items like home-made preserves, a sultana cake, a piece of boiled ham and a bottle of Madeira she quietly eased from the front door and hurried away.

The coach and horses could not essay the narrow track up to the line of whitewashed cottages so Augusta was forced to alight, put on an old pair of pattens to save her slippers and raise her feet from the dirt, and walk to her mother's place. Obviously some sort of farm animals used the path because it was much fouled with dung. Yet the sun glistening on the trees that clustered around and on the rough white walls of the cottages made quite a pleasant rural scene. It gave a feeling of peaceful isolation although in fact it was only a short drive drom Glasgow.

'Augusta! Augusta!' Mrs Cameron flew to meet her with outstretched arms. 'Oh, my dear, how afraid I have been. How dreadfully I have suffered these past few days.'

'Mama, Maureen was here two days ago and I was here only a couple of days before that. We are coming as often as we can.'

'That dreadful common Irish creature. What use is she as a lady's maid? Augusta, I am astonished at your lack of taste and good judgement in employing her. She is rough and vulgar in both speech and manner.'

'I know that, Mama, but she is also very kind and generous-hearted. I have told her to show you how to do necessary tasks, not to do them for you. You must stop forcing her to do everything. That way you will never learn.'

'As for doing my hair, she is absolutely hopeless. She had me in such a state of impatience and frustration with her the last time, I just screamed. I just screamed and screamed.'

Augusta sighed. 'It won't do any good, Mama. You must brush your hair and pin it back the way I showed you. Would you like to come with me for a ride in my carriage? It is waiting at the end of the lane.'

Mrs Cameron's face immediately brightened. 'Oh, yes, dear. That would be delightful.'

'Put your bonnet on then.'

The older's woman's excitement was so intense, however, and her fingers fumbled so much with the tyers of the bonnet that Augusta had to secure it for her.

The drive was a great success. Augusta had risked going through the town as a special treat and her mama had seen much to remark on and gossip about. She never stopped chattering all the way back to the cottage. It was only when Augusta made to leave that Mrs Cameron's lighthearted mood abruptly changed to tragic sobbing and pleading. Augusta had to tear her roughly aside to free herself and run from the house to her carriage. Then as the horses galloped swiftly away she struggled to calm her own distress before reaching Blythswood Square. She patted the beflowered ringlets that peeped from her bonnet, neatly arranged the folds of her dress, then sat with gloved hands on her lap and eyes tightly closed.

Chapter Thirty-seven

Alexander and Samuel were running and tumbling and jumping for joy and even Mary Jane could barely be contained by Nurse's firm hand.

'A wonderful place for children,' Luther said.

Augusta had to agree. Strolling along through the fresh and leafy suburb of Kelvinside by the banks of the River Kelvin was a delightful experience. The fine old trees which stretched along the valley gladdened her eye with their rich soft beauty.

Reaching the tall wrought-iron gates of their new mansion Luther pushed them open.

'I must see that the gardens are properly organized.'

'Yes, an elegant and formal setting is important,' Augusta remarked. 'And of course a good herb garden and vegetable garden are essential too.'

'What about the extra staff you engaged? Are they sufficient to run the place?'

'I may have to make a few changes.'

She was thinking of Maureen. Now that they were settled in Gunnet House and she was handling larger sums of money, in fact everything on a larger scale, it was proving much easier to provide little necessities for her mother without fear of detection. Indeed Augusta now believed that she could risk installing Maureen in the cottage with her mama as a full-time maid.

There were other reasons for Maureen leaving Gunnet House.

For some time now she had sensed a bond between Maureen and Luther and she was convinced for the good of all concerned it had to be severed. Caution and tact were called for, however. Luther had sympathy with the kitchen maid, which was understandable. She was fond of Maureen herself. But the depth of Luther's compassion was embarrassingly improper. The master of a large establishment should have no interest or concern whatsoever with the lower members of staff. The only time the master and the members of the domestic staff should have any connection was when they gathered in the drawing-room on Sundays and the master took family prayers.

For Luther to visit the kitchen and chat to Maureen or order her upstairs to ask how she was feeling was bad enough. The common roots Maureen and Luther shared in working-class society were a danger that Augusta was acutely aware of. Even worse, however, was the familiarity that she suspected might exist between them. She had seen the old devilment return to Luther's eyes and his quick appreciation of a shapely body or slender ankle. Maureen was far too immodestly curvaceous and she had a roguish-ness of eye that matched Luther's.

It was Augusta's duty as his wife and the mother of his children to see that his place in society was properly protected and all the decencies preserved. The more she thought about the dangerous emotion that existed between her husband and her maid, the more she became convinced that Maureen would have to go. She chose a time when Luther was safely away at the diggings before summoning the Irishwoman upstairs.

In the parlour she was sitting at her escritoire finishing off a letter when Maureen entered.

'One moment, please,' she said without turning round.

She penned her signature to the letter, carefully blotting it, folded it, tucked it into an envelope, sealed the envelope and addressed it. When she turned in her chair, Maureen was standing gazing around with interest at the bric-à-nbrac and *objets d'art* that covered every surface of the room.

'I wish to speak to you, Maureen.'

'Sure, Mrs.'

'I must be frank with you. You do not fit in here.'

'Aw, Jaysus, what have I done now?'

'I do not wish you to continue working in Gunnet House.'

'Who's been complaining about my work? Who is it? I'll bate the divil with me own two fists.'

'Lower your voice,' Augusta said coldly.

'I'll throttle the living daylights out of the two-faced . . .'

'No one has said anything about you that has influenced my decision. It is not your work. *You* are not suitable. However I can offer you other employment.'

'Oh, and what might that be, Mrs?'

'You may move in with Mrs Cameron as her full-time servant.'

'Holy mother o' God!'

'I told you to keep your voice down. Shouting and screeching and lack of self-discipline simply cannot be tolerated in an establishment such as this. At least in a labourer's cottage it will not be so outrageously out of place.'

'Will that be why you put your divil of a mother there?'

'How dare you!' Augusta went pale with shock at the Irishwoman's impertinence.

'If you're putting me out, Mrs, out I'll go and there's an end to it. I won't be going to that woman.'

Augusta took a deep breath. 'I would see that you had plenty of time off. Every weekend perhaps. And I would pay you well.'

'I'm sorry, Mrs. I'd rather just pack my box and go.'

Augusta turned back to the escritoire. After a short pause she managed, 'Very well. Here are the wages due to you. I would prefer if you left immediately. One moment.' She penned a few words on a piece of paper. 'Here is a short testimonial to say that you are a willing worker and are honest and goodhearted. I hope it helps you to find other employment, something more suitable – farmwork perhaps.'

'Thank you kindly, Mrs. Ach, haven't I always said you've a heart as big as a bucket?'

After the door shut and Augusta was alone she felt unexpectedly disconsolate. She had not realized how deeply attached she was to Maureen. Quickly she took a grip of herself. She did not regret removing the Irishwoman from Gunnet House. It was not only improper but dangerous for her to remain.

She would have to tell Luther but she hoped this duty could be postponed for as long as possible. There was also the problem of finding other help for her mother. She would of course continue to assist her as much as she could. But with such a large establishment as Gunnet House to run, her time was limited.

An added responsibility was the entertaining she and Luther did and the invitations and engagements they had to fulfil. She enjoyed these occasions of course and Luther obviously revelled in them. He was a most fashionable dresser and all his old swagger and joie-de-vivre had returned. So much so indeed that it worried her. At all times she felt it her duty to keep a discreet but sharp eye on him. At soirées and balls many a flirtatious glance had been fluttered in his direction from above a fan and his wicked grin or outrageous wink had not escaped her notice.

As far as Maureen was concerned, several days elapsed before Luther discovered she had gone. He had been at the stables at the back and entering the house through the kitchen had sought her out. Cook told him that the kitchen maid had been dismissed.

'What the hell's happened to Maureen?'

Augusta looked up from her embroidery. 'Shut the door, please. And I would be obliged if you would refrain from shouting in that coarse and undisciplined manner.'

He lifted his foot and sent the door crashing shut. 'Answer my question.'

'I dismissed her.'

'Why did you dismiss her?'

'She was unsuitable for this establishment. I could have found her other employment but she refused. I therefore gave her money and a testimonial and she left.'

'Why was she unsuitable?'

'Luther, I do not question your judgement regarding the navvies that you employ or dismiss.'

'Where is she?'

'I have no idea.'

'You bitch!'

'I do not see why you should indulge in such an emotional display over a kitchen maid, Luther, and what is worse, abuse your wife because of her. It is most improper.'

'You're always talking about duty. Can't you see we've a duty to her?'

'I have fulfilled my duty to her. I was a good employer, and when she left I gave her full wages and a good testimonial. I could do no more. Nor should I be expected to do any more.'

'Augusta, Boozer was my friend. I slaved side by side with him when I was a navvy. I caroused with him. And

255

when I became a ganger, then contractor, he was one of my best and most loyal workers. He followed me all across the country with his pick and shovel over his shoulder and a grin on his face.'

'Boozer is dead.'

'I owe it to him to make sure Maureen doesn't starve or walk the streets.'

'I do not agree, Luther. But Maureen will neither starve nor walk the streets, I am quite sure. I suggested farmwork. I think she came from a farm in Ireland, did she not?'

'I could have arranged for Tibs to employ her. Then I would have known she was all right.'

Augusta picked up her embroidery again. 'She will be all right, Luther. Try to put her out of your mind. What would people think if they heard you making such a fuss about such a person? They might misunderstand. They might believe there was some serious attachment between you.'

'Do you?'

She widened her blue eyes and stared unblinkingly up at him.

'I believe you are far too intelligent to risk a scandal that would adversely affect your hard-earned social position, or your wife and children.'

He stood with thumbs hooked in waistcoat staring down at her. And suddenly she felt the animal attraction that he could so unexpectedly exude.

Hastily she retreated her attention to her embroidery. It deeply disturbed her to realize that he could still affect her like this. From the first delirious moment when she had experienced his exploring fingers that night of the blizzard so long ago, the intensity of her physical response to him had never waned. If anything it had intensified. It was a weakness, a madness of which she was ashamed.

'Don't try to get clever with me, Augusta,' he said. 'It won't work.'

Chapter Thirty-eight

Easing up her skirts with one hand because she was carrying the flat-ended basket of flowers in the other, Augusta picked her way across the lawn. Dew still sparkled on the ground and she could feel the dampness beginning to penetrate through her slippers. Nevertheless she paused for a few seconds to admire the house. It had a considerable frontage of red sandstone and looked very solid and handsome. Inside, the vestibule supported by pillars led into a marble hall from which opened various public rooms, including a spacious saloon. Luther had said the saloon could be used as a ballroom or for any large social gatherings that they might wish to give. As it happened it was going to prove most useful. The opening of the Glasgow and Edinburgh line was promising to be a most spectacular affair and both cities were to be *en fête* for the occasion. An enormous banquet had been planned in Dundas Street Station. Later that evening the top dignitaries of both cities would be arriving at Gunnet House for a special ball to celebrate the event. There was no doubt in Luther's mind of the importance of this new railway.

'Apart from linking the two major cities of Scotland, Augusta, it's giving us a trade outlet to the sea. The implications are enormous. February 1842 is going to be an important date in the history of Scottish affairs.'

The difficulties in organizing such a social event were enormous too. Not that she would dream of complaining, or of shirking her duty. She was only sorry that on items like floral decoration she could not do better. Flowers in any quantity were not easy to come by at this time of year. Still, she was determined that the ballroom, indeed the whole house, would be most attractively displayed.

'A few more flowers,' she said, giving the basket to a servant. Then she went upstairs to change into dry shoes.

In the bedroom she found Luther examining his wardrobe. She could not help laughing.

'You will be the best dressed man at the opening, and the ball. I fear you will even outshine me.'

'It's the first railroad in Scotland and I built it.'

'You did indeed.'

'Luther Gunnet from the Briggait.' He savoured the words with obvious satisfaction.

'No,' she correctly firmly, 'Luther Gunnet from Gunnet House, Kelvinside.'

He tossed her a sarcastic glance then said, 'I've organized a celebration for the navvies as well. A dinner with boiled hams, bread and cheese and of course plenty of beer and whisky.'

'At the same time as the Dundas Street banquet?'

'No, later. I promised I'd be there to toast them.'

'Luther, that is not possible.'

'I'll be there.'

'But after the banquet you have to return here with me to change into our evening clothes.'

'Everything's ready. I've just checked.'

'Yes, but you must be in plenty of time to receive our guests. Oh, Luther, such important ladies and gentlemen!'

'The banquet's at half-past two in the afternoon. The ball isn't till evening, for God's sake.'

'But, Luther . . .'

'Stop nagging.'

She felt offended. She had only been anxious to ensure that everything would go smoothly on what might be called their day of crowning glory. After all, not only the provost of Glasgow would be coming to the ball but the provost of Edinburgh, the capital city. Military gentlemen like Colonel Fleming and some of his brother officers would be present. There would also be important people like Lord and Lady Hill. It was really too bad of Luther to put a further strain on her already keyed up nerves by disappearing to carouse with thousands of navvies. She went into a huff and did not speak to him again until they were both dressed and ready to leave for the opening. Then he grinned at her, tipped his top hat to a jaunty angle and said,

'How does it feel to be escorted by the smartest man in town?'

'Luther, you are incorrigible!'

She was gratified to see by his quick appreciative look that he thought her appearance matched his in elegance. Her pale blue and white striped skirt was of gleaming silk and set off with a dark blue skirted jacket. Her white bonnet was tied in a large bow under her chin with ribbons the same blue as her eyes.

Enormous crowds had turned out with flags waving for the occasion. They lined the route of the trains and swarmed on the viaducts to cheer the proud and powerful locomotives with their tall chimneys and their ability to pull long trains of carriages packed with many hundreds of passengers.

The Glasgow passenger shed was like a fairy palace. The rails were boarded over and the whole area used as a hall.

'What do you think of it?' Luther asked Augusta.

For a minute or two she was unable to reply. Only someone like Luther could have envisaged something in such a grand style. Three of the walls were stunningly covered with Grecian drapery. The tunnel wall was curtained with enormous lengths of pink calico. The whole place was illuminated with gas jets, some of which formed the outline of a locomotive. A military band was playing in one of the arcades.

'It . . . it . . . quite takes one's breath away.'

There was indeed an exuberance about the whole affair that nothing managed to crush; not even the hitch of the rope breaking on the incline plane at the tunnel before all the carriages had been drawn up. This meant the banquet was delayed until five o'clock but champagne and claret flowed so continuously that nobody was capable of worrying about anything. Augusta took it for granted that Luther would not now think of going to the navvies' celebration. It would take them all their time after the banquet to get home and change and be ready to welcome their guests to the ball.

Fortunately it would not be necessary to offer a dinner to anyone after the sumptuous spread at the station banquet. But she had organized a buffet supper and a bowl of punch in case it might be required.

The banquet tables were served by an army of waiters who dispensed tureens of soup, dishes of potatoes, roast turkeys, each stuffed with a bullock's tongue, boiled rounds of beef richly glazed and ornamented, lobsters and so many other delicacies that Augusta lost count.

Toasts were heralded by a toast trumpet and the first toast proposed by the chairman was 'The Queen' and this was drunk with enthusiastic cheering.

Next came Prince Albert, the Prince of Wales, the Queen Dowager, the Princess Royal and other members of the royal family – all drunk amid loud cheers. Then came the toast to the army and navy, after which Colonel Fleming in the name of Lord Hill and his brother officers begged to return thanks for the honour done to the army.

'To the ladies in particular,' he said, 'we feel deeply indebted for the manner in which they responded to the toast. We flatter ourselves that we have the ladies always on our side for they pity the military for the dangers which they encounter. In return the military men love and adore the ladies because they do pity them.'

This was greeted with resounding cheers.

'The blue jackets of old England,' he went on, 'require no compliment from a soldier. They do their duty nobly and fearlessly on all occasions when their services are required.'

Toast after toast followed but none brought forth louder cheering than: 'Mr Luther Gunnet, the man who made this far-sighted and ambitious project a working reality . . .'

And afterwards, when the proceedings were over and Augusta and Luther were leaving, the company honoured them with a spontaneous standing ovation. Luther acknowledged the applause with a grin and a jaunty wave while

Augusta with a more regal air merely smiled and gave slight movements of her head.

Their carriage was waiting outside and she was settling herself comfortably on its cushions when Luther, instead of following her, nonplussed her by saying, 'See you later.'

'Luther!' she cried out in panic. 'Surely you are not going to the navvies' dinner now?'

'There's still plenty of time.'

'Do not be ridiculous, Luther!'

It was no use. Already he had summoned a hansom and the cab was clattering away over the cobbles.

She felt quite faint. Leaning back in the carriage she tried not to think of the disasters that might occur on this, the most important evening of her life. She failed. Luther could, indeed probably would, arrive at Gunnet House not only late but drunk. He might even arrive in a drunken state after the guests were already in the house and everyone would witness his disgrace. And what disgraced Luther Gunnet disgraced his wife and children. She could not bear to contemplate such a scene. They would be socially ruined. She had a terrifying sensation of déjà vu. She might have known that Luther would always despoil her life. Just as he had despoiled her mother's and father's.

Her mind was so distraught she did not know what to do and on an impulse she called to the coachman to hasten to where her mother resided. Sickened by the prospects of Luther's coarse and disgraceful behaviour she longed for comfort and communion with someone of sensitivity and gentility.

As usual, the coach had to stop at an inconvenient distance from the cottage because the bush and tree-lined road leading to it was too narrow. After she alighted she began picking her way along the muddy track but was soon brought to a halt by the sound of Mrs Cameron's voice raised in anger. Rounding a bend in the lane Augusta was able to see, a couple of hundred yards ahead, a group of women arguing round the water pump. Her mother, as petite and dainty as ever, but with sleeves rolled up and skirts hitched, was giving one of her neighbours a piece of her mind.

'Mercy, the very idea! No, I certainly will not wait in turn for water behind you or anyone else, I know my place all right. The trouble is, you do not know yours! In future you'll keep a civil and respectable tongue in your head when you address me. Never forget that I'm a lady!'

This last warning was delivered in a screech of fury more akin to that of a fishwife.

Even more shocked and confused, Augusta retreated back to her carriage without being seen. The unexpected picture of Mrs Cameron with sleeves rolled and arms akimbo, coupled with such piercingly uninhibited sounds, increased her feelings of agitation and general insecurity. Trembling from head to foot she collapsed back against the carriage seat and allowed herself to be transported to Gunnet House.

Once there, she had to lean heavily on the footman as he helped her to alight. It was only with a supreme effort that she managed to walk into the house without assistance.

Upstairs in the master bedroom all the evening clothes had been laid out in readiness by the maid. She sat down in front of the dressing-table, willing herself not to give way to panic that could so easily tip over into hysteria. The vision of Luther arriving home and causing a disgraceful scene kept returning to terrify her. How dare he torment her like this! He was always the same. He took positive delight in tormenting her. It was a sadistic streak that she was only too well aware of. It took different forms, some so subtle and devious she had not realized his intent at the time. On other occasions he was purposely and crudely obvious.

She removed her bonnet, jacket and skirt with vague, fumbling fingers. Her concentration was so splintered it never occurred to her to ring for the maid. It was a much as she could do to grope into her dressing-gown. The beautiful evening dress lay untouched. She was suspended in such a state of anxiety she was incapable of contemplating anything except Luther's return.

The moment she heard the horses' hooves and the clatter of the carriage her whole being tightened with apprehension. Yet as always when he entered there was the strange thrill of excitement she experienced in his presence. She turned to face the doorway at least outwardly calm and composed, her dressing-gown ribbons tied neatly up to her neck. He seemed perfectly sober. Yet there was something wrong. His face was pale and hard set. Peeling off his coat he tossed it aside and began unbuttoning his waistcoat. Even in the way he performed this simple task she detected something ominous.

'I met an old friend,' he said.

'I am not interested in your navvy friends at the moment. We have a duty to our guests. A duty that already you have made extremely difficult to fulfil with propriety and decorum.'

'What about your duty to me?'

She raised an eyebrow as he approached her. 'What do you mean? I have always been a good wife. I have always obeyed your wishes.'

To her astonishment he lashed out at her with the back of his hand. Instinctively she averted her face, but the blow caught her on the side of the head, stunning her as much with amazement as with the force with which it was inflicted.

'Luther, our guests!' she cried.

'To hell with the guests.'

'You are drunk.'

'No, but Maureen had a few glasses. She turned up at the navvies' celebration, and very talkative she became. I have also spoken to the coachman and the footman and they confirmed what she told me.'

'Oh, and what did she tell you?'

'You know damn well what she told me. You were supposed to have nothing more to do with the Camerons. Yet I find that Maureen and other members of my staff have been ordered by you to dance attendance on your bitch of a mother.'

'No, that is not true, Luther.'

'She has eaten my food. Employees whose wages I pay have cleaned her house, washed her clothes, taken her for jaunts in my carriage.'

'Luther, for pity's sake, let us discuss this at some other time. It is imperative that I am not flustered and upset. It is my duty to create a dignified and pleasantly welcoming atmosphere in which to receive our guests. They will be arriving at any moment. I must ring for my maid to help me into my ball gown.'

She gasped in pain as he roughly jerked her away from the bell-pull.

'Augusta, have you ever known me to go back on my word?'

'No,'

'If I make a threat or a promise, I keep it.'

'Yes.'

'Well, listen carefully because I mean what I say. If you ever defy me again by going to visit Mrs Cameron, you can stay there. You will not get back in this house. If you choose to remain here as my wife you must promise never to have any contact with that woman again.'

'But I am her only daughter, her own flesh and blood. How can I allow her to suffer? How could she survive on her own?'

'She'll just have to.'

Her face was a colourless mask and she stared at him for a long time in silence.

'Well, Augusta,' he said eventually, 'what is it to be?'

'You are a wicked man.'

'So you keep telling me.'

'You take sadistic delight in tormenting me.'

'Come now!' His words, half reprimand, half denial, were honeyed with sensual overtones.

'I hate you and I do not want you to touch me ever again.'

He tutted and shook his head. 'You don't mean that.'

Slowly, deliberately, he began loosening the top ribbon of her dressing-gown.

'I had better ring for the maid,' she faltered.

Hard fingers dug into her arm preventing her from doing so.

She eyed him with cold dignity. 'You know that I am staying.'

'Yes, I know you're staying.'

'Well, kindly remove your hand from my arm. There is no need to use force.'

'Let me see your arm.'

'What?' Surprise scattered her defences and before she could recover, he was easing the dressing-gown from her shoulders.

'Let me see it.'

'It is all right. It is not bruised.'

She stepped back, her legs jamming against the dressing-table. He moved closer, his fingers caressing her shoulder while his eyes flowed over her, exciting her against her will, even through her distress.

So often Luther's gaze held a barely hidden obscenity when he looked at a woman.

'Luther, please allow me to get dressed.'

'You know you like me to look at you, and that's not all you like me to do.'

'Luther! The guests!'

'I told you,' he said quietly, 'fuck the guests.'

'Ohl Luther, please. I feel quite faint with apprehension and it is imperative that I retain a ladylike decorum to greet them.'

'Every inch of smooth skin. So peachy I want to bite into it. You even taste like a peach. Sweet and soft . . .'

'No, Luther. Don't. You are hurting me.'

His mouth softened and his tongue moistly caressed her as he removed her under-garments, fondled her breasts and slid his lips round and over them.

A vision of every person of rank and importance for miles

around arriving at any moment battered like madness at the door of her mind. The horror of it see-sawed with her physical rapture. And when he lifted her into his arms and carried her towards the bed she raged and struggled against him.

'You bastard!' she said.

His laughter held a note of mock surprise. 'That wasn't very ladylike.'

'You want to bring me down to your level.'

'Where is that, Augusta? Here in bed lying beside me?'

Despite her rage her voice broke. 'I know what you are trying to do.'

He cupped her face in his hands and whispered: 'I'm going to look at you. At every part of you from the gold silk of your beautiful head, and the feathery tufts deep in the warmth under your arms . . .'

'Luther, I beg of you . . .'

'Yes, beg me.'

Her ear tuned into footsteps in the corridor and on the stairs, acutely sensing the anxiety in the quickness of them.

'The servants will be wondering what's happening. They will be getting worried and . . .'

'And your breasts are just big enough to cup in my hands like this so that I can caress and kiss them. And look at them. And your soft belly and the downy blonde hair at your groin.'

'Luther, please, oh, please . . .'

'And every warm, moist fold of you.'

Her bemused brain thought it detected the sound of carriage wheels. Her mind was deranged with anxiety yet her body slackened and accommodated his every touch. Gradually her mental delirium infected her body and she was no longer in control of her physical movements. All she knew was that he excited her beyond words.

Then he said in a cool, quiet voice next to her ear:

'They're arriving. Listen! There's a carriage.'

She began to moan louder and louder as his lovemaking increased in force.

'Listen,' he kept whispering, 'they're here! They're here!'

Afterwards she lay shattered and helplessly weeping while he with his usual vitality arose, washed and dressed, and in a matter of minutes was plucking her from the bed as if she was no more than a feather. His speed bewildered and confused her.

'Get washed and dressed. Come on!'

It was as if he was rasping a command to one of his navvies. She fumbled with the sponge and water. He flung the towel at her.

'Move!' Then snatching at her clothes he pushed and pulled and jerked her into them. 'Stop that snivelling and sit down at the dressing-table. You put on your earrings, I'll fasten the necklace.'

'My God,' she said, 'I cannot go downstairs like this.'

'Like what?'

'For pity's sake . . .' She gazed imploringly up at him through the mirror.

'You're beautiful,' he said. 'Look at yourself, woman! You've never looked so radiant. Flushed cheeks, shining eyes, quivering little rosebud of a mouth. I could take you all over again.'

The fear in her eyes made him grin and bend over to kiss her ear.

'Come on.'

She wandered after him across the room.

'Take my arm,' he said. Already he had opened the door and was leading her down the stairs to the saloon.

A gaggle of distracted servants looked as if they wanted to faint with relief at the sight of her.

'Oh, ma'am,' Kennedy hurried forward. 'People have arrived. They are in reception taking off their cloaks. The rest of the staff are attending to them but we didn't know when to – '

Luther interrupted her. 'We're waiting to welcome our guests. Show them through.'

Then he signalled to the orchestra at the opposite end of

the long room. Suddenly everything burst into life and gaiety. The chandeliers brilliantly sparkled. The servants stood ready with trays of glasses shooting up bubbles of champagne. The musicians enthusiastically swayed from side to side. Lady guests came swooping forward, their gowns a riot of colour, their hands outstretched in happy greeting. The gentlemen followed behind, immaculate in military uniforms or cravats and tailcoats. But none smarter than Luther, his white silk waistcoat, frilled shirt and high cravat a brilliant contrast to his luxuriant black hair.

Augusta, her cheeks still flushed, stood beside but a little behind him, the rich gold glimmer of her ballgown accentuating her look of suppressed excitement as she held out her hand to each guest. Luther pushed his out firmly, confidently. When everyone was rainbowing the walls of the saloon with colour, and glasses were clinking merrily above the rhythm of the polka, he turned to Augusta and looked down at her with narrowed eyes.

'My dance, Mrs Gunnet,' he said. Then, with a hint of mockery in his smile, 'May I have the pleasure?'

'Mr Gunnet,' she murmured, before allowing herself to be led into the centre of the floor and whirled triumphantly away.

THE END

STAR BOOKS BESTSELLERS

	JAY ALLERTON	
0352320184	**Mothers and Daughters**	£3.50*
	TESSA BARCLAY	
0352319321	**The Last Heiress**	£2.50
0352315520	**Garland of War**	£1.95
0352317612	**The Wine Widow**	£2.50
0352304251	**A Sower Went Forth**	£2.25
0352308060	**The Stony Places**	£2.25
0352313331	**Harvest of Thorns**	£2.25
0352315857	**The Good Ground**	£1.95
035231687X	**Champagne Girls**	£2.99
	JOANNA BARNES	
0352316969	**Silverwood**	£3.25

STAR Books are obtainable from many booksellers and newsagents. If you have any difficulty tick the titles you want and fill in the form below.

Name _____

Address _____

_____

Send to: Star Books Cash Sales, P.O. Box 11, Falmouth, Cornwall, TR10 9EN.

Please send a cheque or postal order to the value of the cover price plus:
UK: 55p for the first book, 22p for the second book and 14p for each additional book ordered to the maximum charge of £1.75.

BFPO and EIRE: 55p for the first book, 22p for the second book, 14p per copy for the next 7 books, thereafter 8p per book.

OVERSEAS: £1.00 for the first book and 25p per copy for each additional book.

While every effort is made to keep prices low, it is sometimes necessary to increase prices at short notice. Star Books reserve the right to show new retail prices on covers which may differ from those advertised in the text or elsewhere.

*NOT FOR SALE IN CANADA

STAR BOOKS BESTSELLERS

LOIS BATTLE
| 0352320958 | **A Habit of the Blood** | £3.50* |

| 035231270X | **War Brides** | £2.75* |

| 0352316640 | **Southern Women** | £2.95* |

PAULA BLAKE
| 0352320753 | **Just Good Enemies** | £1.95 |

MAGGI BROCHER
| 0352321733 | **Kathleen** | £3.50* |

CHARLES BUKOWSKI
| 0352309679 | **Women** | £2.25* |

| 0352310499 | **Factotum** | £1.50* |

| 0352315989 | **Post Office** | £1.80* |

STAR Books are obtainable from many booksellers and newsagents. If you have any difficulty tick the titles you want and fill in the form below.

Name _____

Address _____

_____

Send to: Star Books Cash Sales, P.O. Box 11, Falmouth, Cornwall, TR10 9EN.

Please send a cheque or postal order to the value of the cover price plus:
UK: 55p for the first book, 22p for the second book and 14p for each additional book ordered to the maximum charge of £1.75.

BFPO and EIRE: 55p for the first book, 22p for the second book, 14p per copy for the next 7 books, thereafter 8p per book.

OVERSEAS: £1.00 for the first book and 25p per copy for each additional book.

While every effort is made to keep prices low, it is sometimes necessary to increase prices at short notice. Star Books reserve the right to show new retail prices on covers which may differ from those advertised in the text or elsewhere.

*NOT FOR SALE IN CANADA

STAR BOOKS BESTSELLERS

	ASHLEY CARTER	
0352317264	**A Darkling Moon**	£2.50*
035231639X	**Embrace The Wind**	£2.25*
0352315717	**Farewell to Blackoaks**	£1.95*
0352316365	**Miz Lucretia of Falconhurst**	£2.50*
0352318503	**Mandingo Master**	£3.50*
0352320885	**Sword of the Golden Stud**	£3.50*
0352320990	**Flight to Falconhurst**	£3.50*
	KYLE ONSTOTT	
0352320664	**Drum**	£3.95*
	KATE CAMERON	
0352321175X	**As If They Were Gods**	£3.50*

STAR BOOKS BESTSELLERS

| | LOUISE ELLIOT | |
| 0352319437 | **This Side of Christmas** | £2.50 |

	THOMAS FLEMING	
0352316950	**The Spoils of War**	£3.95*
0352313986	**Dreams of Glory**	£2.95*
0352312750	**Promises to Keep**	£3.25*
0352310634	**The Officers' Wives**	£3.95*

| | DORIS FLOOD LADD | |
| 0352316977 | **The Irish** | £2.95* |

| | RICHARD FREDE | |
| 0352318716 | **The Nurses** | £3.95* |

| | EDITH FREUND | |
| 0352319992 | **Dare to Dream** | £3.50* |

STAR Books are obtainable from many booksellers and newsagents. If you have any difficulty tick the titles you want and fill in the form below.

Name _____

Address _____

_____

Send to: Star Books Cash Sales, P.O. Box 11, Falmouth, Cornwall, TR10 9EN.

Please send a cheque or postal order to the value of the cover price plus:
UK: 55p for the first book, 22p for the second book and 14p for each additional book ordered to the maximum charge of £1.75.

BFPO and EIRE: 55p for the first book, 22p for the second book, 14p per copy for the next 7 books, thereafter 8p per book.

OVERSEAS: £1.00 for the first book and 25p per copy for each additional book.

While every effort is made to keep prices low, it is sometimes necessary to increase prices at short notice. Star Books reserve the right to show new retail prices on covers which may differ from those advertised in the text or elsewhere.

*NOT FOR SALE IN CANADA